REMO WAS ON HIS FEET

The crowd was screaming. People were bloodied. One man was flat on his back with a gash in his head. Amazingly few casualties, Remo thought, in a small corner of his brain that was still capable of being rational.

Most of his brain had stopped being rational many, many jiffies ago. Most of it was screaming.

Remo ran like something white-hot that is propelled from a volcanic crack in the earth. When he caught up to the next car he hit the part in the middle—the soft, human part. That stopped the car just as well, and nothing exploded into the crowds except for a few flecks of brain matter.

Remo kept moving. Fast. Still screaming silently.

Idiot! Idiot! How many people had he wounded? How many would die because of him?

Other titles in this series:

CREATED BY MURPHY & SAPIR

THE DESTROYER

DARK AGES

A GOLD EAGLE BOOK FROM
WORLDWIDE®

TORONTO • NEW YORK • LONDON
AMSTERDAM • PARIS • SYDNEY • HAMBURG
STOCKHOLM • ATHENS • TOKYO • MILAN
MADRID • WARSAW • BUDAPEST • AUCKLAND

First edition July 2005

ISBN 0-373-63255-X

Special thanks and acknowledgment to Tim Somheil for his contribution to this work.

DARK AGES

And for the Glorious House of Sinanju,
sinanjucentral@hotmail.com

1

The castle was burned to the ground.

Funny thing about that. Stone castles aren't supposed to burn to the ground, but there was no denying that Loch Tweed Castle was reduced to ashes. The local gossip placed the blame on the late Mrs. Tweed-Smythe, who had taken to collecting newspaper clippings during the Second World War. What started as a hobby, the locals claimed, became an obsession. Mrs. Tweed-Smythe tried to keep it secret that she was filing away a copy of the newspaper, each and every day, year after year.

The locals who were employed by the late Mr. and Mrs. Tweed-Smythe reported on the unusual volume of newspapers received by the old couple. The *London Times*, the *Peebles Shire News,* plus the *Edinburgh Evening News* and some others. No one could explain the need for all those newspapers.

There had to have been twenty or thirty thousand daily newspapers stored in the old cellars of the castle. With that much fuel, the fire would burn on and on, until even the stone walls crumbled. It was the only reasonable explanation for the extent of the castle's obliteration.

"So there's no chance of finding any bones," the locals decided as they discussed the matter endlessly. "There's nothing left but dust."

This made the tragedy even harder on the good people of the little Scottish village. Many of their sons and husbands and fathers—and a few wives—were driven mad during the recent troubles. They had stormed the castle, for reasons that were too foolish to believe and best left unsaid. They killed the poor old Tweed-Smythe and his helpless, daft wife, then burned the castle down around them. Nobody understood why it had happened. All they knew was that their loved ones were dead and gone, without even bones to bury.

The simple, mourning villagers were wrong. Old Mrs. Tweed-Smythe was as crazy as they came, but she didn't hoard newspapers, and it wasn't a stash of six decades of the *Strathspey & Badenoch Herald* that fueled the flames. The cause was the strategically placed phosphorus tablets. The secret researchers who worked below the castle placed the phosphorous to be sure that, if the castle burned up, it burned up real good.

The villages were also wrong about there being no bodies.

"Fuh! Christ!" The English gentleman got a face full of putrid air when he wrenched open the trapdoor. Something inside was decomposing.

The Englishman staggered away and vomited into the ashes, then rested with his hands on his knees.

This was awful. He shouldn't have to do this kind of thing. There should be people to do it for him. All his life there were people to do it for him, whatever it was.

But he couldn't trust anyone else, friends, family or coconspirators. *Not with this.* And he had to do it now, because surely some sort of a cleanup detail would be here soon to make absolutely sure the place had burned completely. Then his prize would be lost forever.

But did he have what it took? Of course he did! He was an Englishman—a true, old-fashioned, unflappable Brit.

But could he *really* do it?

Well, certainly. He had faced unpleasantness before and come through with flying colors. There had been the bit of murder down in Africa a few years back, and then the other bit of murder, also, coincidentally, in Africa, also a few years back. His constitution had been fully tested and hardened. Or so he had thought, until he had breathed in the fumes of the rotting corpses down there.

"You must do it, old man, or you'll never get the empire off the ground," he stated aloud, using his haughtiest tone. Arrogance always lifted his spirits. Arrogance was his best character trait.

He made for the trapdoor, covered his nose and mouth with a handkerchief and stepped into the blackness. He felt his way down the steep emergency stairs, which had buckled from the heat, and didn't turn on the flashlight until he reached the bottom.

After more vomiting, he picked his way among the corpses. They were charred from the initial blast, but the stone-crumbling heat had missed this place and left more than enough human flesh to putrefy. He hoped that was a good sign. Maybe his treasure would have survived, too.

Then he saw the state of the containment boxes, the steel walls black and pitted from the heat. The things that had once been inside would be nonfunctional. Dead.

He followed the only corridor, going deep into the earth, until he came to the emergency-isolation development room. Oddly the aluminum containment chamber was open and burned. The corpse on the floor smelled to high heaven, but he wasn't burned at all. The fire that destroyed the castle hadn't touched this chamber, and yet the containment cell showed signs of superheating.

In the congealed blood on the floor, the Englishman found a thin crust of opaque crystal.

They had escaped, and *then* they were burned. Tiny crystal splotches indicated that the fleeing entities had been assassinated, one colony after another. They didn't get far.

His worry grew, but there was still one last place to look. The drunken American—the same man who secretly removed the phosphorus incendiaries from this wing of the laboratory—had provided him with this secret.

By virtue of his renowned patriotism, unquestioned loyalty and distance from London politics, the Englishman had been asked to lead a security probe into assorted secret projects. That was how he found out about the secret work at Loch-Tweed Castle. It was a joint American and British weapons-development effort. Those very few British who were aware of the project were worried about the security measures at the laboratory.

After gaining his confidence, the Englishman wheedled the truth about the security out of the American researcher. About the sabotaged self-destruct system—and about the hidden sample.

"I couldn't bear it if all my work was burned alive," the American slurred after five big gin and tonics.

"Oh, I agree. Good work," the Englishman said. "I assure you, this is between the two of us."

Soon afterward, it was the Englishman's secret alone. After two more gin and tonics, the American had passed out. The Englishman put him in his car, started it and put the transmission in Drive, then slammed the door as the vehicle began rolling away. It rolled directly off the road into the Thames. Windows open, the car went down in seconds and wasn't hauled out again until morning.

The American researcher's hidden sample was right where he said it would be—buried two feet under the earth, directly beneath the destroyed aluminum cube. The Englishman unearthed it in minutes. The insulated box contained twenty-four stainless-steel straws, each of which could wipe out a city.

The tiny glass capsule in the bottom of the box was green. The chemicals inside the capsule would react to damaging heat by turning red, permanently, but the capsule was still green.

Which meant the creatures—things, devices, whatever—inside the steel straws were still alive. Viable, functional, whatever.

The Englishmen had just become the most powerful man on the planet.

This was only right and proper.

2

His name was Remo, but around these parts folks knew him as the Big Rig Bandit of I-44.

"You're him, ain't you?" asked the terrified driver.

"Who?" Remo asked.

"The Big Rig Bandit of I-44. You're him."

"Never heard of him. But I'm him."

The driver was no longer driving. She had been a minute ago, barreling down the interstate and listening to the CB chatter about the bandit. There was a lot of chatter. People were scared.

"You been stealing rigs up and down this stretch of road," the driver said. "Got yourself a peculiar reputation."

"How'd my reputation get peculiar? I only started hijacking eight hours ago."

"You ain't gonna hurt me, are you?"

Remo frowned. He didn't like having a reputation. "They say I *hurt* people out there?"

The driver cranked her head to look at Remo, but it did her no good, what with one of her own grease rags tied around her head to make a blindfold.

She had never heard him, never sensed him. All of a sudden, she felt a tiny pinch on the neck and felt her arms and legs stop working. In a flash she was scooted into the passenger seat and belted in, and only then did she realize she had been blindfolded. She had expected to feel her vehicle veer out of control and crash, but it drove on as if nothing had happened.

His first words to her had been, "Just consider me your relief driver."

Now he said, "Well? Who says I hurt people?"

"Nobody," she admitted.

"What do they say about me?"

"That you're some sort of a weirdo. You hijack 'em, then strand 'em. You ain't hurt a single soul. But what're you doing with all those rigs, I wanna know?"

"If I told you, then maybe you'd be the first one I had to hurt."

The driver tilted her head like a curious mutt. "Naw. I think you're a nice guy."

"No way. I'm bad."

"You're a pussycat."

"Hey, no. I'm a killer. I killed lots of people. I could kill you, too, just like snapping my fingers."

The driver laughed. "You're a funny. I like you, kid. Name's Penny."

"Hi, Penny. I'm Darren 'The Decapitator' Dougally."

Penny laughed. "Yeah, right."

Remo had to admit Penny was a cool customer. She wasn't just putting on a brave front, she truly wasn't the least bit concerned about being hijacked and paralyzed. Maybe she was bonkers.

"So? Where you gonna leave me, Triple-D?" she asked.

"How about the access road back of the Neosho Truckers' Campus?"

"That'll be just fine," Penny said. "Give you lots of time to get to wherever you got to go while I hike on in. You're going to unfreeze me so I'll be able to hike, right?"

"Sure," Remo said easily, but now he had an itch in his head.

Penny was cool, but she couldn't be *that* damn cool. He could sense her pulse, and it was suspiciously modulated. So was her breathing. She was cool in a practiced way, and why should she practice being cool unless she was some sort of an undercover agent who needed to be cool in extreme situations?

"You're from Langley, huh?"

Her heart rate rocketed, even as she replied easily, "Nope, I'm a Texas girl from Angelina."

"The Bureau?"

"Pardon?" she asked.

She was still tense, but her pulse didn't spike again. Remo could tell such things. "You know, the Company's not supposed to do intelligence-gathering inside the U.S."

"What are you talking about?" Penny chuckled, but she did it like an expert. Only Remo's highly tuned hearing picked up the slight quavering of her nervousness.

"So. CIA it is. You people tracking the Big Rig Bandit of I-44 or this vehicle specifically?"

"Triple-D, I got no clue—"

"Can it, Agent," Remo said. "You're with the CIA and you're operating on U.S. soil. That's the facts I know so far."

"Boy, you're crazy," Penny replied, her heart now in her throat. "You've hijacked one too many rigs today, and the stress is making you a little, you know, paranoid, like."

"Maybe," Remo said. "Here's an idea. I drive you on into Springfield and turn myself in to the news station and they broadcast live. You and me. And I tell them how I think you just might be a CIA agent. I'll look totally crazy, right?"

Penny said nothing, but her heart was racing like a marathon runner.

"So, think about all the publicity when they do a little checking and find out you *are* a CIA agent. Operating illegally inside the United States."

"You'll go to prison," Penny protested.

"Naw. I have legal title to this particular vehicle," Remo said. "I didn't leave any physical evidence at any of the other hijacks. Fact is, you—meaning the CIA—stole my RV."

"Ain't your RV," Penny snapped. "I was hired to take it to its rightful owner in Indianapolis."

"I'm the rightful owner, and I have the papers to prove it. But never mind that. We'll let Fox News sort it out. In fact, we'll make it in time for them to get us on their 5:00 a.m. program."

Penny stewed. Remo drove. The mile markers decreased by fifteen.

"Okay. Fine. I'm with the Company," she admitted.

"What's your purpose?"

"Figure out about this vehicle."

"What about it?"

"What do you mean, what about it? If this is really your recreational vehicle then you were the guy who was driving it on national TV, right? You got half the military in the Southwest U.S.A. mobilized around it, and then you just disappeared. Nothing left but questions about who gave the orders to the military and where y'all vanished to."

Remo hmmed. "There should have been a note that made it all okay."

"Huh?"

"You know, like from somebody high up in the government?"

"Yeah. There was all kinds of authorization. So?"

"What do you mean, so?"

"I mean *so what?* Just because somebody high up says it's okay don't make it okay at all. Makes it more suspicious than ever. We gotta know."

"*Who* has to know? *What* do you have to know?"

"Who's behind the hijackings and what your purpose really is, of course."

"Why?"

"Because we don't know, why else?"

"I see. So you're with some sort of a supersecret club inside the CIA, right?"

"No," Penny shot back, her heart rate leaping.

"I'll take that as a yes. So what do you think you know about all of this already?"

"Just what I told you. Ain't that enough?"

"Liar. Did you know your nostrils flare when you lie? Even in the dark I can see it."

"They don't flare!" Penny protested. "Not anymore! I trained 'em not to."

"Hey, it's just a little bit, hardly enough to be noticeable. Now, what do you know about all this?"

"I said, nothing."

"Nostrils! Start talking or I get Walter Jacobson on the phone."

Penny sulked. "After the network morning-show fiasco, we tracked the RV being hauled to a chop-shop in Tucumcari. They did a butcher job on it, then hauled it to a private garage out in the sticks, where it got smashed up like it was in a wreck. Damn thing changed hands three more times with the SUV it used to be attached to, then it ended up in a RV body shop in Flagstaff and both was restored to what they are now."

"Keep talking."

"The RV looks like a vintage Airstream again and the SUV looks like any other SUV," she pointed out. "They're not welded together like some oddball vee-hickle like you expect to see at a monster truck show."

"Tell me the stuff I don't know already."

"Okay. All we knew was that somebody was working the system better than even we knew how to. Legal title on the RV and this here SUV was held by the military, the State of New Mexico and then Vintage RVs of Santa Fe, all in the course of two weeks. Even the U.S. Postal Service had legal possession of the thing for a few hours on Wednesday. Damn, it was beautiful how you people worked it. How'd you do it?"

"Beats me. I just do grunt work. You try to put some sort of electronic tracking doohickeys on it?"

"Didn't dare," Penny said. "We saw the thing being scanned for bugs every day and every night. You folks were sending orders to the FBI to do the scanning. One time it was the Flagstaff PD. Once it was BIA!"

"What's BIA?"

"You don't know?"

"Told you, I'm just the grunt."

"Bureau of Indian Affairs. Anyway, you people had it zipped up tight. So we took the human approach. When they went to hire a driver to take it to Indy, I applied and managed to get the job instead of the regular relocation service."

"How'd you get the job, exactly?" He could feel the interior heat up from Penny's radiating face. "I see. A little puttin' out."

Penny was too embarrassed to even try denying it.

"Well, hell, what am I supposed to do now?" he demanded.

"Tell me who you are," Penny said.

"Aren't you supposed to leave the questions to the professional interrogators?" Remo asked. "I assume they're tracking us. I can hear your cell phone working its little chips. They must be listening to everything we say. That's why you're stalling and telling the whole long story." He snatched the phone from the breast pocket of her denim shirt. The display was dark, but there was a lot of electricity zipping around inside. Remo squeezed it flat in one hand, which took more effort than smashing a typical mobile phone. He crumbled the remains like Roquefort cheese.

Penny felt the chunks placed on her lap. "That phone was armored with steel plate."

"Felt like it."

"It's too late to get away. They'll swarm this vehicle in minutes. They won't let you slip the net."

"Why not?"

Penny glared sightlessly in his directly. "Because. Whoever you are, you're not under control."

"Not under *your* control, you mean?" Remo asked, his hackles rising. "And who are you people exactly?"

Penny got stubborn. "Don't ask me. I'm just a grunt."

THE TRUCK STOP was lit as bright as Las Vegas, but there were just two customers in the entire place—two truckers sipping coffee in a booth at the restaurant. They stopped sipping when they heard the sound of propellers.

"Sounds big," said the trucker with the mustache.

"Yeah," said the trucker without a mustache.

They were identical twin brothers, separated at birth, raised on opposite sides of the country. They barely knew each other while growing up. They had both chosen to make a living as long-haul truckers and met up for a coffee every few months when their paths crossed. Despite their disconnected lives, they shared that amazing bond that all twins shared, in which each seemed to know what the other was thinking.

"Real big," said the brother without the mustache, as the black shape swooped out of the dark sky and thundered to a touchdown on the empty interstate, roaring by the truck stop without slowing much.

The racket brought the waitress stumbling out of the ladies' room with her skirt tucked in her underwear. "What is it?"

"Hercules," said the brother with the mustache. "C-130. Heavy-lifter."

"Worked on one in the Army," added his brother.

"Don't say?"

"Great big sucker."

"Yeah."

"Oh, my God!" The waitress ran into the parking lot, waving her arms at the headlights that had appeared on the highway, closing fast on the taxiing aircraft.

"Herc pilot ought to put on some lights if he's gonna land on the road," said the man without a mustache.

"That goes without saying."

"I apologize, then."

There was no chance the shrieking waitress was going to reach the highway in time to warn the approaching vehicle, which wasn't slowing. The gigantic aircraft had to have been visible, even with its lights off, but the approaching headlights didn't reduce speed.

As it flashed by the truck stop, the brothers could see the perfect gleaming profile of a restored Airstream towed behind a big SUV.

A quarter mile later it was about to rear-end the Hercules, but the airplane lowered its ramp. The SUV accelerated, then drifted up the ramp and disappeared inside the aircraft. The Herc accelerated and lifted off.

The waitress watched it vanish, which didn't take long in the dark of night, then she turned and stared at something far down the highway. It was a woman, running wearily to the truck stop.

"Are you hurt? Were you raped?" the waitress shouted as she followed the haggard jogger into the restaurant.

"Would you shut up? I'm fine. I'm gonna use your phone." The jogger barked some sort of code words into the telephone, then turned on the twins. In minutes, the sky filled with helicopters. Unmarked cars arrived next. The state police came last, demanding explanations.

"Got away?" shrieked the woman who had jogged to the truck stop. She was getting some sort of update on a walkie-talkie. "It's a freaking flying football field! Half the state must have seen it!"

"Running dark," pointed out the brother with the mustache.

"Above the cloud cover, and it'll cushion the sound," his brother explained.

"Shut up!"

The brothers were questioned. They told the same story as the waitress, and when they asked to see the Feds' badges they were rebuffed. They helped themselves to more coffee. The woman jogger asked them one last time, "You sure you didn't get the numbers off that aircraft?"

"'Course we didn't. It was running dark."

"Goes without saying."

3

There were no sacred cows left. Even the highest of all honors had become polluted with the political realities of the modern age. These days the monarchy was symbolic, and when the British crown bestowed the honor of knighthood it wasn't necessarily to recognize great accomplishment. Sometimes it was, quite simply, politically expedient.

It all started with a zealous reporter on the local paper. He needed a story and there was no news to be found, so he scrounged some up. There are always problems, he was known to say, that have yet to be brought to the attention of the people.

This problem wasn't likely to stir the masses, but it filled half a front page. Newfoundland Is Knightless! the headline screamed.

It reported that not one citizen of the Canadian province of Newfoundland had received knighthood in a decade. The queen had knighted a few citizens of Ontario, a couple of English-speaking Quebecers and a handful of Albertans and British Columbians. There was even a man from the Yukon who received a knighthood a few years back for rescuing a Royal Navy ship from pack ice.

"Why have the good people of Newfoundland received no such honor?" the paper asked.

"Why No Newfie Knights?" asked the TV promos when the Newfoundland news programs latched on to the scandal.

A marine environmental study was released the next day, and anything that concerned fishing was *real* news. The business about the knights was forgotten, but the PR strategists for the royal family had noticed the uproar.

"We need to act now," explained the royal administrator of Her Majesty's public relations. "The next time the story surfaces it could create ill will."

So they tossed a knighthood at the first semiqualified candidate from Newfoundland. Good public relations were ninety percent forward thinking, after all.

To be fair to the royal administrator of Her Majesty's public relations, he couldn't possibly have foreseen the disaster that resulted from bestowing knighthood on Regeddo Tulient.

Her Majesty's army of honor arrived at the Confederation Building in St. John's, Newfoundland, in a fleet of taxis, then gathered in formation on the front steps.

Regeddo Tulient circled to the head of the formation and looked around.

"Take control, Sir Tulient," barked the voice in his ear.

"I don't know if they'll even listen to me," Tulient whined.

"They're paid to listen. You're their boss. Start acting like it."

Tulient wasn't sure he was cut out for this. He didn't like telling people what to do. He wasn't a people person. He was an archaeologist. Not even a good one. He had happened to discover, through no fault of his own, the remnants of the earliest Viking settlement in Newfoundland. To his astonishment and embarrassment, they knighted him for it.

"I don't think I deserve it," he confided to Her Majesty's representative.

"You made a great find that proved the English were on this soil a thousand years ago. It's a monumental discovery."

Actually, he had been looking for the remains of a hundred-year-old railroad spur. His expertise was in the recent history of Newfoundland and Labrador, and he later realized he had been looking for the railroad spur on the wrong side of a certain hill. The Viking find really had been a blunder. And the proof that the Vikings were "English" was based solely on a few pieces of wrought jewelry found at the site, which had originated in England. Only the British nationalists saw it as evidence that the Vikings were, somehow, English. Still, it was a boost to English and Newfoundland pride, and after a few deeply embarrassing ceremonies and a horribly uncomfortable trip to London, it was over with.

Until the knock that came on Tulient's door a few

months back, along with an opportunity that was beyond belief.

"Follow me," Regeddo Tulient stammered, and the mercenaries *did* follow him.

At the entrance to the mezzanine of the Confederation Building was the main security checkpoint. The commander of the mercenaries, a man named Hare, presented a sheaf of papers.

The chief of mezzanine security weighed the stack of forms in his hand and skimmed the first page, then looked incredulously at Tulient and Hare.

"Financial planning conference in the Gilbert wing," Hare explained tersely.

"All of you?" the security chief asked, eyeing the rows of men in badly fitting suits, skewed ties and matching vinyl briefcases.

"We're cleared. Check the paperwork."

"Heh. Yeah." The chief of security pushed them back at Hare and waved the mercenaries through.

"You—you're supposed to clear us," Tulient said, suddenly panicking. He had been expecting the security staff to catch the forged papers. He had been hoping for it.

"No, thanks. I got better things to do."

One of the mercenaries dropped his briefcase, and it clattered noisily on the steps. It burst open, and paperwork began flying away in the breeze. The man cried out and scampered wildly after the papers, and for a moment, nobody was looking at the metal detector.

Hare flicked a tiny pellet at the detector. It hit on the

inside and a tiny puff of powdered steel covered the inside panel. The metal detector began whooping, even with nobody inside of it. The security staff puzzled over it and cursed as the whooping continued and the entrance became crowded with more visitors.

"Can't you just do a pat-down search?" Hare demanded. "We're expected upstairs in two minutes."

Nobody had a clue why the metal detector was acting up. Not only was it making a racket, but also the video screen was all white. The tiny powder particles were still unnoticed on the inside of the walkway. The crowd was getting ugly, and the whooping wouldn't stop.

"Aw, just go," the security chief said, and with a wave of his hand he ushered the mercenaries into the Confederation Building. They hurried through the metal detector, looking at their watches, like all harried accountants and bureaucrats. The metal detector just kept whooping and the security chief started kicking it.

The Confederation Building had 675 rooms when it was built in the 1960s, and it had been expanded at least twice. Tulient was hoping now that they would just get lost. But no such luck. Hare knew the way. On the sixth floor of the tower, Tulient and Hare left the elevator with eight other mercenaries. More climbed the stairs on either end of the building. They took out their automatic rifles and unfolded the stocks, leaving the Wal-Mart briefcases scattered in the hall.

"Maybe we should rethink this," Tulient suggested.

Hare ignored him and pushed through the doors into

the office suite of the premier of Newfoundland and Labrador.

His secretary looked up. "Can I help you?"

"Uh, yes, well," Tulient said, but Hare was already pushing through the doors into the office of the premier.

"Hey!" said one of the honor guards, who stood outside the door to the office.

"Halt!" said the second guard.

The men in suits took away the guards' rifles. Each of the guards came to the late realization that there was real trouble brewing, and they went for their handguns, only to be bashed in the skull with the butt of their own rifles.

"What's going on here?" It was the premier himself, on his feet behind his ornate antique desk.

The mercenaries parted before him, and Tulient was deeply embarrassed to find himself the focus of everyone's attention. He had no choice but to move forward.

"Give the speech," someone shouted. Tulient had forgotten about the headset. "Use your authority. You have the right and the obligation to do what you do."

"Mr. Tulient!" the premier exclaimed.

"He knows who I am!" Tulient hissed as terror fought with embarrassment. "I'm getting out of here!" But when he turned, he found that the mercenaries had closed ranks behind him. They looked grim.

"Tulient, you can't back out now," the voice said. "Give the speech."

"Aren't you Mr. Tulient, the archaeologist?" the premier asked. Of course, the premier had been present for the knighting of one of his citizens.

"Yes, sir, Premier," Tulient squeaked. "Ahem."

"Yes?"

"Uh, I, Sir Regeddo Tulient, humble servant of Her Royal Majesty the queen of England."

The premier nodded. "Yes?"

"Under the authority and obligation vested in me by the Proclamation of the Continuation of the British Empire…"

Someone coughed.

"Get on with it," the premier said.

"—I reassert the authority of the Crown on this New Found Land for her Majesty the Queen and assume control and rank of governor of all the territories and assets of this province."

The premier squinted. "Okay, I am trying hard to understand this. Sorry if I'm a little slow, eh, but what the hell are you talking about?"

Tulient felt better now. The declaration was made.

"Under what authority again?" the premier asked.

"The Proclamation of the Continuation of the British Empire, written in 1655, provisionally altered in 1702, 1709 and 1742," Tulient lectured. Lecturing was one of his few skills. He enjoyed talking at people, at least until they started asking questions.

"Are you sure there is such a thing? I've never heard of it."

"There is," Tulient stated flatly, his ire finally elevating.

"So you're here to seize authority of Newfoundland and Labrador?" the premier continued. "Newfoundland's already subject to the queen."

"Newfoundland has illegally distanced herself from the authority of the Crown, disregarding the edicts of the Crown, ignoring its obligation to support the Crown monetarily," Tulient retorted. Oh, he was enjoying himself now.

"There's nothing illegal about it. The Crown bestowed independence upon us. You're a Canadian historian. You ought to know this."

"The Proclamation of the Continuation of the British Empire makes it illegal, regardless of the implied sanction of the Crown," Tulient explain, feeling haughty. Him! Feeling haughty! Who would ever have believed it? "As a knight of the realm of the British Empire, I have the right and the duty to reassert the authority of the Crown on this territory, effective immediately."

The premier laughed. "Is this some sort of a prankster television show?"

The mercenary commander had been patient for about as long as he could stand it. "May I shoot him, Premier?" the mercenary asked Tulient.

"I'm the premier!" responded the man behind the desk, trying to stop laughing.

"Not anymore," Tulient snapped, and he nodded to the mercenary, Hare.

Hare shot the man behind the desk, right in the chest.

The secretary screamed and security teams were running here and there and Tulient felt like Odin or some other powerful being that could look down on the chaos of mankind and feel utter calm and confidence. After all, he and only he had power over this chaos.

"You have a choice," he announced to the prim executive assistant. "You may stop screaming and go back to your desk and continue to serve the new governor of Newfoundland, or you may join the ex-premier."

The woman swallowed her scream as the body was being carried out on a woven carpet.

"The rug is ruined," she said tearfully.

"We'll get another rug," Tulient said, giving her a comforting smile. She sadly smiled back.

"He was sort of a jerk." She was almost asking Tulient for permission to rationalize being okay with her boss's murder.

"Everybody thought so," he said, although he had no idea if this was true.

The secretary sat at her desk. Tulient nodded for his soldiers to lower their automatic weapons.

All at once, he had people skills! A little confidence was all he had ever needed. He felt wonderful.

The shooting started on the lower floors, and the infrequent voice came on in his ear. He kept forgetting he wasn't alone. "You're doing quite well, Sir Tulient. Now it is time for you to show the rest of the province, and the world, that you are in control of Newfoundland and Labrador."

"I shall." He sounded different—even he could hear it. He marched with his guard to the executive security booth and addressed the entire Confederation Building on the emergency public-address system.

"This is your new governor," he announced. "I don't wish there to be any more fighting. Lay down your weapons. Your resistance will make no difference."

At that moment, as planned, the mercenaries engaged in the various gun battles put down their automatic rifles and let loose with a trio of portable machine guns that packed quite a wallop. Their opponents withered.

The survivors saw the stark contrast in their two choices. But if they did stop fighting...?

"You will be permitted to return to your jobs or simply go home," the new governor announced on the PA.

Well, that settled it. The security forces dropped their weapons as if they were red-hot. Hands went skyward in surrender, and the Canadian province of Newfoundland and Labrador became the first territory to be retaken by a twenty-first-century knight. And imagine, Tulient was thinking, I was just an archaeologist who happened to like old trains.

The reports came from all levels that the Confederation Building was taken. "Remember, I want every one of the former employees to be treated kindly," he said. "Offer all of them triple their former salary to stay on the job. Payable in U.S. dollars."

"Yes, Governor," replied Hare, who seemed to be

having as much fun as Tulient. His soldiers had reported no casualties.

"At this time," Tulient spoke into the PA again, "would the minister of finance please report to my office?"

4

Remo didn't take orders from overgrown parakeets.

"I'm not going in there," he told the bird. "It smells."

The big violet parrot screeched in his face, then jumped off his shoulder and flapped into the trees to perch on a dead branch.

"He knows the way to go. You do not." The man who spoke was tiny and ancient, an Asian dressed in a fine robe. Despite their trek through the rain forest, the Korean kimono was unsoiled, and not a single stitch of the priceless embroidery was snagged.

Remo was younger, taller and less finely dressed, wearing his standard uniform of Chinos and a T-shirt. His shoes were hand-stitched leather, made in Italy just for him. The shoes, T-shirt and Chinos were just as amazingly clean as the old man's kimono.

"What makes you think Purple Polly knows where to find Burgos?" Remo asked the old man.

"Finding the dope fiend is not the reason we came."

"It's the reason I came."

"We came to return this creature to its home, sparing it the rigors of journeying halfway around the world."

"Uh-huh," Remo said. "I have my doubts about him coming from this place, Chiun. I don't think this bird has a clue where he even is."

Chiun, the ancient Korean man, glared at Remo Williams. "He told Sarah that this is his home."

"He told me he had a program to get rich in the real-estate market with no money down," Remo said. "I didn't fall for that one, either."

The old man sniffed. "I shall accompany this creature to its home. If you would go elsewhere, and abandon your elderly, frail father to the terrors of the jungle, so be it. Remain here where it is safe."

Chiun glided away, into the vast brown remains of the dead section of the rain forest, and the bird delightedly took to the air to swoop on ahead of him. Remo sighed and followed.

Chiun was certainly elderly, but he was as frail as a cast-iron locomotive. A Master of the ancient martial art called Sinanju, the elderly Korean had trained Remo. Remo was a Master of this martial art himself. In title, at least, he was *Reigning* Master of Sinanju. Chiun had given up his Reigning Master status to become the Master of Sinanju Emeritus, which implied some sort of retirement and surrender of authority.

In practice, Remo still did what the old man told him to do a lot of the time. Chiun had an air of all-encompassing wisdom and a goatlike stubborn streak, both hard to ignore.

Remo caught up to the old man in seconds. "I couldn't let you go on alone, you being so frail and all."

"Hush," the old man said. "This is a place of death."

Remo looked around, then felt what Chiun was talking about. They had entered a vast tract of Brazilian rain forest that was recently engulfed in a cloud of superheated steam, which killed everything. From tiny gnats to the giant upper-canopy trees, the steam killed them and left their cooked remains where they had died.

It was unlike the clear-cutting of the rain forest. This forest was still there, but dead. The earth was littered with the carcasses of the forest creatures. The smell was overpowering, but the aura of the place was even more unsettling.

"It's worse than a battlefield," Remo observed. He had been on jungle battlefields. "Everything is dead here."

"Yes," Chiun said somberly.

"Everything," Remo added, sounding lame.

Chiun seemed to understand. He turned to Remo and nodded. "Exactly."

Remo and Chiun were no strangers to death. Delivering death was their job. The Masters of Sinanju were assassins—the world's preeminent assassins. Working for the U.S. government, Remo and Chiun had encountered and delivered more death than they cared to remember—but not like this. Remo had never been so immersed in the smells and stillness of so many dead things…

He tried to think of something else. He really ought to be looking for the drug lord, Burgos, not tagging after a fast-talking parrot. Burgos was intent on establishing a system of coca farms in the territory stricken by the geothermal disaster. He could easily clear narrow, miles-long strips of land among the decimated rain forest. The dead trees and the new growth would hide the cultivation, and this patch of land was so far away from everything it would be expensive to monitor from the air. Burgos would be less harassed here than in Colombia, making for better harvests.

Burgos himself was on a personal tour of the parboiled rain forest. As far as Burgos knew, his plan was still a cartel secret.

Remo and his employer were determined to nip Burgos in the bud—as long as Remo was in the vicinity anyway.

"Wouldn't it be cool if the bird *did* lead us to Burgos?" Remo suggested, trying to lighten his own mood. "Maybe that's why he brought us here."

"I think not," Chiun replied, not even breathing hard as they skimmed through the detritus of the jungle floor.

"Who can tell? Maybe he can be our crime-sniffing sidekick. You know, he points us to the bad guys and we go take them out."

"Like Rin Tin Tin?"

"Sure. But in color."

"You speak nonsense. His globe-trotting days are done, and he desires the serenity of his home."

"Is that what he told you?"

"That is what I know to be true."

After another few miles, Remo said, "I'm not so sure, Little Father. If this was my home, I don't think I'd want to come back to it."

Chiun said nothing.

The bird stopped on a dead branch high above them, peered ahead and screeched in alarm. He flapped strongly into the trees and was gone.

Remo and Chiun reached ahead with their senses. The smell of human remains now tinged the air.

Someone shouted in Spanish. Another voice spoke in a language totally foreign to Remo Williams. Far away, the bird cried out in pain.

At that, Chiun slipped away like a racing breeze, Remo close behind. They moved faster than any other man on Earth could run, and yet they didn't disturb the litter that carpeted the jungle floor.

In seconds Remo found himself at the edge of a jungle clearing. Some sort of a native village had recently stood here. The putrefying corpses of the villagers were still scattered about the village.

One of them was alive. It was an older male figure in a brief loincloth, his face smeared with symbols painted in mud. He was standing against a hut wall, bloodied from a beating.

His torturer was bloodied, too. There was a fresh gash across his face and the huge parrot was flapping around above him, screeching.

The man yanked out a handgun.

The villager's stiff-back pride melted. He collapsed at the feet of his torturer, begging him to spare the bird. The gunman delivered a quick kick to the man's temple and shot at the hyacinth macaw.

A target that big, that close, that *purple* should have been hard to miss.

But the torturer missed. Chiun had slipped across the clearing with all the speed and commotion of hawk shadow, coming alongside the torturer before the man knew Chiun was even there. The elderly Asian man snicked his long fingernails at the gun hand as the trigger was squeezed.

Chiun's fingernails were strong and sharp as the finest sword blade. They detached the hand from the wrist, and the bullet went wild.

The torturer fell down, his lifeblood pouring out, which didn't make his friends happy at all.

Remo was on the attack, skimming among the other gunmen. Armed guards had been standing by with automatic rifles ready. Remo snatched the rifles and sent them arcing away into the jungle.

Then he went for the others. Every one of them was armed, and he took their weapons away from them in whatever way was most expedient. He slapped their pistol hands, shattering their hand bones in the process.

He shoved the rifles like battering rams into the rib cages of the owners.

Chiun was helping the villager to his feet. The man cared only about the huge macaw, now standing on his wrist and nuzzling his chest. The bird became stained with the old man's blood, but neither of them cared.

"I guess they know each other," Remo observed. "How bad is he?"

"If he ceases squirming, I shall be able to inspect him. I think he shall live. I believe we have also found what you were looking for, Remo. I suggest you deal with them while I tend to him."

Chiun barked at the villager in a strange tongue and pushed the bird away. The old Korean didn't have the gentlest bedside manner.

"Notice I did not kill a single one of you," Remo announced grandly to the others, most of whom were on the ground holding some injured part of their body.

"You killed him," snarled a man hugging a broken arm.

"Not me. It was the elderly fella. You gentlemen happen to be friends of Juan Burgos?"

"No," snarled the man with the busted arm.

"Liar," Remo announced, and touched the man on the forehead. A deep pit appeared there, and the man collapsed.

"I bet one of you is Juan Burgos," Remo said. "And you're just too chickenshit to make yourself known."

Remo loved to humiliate a high-up slimeball in front of his subordinate slimeballs. They were usually too stupid and too concerned with their own masculinity to ignore the gibe.

"I am Juan Burgos and I am no coward."

Remo looked him up and down. "I believe you because you have the most expensive-looking suit and the greasiest-looking hair."

"What do you want from me?"

"Nothing. I just had to be sure I had the right piece of human trash before I put the garbage out."

"You're outnumbered. We can take you down before you know what hit you. *You* are going to be the one floating down the river."

Remo nodded agreeably. "I meet people like you all the time. You're so full of yourselves, you just can't accept it when somebody is tougher than you are. I just took away all your guns and you still think you can kick my ass."

The surviving Colombians had to admit to Remo's point.

"On the other hand, you might as well give it a shot. You've got nothing to lose. I'm not here to arrest anybody."

"Remo," Chiun called, "must you play?"

Remo turned to Chiun. The villager was looking cautiously optimistic at the turn of events. "Be done in a jiffy."

Juan Burgos decided this would be a good time to strike. He aimed for the back of Remo's head with the fist-sized rock he had sneaked into his pocket.

Remo took the rock away just before it would have

cracked his skull, then wedged it inside Burgos's mouth. The rock was bigger than the mouth. Burgos's jaw hinges crackled. It all happened too fast for Burgos or his men to react.

Burgos whimpered, prying at the rock with his fingers while Remo again made the rounds among the drug thugs. When Remo returned, Burgos saw through his agony that all his men were dying fast from new assorted wounds. It had taken the American seconds to wipe out his entire senior security staff.

Chiun spoke in a singsong. "This is taking much longer than a jiffy."

"Maybe my jiffy is longer than your jiffy."

"A jiffy is not arbitrary. It is ten-thousandths of a second, and you have used up many jiffies."

"You're making that up."

"You accuse me of telling lies? Ask Prince Howard to look this up for you in a book when we return home. Meanwhile, spare the dope fiend for the time being."

Remo pondered. "Exactly how long is a time being?"

Chiun glared at him.

"My father says you don't get to die for at least one time being," Remo informed Burgos. "Says there's something we need to see."

The villager led them through the rain forest. The drug lord, his face still wedged full of rock, walked in the middle with the macaw perched on his head. When he tried to shoo the bird, Remo chopped him in each shoulder and made his arms stop working.

They came upon a sea of putrefying animals. They were piled atop one another inside a rock formation. Fleeing from the tide of steam, they had been trapped by the rock and died together by the hundreds.

"This is not it," Chiun said, and the villager led them on, until they found more dead people, fresher than the rotting villagers.

They were with some sort of an ecological research group out of Rio de Janeiro. Their crates of equipment said they were on-site to assess the damage done by the geothermal event.

Deep in the remote Amazon rain forest was not where one expected to encounter gangland executions, but that's what happened. They were all on their faces, hands tied behind their backs, shot in the back of the head.

"You did this, I guess," Remo said.

The billionaire Colombian had blood and drool dripping from his chin. He couldn't decide what would benefit him most—lying or telling the truth. Finally he just nodded.

"It was a rhetorical question. I knew you did it."

"I shall go into the mountain with this one," Chiun announced, waving at the villager. "You may honor this man by tending to the proper burial of his slain People."

"What? Why me?" Remo asked.

"This man had benefited us in ways you cannot know," Chiun informed Remo. "The least that we can do is offer him help in this grim task."

"We?"

"I mean you."

"Okay if I delegate?" Remo asked, thumbing at the drug lord.

"I care not how it is done. We will be gone one night and half of tomorrow. Consider this free time for you to spend in whatever idleness catches your fancy—after the People are buried."

Chiun and the villager strode off into the brown jungle. The macaw cocked his head, then soared off in a different direction.

"I guess it's just you and me," Remo said.

Burgos ran as hard and as fast as he could, then slammed face-first into the ground. Something had tripped him, but Remo was now on the other side of the researchers' camp, rummaging in the supplies. He came out with a foldable shovel, which he tossed at Burgos's feet. With a couple quick pinches Burgos's arms started working again—although they still hurt as if they were on fire.

"Start digging, dope dealer."

Burgos dug until the blue sky turned orange. The flies and the mosquitoes had migrated into the lifeless zone and they swarmed him, some even wriggling past the rock into his gaping mouth. Still he labored, out of desperation, praying that he might earn a reprise from death.

The American named Remo lounged in the trees overhead, where Burgos couldn't see him. "Air's fresher up there," he explained when he came down briefly. Burgos had tried to run but made it less than twenty paces. Remo applied a little pain, making Burgos's previous pain seem inconsequential, which convinced Burgos to return to his digging.

Soon he had six shallow graves dug, but when he began hoisting the bodies into them he became sick, then choked on what came up. Remo had to descend from the tree to dislodge the rock; he achieved this by pounding Burgos on the back of the head.

"Happy vomiting," Remo said, then went back up into his tree. As night closed in, the last slain researcher was buried in the jungle soil.

Burgos was exhausted, every joint was a point of pain and he craved sleep.

"Hey, no way, Jose," Remo said, appearing out of nowhere. "That's just phase one."

Burgos was marched back to the village. The place was filled with rotting corpses.

"I suffered enough," he slurred through his dangling jaw.

"Ha. You haven't suffered nearly enough. You'll *never* suffer enough. When you add up all the misery you caused—hell, maybe Smitty's computers could come up with an answer."

"I cannot go on. Kill me."

"Too good for you."

"You can't make me do anything." Juan Burgos lay down on the ground to sleep. "What can you do to a man who wants to die?"

"Let me show you." Remo took the Colombian by the

hand and squeezed the ball of his thumb, and the pain was like nothing Burgos had ever dreamed of—as vast as the universe.

"If you work hard, you'll only get three of those an hour," Remo said.

By dawn, Burgos's strength was sapped. He flopped in the dirt and didn't get up again.

"Good riddance," Remo said. He did the last of the manual labor himself.

The macaw flapped noisily onto Remo's shoulder and regarded the finished graves. It looked sad.

"The People," the bird murmured.

Remo didn't know what to say. "The People," he agreed. How do you comfort a bereaved parrot?

"The People are coming," the bird said. "Get ready!"

CHIUN AND THE VILLAGER returned after noon, and they stood in silence before the long line of graves. The stench was diminished.

A few hundred paces away, Remo had just finished replacing the support poles holding up the roofs of the village huts—the old poles had turned to rubber when the steam came.

"I sent the drug lord upriver with all his buddies."

"Downriver," Chiun corrected him.

"Whatever. They're piranha food."

"My son, why have you repaired these buildings—and how?"

"How is easy. I jogged out of the steamed part of the

jungle and got good wood from the uncooked part," Remo explained. "Hey you, come look at this."

He took the elbow of the sole surviving villager and led him through the huts. There was a place where a body had lain since the moment it fell in the catastrophic surge of superheated steam.

Now the body was buried, and green plants were sprouting.

The villager was stunned.

"Come on." Remo guided the man to another spot, where another body had lain. It was small, the outline of a frail young person. Remo knew a skinny girl had died here—and now grass was pushing into the world where she had lain.

The villager was weeping.

"See, Chiun, this place never died. Because even when they died, their bodies were protecting some of these plants, so the plants lived."

Chiun started to say something, but Remo held up a hand. "Wait a second. Come look at this." He led Chiun and the weeping villager into the jungle for a hundred paces, where the rock formation had trapped countless jungle creatures.

The carcasses were gone and it was an oasis of green, thriving plant life.

"Slimy, but nice," Remo said.

"You cleared all this away yourself?" Chiun asked.

"Had to. Burgos dropped dead on me. Ever hear the saying that a little hard work never killed anybody?

Well, guess what? It killed Burgos. Is your skinny friend happy or sad?" Remo nodded at the villager, who was weeping and opening his arms to the sky.

"He is both. Remo, this has lifted his spirits to heaven. He sees now that the world will continue, and he hopes that he may be taken up now to be with his People."

Remo shook his head. "Hey, no way. After all the home repairs I made?"

Chiun looked strange. He looked sad. "My son, do you not understand? The village is gone. All the People were killed."

"No." Remo walked away a few steps, turned and raised one finger. Very distinctly he said, "No."

"No?" asked the villager.

"Come on."

Remo led the way this time, and the villager trotted to keep up. He reached a tree that was near the edge of the brown jungle, where the steam cloud had finally lost its murderous heat. The sky-scraping upper branches were alive with a smattering of green leaves—and a flock of noisy purple birds.

At the base of the tree was a sleeping boy no more than eight years old.

The villager looked at the tree with wide eyes, muttering to Chiun.

"It is a tree of some significance," Chiun said.

"Yeah. It's the highest one around—you can really see for miles. They're coming this way."

"Who is?" Chiun demanded.

"The new People." Remo shrugged.

The villager grabbed Remo by the biceps and looked into his eyes like he was seeing a vision. "The new People?" His English was imperfect and tremulous.

Remo smiled. "He's one." The boy was awake and looking at the three adults shyly. His gaunt face was covered with the sticky remains of fruit. Rinds and cores littered the ground.

"Who is he?" the villager demanded.

"He's one of the People," Remo said. "They're all over the place. They're survivors, like you. There must have been twenty villages affected by the catastrophe. This kid was out wandering the jungle all by himself, eating gross steamed vegetables. Everybody he ever knew is dead."

Chiun held up his hand, and no one spoke. Remo heard what Chiun was hearing—other voices, fearful and hopeful, coming closer. "Remo, you did this?" Chiun asked.

"Not me. It was the bird. He's been out looking for them all night. He told them to head for the tree with the purple parrots."

Soon the newcomers began to straggle, singly or in pairs, out of the forest, converging on the tree of the purple parrots. They were mostly young adults, some children, and they all looked like hell. They were filthy, naked, covered in wounds, their arms and legs splotched with bruises. They gathered about the base of the tree, not sure what to expect.

"Lunch is on me." Remo pulled bags of supplies out of the bushes, all salvaged from the researchers' camp. The people were soon opening packages of hermetically sealed beef stew and chop suey. "Later you folks can help yourself to whatever's on the Burgos boat—it's a few miles upriver. Or maybe downriver. That way, whatever it is. Hey, look, everyone! Spam!" He held up a box of meat cans.

The villager grabbed the food from Remo's hands and took it to the newcomers. More were coming out of the trees, all of them shell-shocked victims of a catastrophe that they had never expected and didn't understand.

The villager was crying, but now they were clearly tears of joy. He deftly used the can key to open the lunch meat and present the food to the famished survivors. He laughed as he cried, and he gave words of encouragement to each and every one of them. He busied about them with more stocks from the supply packs. He spooned food into the mouth of a woman whose fingers were worn raw from whatever she had endured.

The young boy, the first to arrive at the tree, ate just a little of the new food, then followed on the heels of the villager, helping him feed the People. One last survivor stumbled out of the trees, his face shrunken. The villager, and others, raced to him, took hold of him as he stumbled and carried him to the tree. Soon he was eating and looking stronger by the minute.

"This is a pretty nice picnic, huh?" Remo asked.

Chiun was detached and silent, but not in his usual obstinate way. Remo didn't know what to make of it.

"You have accomplished something worthy of the scrolls, Remo Williams," Chiun said at last.

"What are you talking about? I just cleaned up the corpses."

"You have restored the People," Chiun said.

"That was his doing," Remo said, pointing at one of the purple parrots that was diving on them. It landed on the ground and waddled to Remo and Chiun.

"He rounded them all up," Remo explained.

"Rounded them all up," agreed the macaw.

"You do not know what have you done," said the villager, coming to them with the boy at his heals. "This be way the People came to be—the *old* People."

"Talk to the bird."

The villager ignored the bird and wrenched the difficult English tongue from his brain with great intensity. "Now I know why all have I been made to do. I lived when all died so to guide *new* People—just as did one who was Caretaker lifetimes in the past. This the tree where bird hatched. This the tree where little father died fetching the great gift for me—the egg of purple bird. It all comes to a circle you closed."

Remo was getting uncomfortable. "Really, all I did was cleanup. I just wanted to bring back some green. And fetch the feedbags. Janitorial work and gardening and grocery shopping."

"You have remade the People and made me the Caretaker again."

"Bird," Remo said, "tell 'em it was your idea."

"Trail mix!" the bird demanded.

"Remo," Chiun said quietly in Korean, "accept graciously this high and deserved praise."

"I don't deserve this. I didn't save these People."

The Caretaker nodded, and nodding still he looked back at the quiet gathering of survivors, who had eaten well for the first time since the catastrophe. They were resting, finally abandoning the fear that tomorrow would offer them only continuing uncertainty.

"There is a story of one named Qetzeel," the Caretaker began.

"You don't say?" Remo said, then felt a sharp pain in his elbow. Chiun was holding it, but listening to the Caretaker attentively.

"Qetzeel is the Unmaker, the Destroyer," the Caretaker continued.

Remo felt the blood trickle like ice water down his spine.

"Qetzeel is also the maker of the new world. When he destroys, he cleanses the world and makes it ready for rebirth. Friend, you have fostered the rebirth of the People through your symbol of new life."

"Hey, buddy, get it straight," Remo said. "I'm just the manual labor. I didn't destroy your people, and I didn't make the new ones. Talk to the damn bird."

Chiun was aghast, but strangely the Caretaker was not shocked. He still wore his smile of contentment, as if everything was once again right in his world.

Remo was out of there.

5

The pilot was waiting for them up—or down—river, but he was surprised to see them again.

"I left a voice mail for your supervisor and told him I thought you was dade." He was from Alabama and had found a market for his pilot services in the less accessible reaches of the Amazon River basin in Brazil. When Americans came here and had a reason to get into the rain forest—usually university researchers and such—they were drawn to the American-speaking pilot. He charged a premium for friendliness.

Remo didn't want friendliness or any other kind of social interaction.

The pilot was sitting on the pontoon of his water-landing helicopter and watching them come. The silence was uncomfortable. These two seemed mad at each other. The pilot tried hard to lighten the mood. "But you ain't dade!"

"No. We are not." The dark-haired younger fellow was the grumpy sort. The old Far Eastern man was off in his own world, but a young white fellow had no business being so off-putting.

"You all ready to head on home?"

"Yes." The young man stepped off the shore onto the pontoon—no small thing, since the helicopter had drifted eight feet or more out into the sluggish waters of the small Amazon tributary.

"Man alive, you a track star or something?"

Then the old man, who had to be in his nineties, made the same leap, as if it were nothing. The pilot decided his eyes were playing tricks and he had to be a lot closer to the bank than he thought.

"Let's go," the young one griped. He was twisting his hands as if he was nervous or mad or something. The man had wrists as fat as a skinny girl's leg. He slipped into the rear of the helicopter. They moved smooth, those two. The chopper wasn't exactly stable on the water and usually it was rocking and rolling when passengers came aboard.

"I'll just get the line," the pilot said.

The old man waved his hand at the taut cable, and the cable snapped with a twang. The old man got in; the pilot concluded the geezer had to have been packing some sort of Ginsu knife up his sleeve.

There was definitely more to these guys than met the eye.

"Find what you was looking for?" the pilot asked as he went through the start-up routine.

Nobody answered. The pilot shut up and took off.

"You were obstinate and childish. I tire of your tirades." Chiun spoke in Korean, the one language besides English in which Remo was fluent.

"I'm tired of being the brunt of everybody's myths and legends. Did you set me up for that, Chiun? Were you trying to teach me some god-awful lesson?"

"I set nothing up."

"Seems like everything fell right into place."

"Nothing fell into anything. I am not playing puppeteer."

"What were you doing on that mountain all night?"

Chiun sighed. He was looking out the windows, watching the jungle below them and the rotors above. One of the rotors had a slight vibration that was probably harmless, but Chiun intended to monitor it carefully. "I went with the Caretaker to see the place from which he spoke to Sa Mangsang. You recognized his voice, I assume?"

Remo had recognized the voice of the Caretaker. It had been the voice he heard chanting, arising from the living rock of a basalt island in the Pacific Ocean. It had been the Caretaker's lullaby to an elder god, which lulled the great being and helped Remo and Chiun send Sa Mangsang back into his comatose state.

If they had not done so—if Sa Mangsang had gained sufficient strength to exert his will over Remo—then the world would not be carrying on in its typical, heedless fashion. In fact, there might not have been a world left. Remo pondered for a moment how the Caretaker's voice was heard a half-world away. He seriously doubted this fellow had been vacationing in the South Pacific lately.

Then he mentally waved away the thought. It was just one more minor mystery. He'd had enough of all mysteries, great and small. He wanted to think about earthly things.

Remo and Chiun had gone to the island, newly risen from the ocean and serving as the apex of a drain in the ocean floor. Somehow, Sa Mangsang had opened a channel for the water into the mantle of the earth. The water became superheated and flowed back to the surface, exploding out of the earth's crust in the form of miles-high geysers of boiling steam. The geysers had come from the ocean near the Hawaiian Islands and from a place in the Rocky Mountains. And it had erupted from the Amazon jungle, where it killed every living thing for miles around it.

But these geysers were only the side effect. Two geysers also formed in the Antarctic, where the millions of gallons of water froze—and stayed. In its solidified form, it didn't return to the oceans like the water from the other geysers. It just kept piling up as more and more ice. Sa Mangsang, true to his prophecy, was draining the oceans dry.

Desperate scientists had come up with a hundred different eventual outcomes—none of them good. Some said that Earth would shift in its orbit. Some said the climate would become radically unstable. Some said the weight of the ice would build up to such a degree it would impact the actual drifting of the continental tectonic plates.

Whatever the outcome was, they concluded that the human race would not be around to see it all happen. Climate extremes would have wiped out everybody soon enough.

There was more to the looming catastrophe, of which the world knew nothing. Sa Mangsang would feed off the "sensitive" people of the world, consuming them for the vital nutrients their specially tuned minds gave him.

Remo might have been used as the delivery boy. If Sa Mangsang had succeeded in holding Remo in his thrall… But Sa Mangsang failed—with the help of the gentle chant of a man in a cave in the Amazon rain forest.

"You're right," Remo said. "I should have thanked the Caretaker. If it weren't for his chanting, Sa Mangsang would have turned me into his gopher."

Chiun said, "On the mountain, the Caretaker showed me the cave where his legend is engraved. There was a speaking tube there. I did not know of its existence."

Remo wanted to stay irritated, but he was also curious. "How'd the bird fit into all of it?"

"The bird was a gift to the Caretaker from his grandfather, who mentored him. The grandfather fetched the egg for his protégé and was killed from the fall. The bird hatched, and the people believed it was the reincarnation of the dead Caretaker."

"Maybe he's in there, but he's not alone. When he

was talking sense, the bird spoke like the head of a committee. What about the dirty ditties?"

The parrot had displayed a vast repertoire of bawdy limericks—in English.

"The legacy of an anthropologist who lived with the People many years ago."

Remo nodded absently. "You know I didn't fulfill any stupid prophecy."

"I know nothing of the kind."

"Look, I was bored. I had no clue how long you were going to be hiking the foothills. Call me a neat freak—I just wanted to tidy up the place. When I started seeing all the greenery under the bodies, it made me feel good. After the drug lord ran out of steam, I buried the rest of the villagers and buried all the dead animals. I had to stand under a waterfall for an hour to get the smell off."

Chiun nodded. "You should have stood under it for two hours."

"The point is, I was just passing the time."

"What of the new People?"

"That was a hundred percent the bird's doing. I found him flapping around the tree about midmorning with the kid. The bird told me he had more People on their way. Of course, you can't put faith in what the bird says, so I climbed up the tree and watched him until I spotted more People. He was leading them to the tree where the boy was. I figured I might as well fix up the village, feed the kid, get the supplies."

"Restore the village for the new People," Chiun concluded.

"So call me Suzy Homemaker. But don't call me Qetzeel the Destroyer."

"I did not call you Qetzeel."

"You believed the old man."

"The Caretaker's faith served him well, Suzy. Why should I not believe what he believes? He has seen the legend of his creation reenacted before his eyes. The People are made anew. They were gathered together around the only survivor, the Caretaker, and this is precisely how the People came into being in their previous incarnation. And in the incarnation before that."

Remo saw green under the helicopter. It went off in every direction. The jungle was huge. But when they were on the ground, in the midst of the dead zone, it had felt like the entire world was dead.

"What do you mean, the time before that?" he asked suddenly. "You mean this happens over and over?"

Chiun was still staring out the window. "That is the legend of the People."

"And the Caretaker is always the one who survives to reform the new People?"

Chiun nodded. "So the legend says. I know not if it is true. I do not know what catastrophe comes to slay the people—if it is not always Sa Mangsang."

Remo became angry again. "So why didn't you tell the Caretaker to move the damn People somewhere else? Obviously, that patch of real estate ain't safe. Maybe if they moved away from the cave with the speaking tube, they wouldn't get wiped out over and over."

Chiun considered that. "The Caretaker's role is not to care for the People, Remo. Even the man himself does not realize the scope of his destiny. He is the Caretaker of Sa Mangsang. He lives to do what this man did—speak to Sa Mangsang—or to train a protégé to carry on for him. The People's purpose is to sustain the lineage of Caretakers."

Remo chewed on that and he didn't like the taste of it. "So, we just set those People up to die?"

"Not this generation, or the next, but some generation in the future."

"That stinks. They're pawns. They ought to be told what they're being used for."

"Used by whom?"

"I don't know," Remo said. "Somebody."

"And if there were no People?" Chiun asked. "There would be no Caretaker. If there was no Caretaker, there would have been no voice to lull Sa Mangsang into slumber. Where would the world be, Remo, if not for this band of orphans adopted into this special purpose?"

Remo twisted his fists and clenched his lips. "Dammit! I hate all this crap. What's it supposed to mean? I'm just like one of the People, Chiun?"

"I did not say this," Chiun replied.

"I'm an orphan. I'm destined to serve some great purpose and fulfill some old-time prophecy. I'm just like the People, huh? Dammit all to hell, what's it take for a guy to get a little bit of control over his own life?"

Chiun frowned. "Few men control their own destiny."

"But most people have real-world problems. They don't go running around having their sailboat blown off course by Zeus in heaven. Or whatever high-and-mighty deity of the day is meddling in my affairs."

Chiun pointed out, "But look at the greatness such destiny has bestowed upon you, Remo. You have achieved what no other white man before you ever achieved—you are blessed with the mastery of the art of Sinanju. It is a rare and precious gift."

"Yeah."

"You doubt this?" Chiun demanded.

"I'm just wondering what life would have been like if I hadn't been the answer to everybody's myths and expectations." Remo saw the glimmer of an outpost of civilization in the distance. "What if I'd had a regular life?"

"Fah!" Chiun dismissed it with a wave. "You would be dead. Or obese and filthy."

"But I'd be master of my own destiny."

"You would be master of a hovel on a rank street in the city of New Jersey. You would doubtless be cuckolded by your strident wife and disdained by your belligerent children. You would spend your days directing traffic on street corners and your weekends watching sports programs on the television."

"Sounds okay."

"It sounds repulsive. You would probably shoot yourself in the head with a clumsy firearm out of sheer boredom."

"Maybe."

"You would never have found your sire. You would never have known you were linked by blood to the Sun On Jo people. Thus, you would never have known that you are blessed with the greatness of the glorious lineage of Sinanju. Blood much polluted by other strains of humanity, yes, but still tinged with a measure of excellence."

Remo felt the world cloud his thoughts. "Fate *did* have it in for me."

Chiun looked out the window, watching the ugly Brazilian outpost loom large underneath them.

6

"Tulient is using banks, credit cards, international credit lines, all for the purpose of converting any and all Canadian currency in the province to U.S. dollars. The Canadian government is taking measures to keep the value of the Canadian dollar stable." The old man sat back in his creaking chair, but didn't take his eyes off the vivid computer display under the glass top of his desk. "He's creating a scarcity of Canadian dollars inside Newfoundland and Labrador."

The younger man in a nearby desk was looking at his own screen, which was elevated from the onyx surface. "What's his purpose? He's taking huge losses in the process." The man looked up. "I suppose he isn't the one losing the money on the exchange."

"The provincial government, the people of Newfoundland, they're taking financial losses," agreed the old man sourly. "However, I believe it is the Canadian government that will lose in the end. It won't risk allowing its dollar to become destabilized, so there is no real incentive for him to *not* make the exchange. And in the end, the province ends up with a currency that the federal government of Canada cannot control."

The young man nodded. He understood the concept, but he still wasn't sure about the *why* of it all. He should have been able to wrap his mind around it. His expertise was in understanding the motives of criminals, terrorists, politicians and bureaucratic systems. It was what he was trained for —and what he was born to do.

Mark Howard had been regarded as a brilliant, if quirky, investigator for the U.S. Central Intelligence Agency. A few years ago he received an order, from the President of the United States, no less, to move into a new position. Now he was the assistant to the director of Folcroft Sanitarium, a private convalescent hospital in Rye, New York. He was also assistant to the director of a highly classified government agency known as CURE.

The director of Folcroft, and CURE, was the old, sour man at the next desk.

Harold W. Smith had also been recruited from the CIA to CURE by a U.S. President, but it had been long before Mark Howard. It was decades ago, when a young and idealistic President had come to the shocking revelation that the U.S. was doomed. The Constitution of the United States, which promised freedom and due process to every crook and killer, tied the hands of those who would enforce the laws of the land. For every murderer who got jail time, another killer was set free by the machinations of a clever attorney. For every rapist who served hard time there was another who spent a few token years behind bars and then walked out into the streets again, free to resume his predatory ways.

The solution was easy enough to formulate. Create a law-enforcement agency that operated beyond the law, just as the criminals operated.

For that young President, it was a pill he almost could not swallow. When he finally decided to take this drastic step, he knew the new agency would need an exceptional individual to organize and manage it. It would have to be a man of unquestioned loyalty—and maybe someone a little lacking in imagination. Someone with a ramrod sense of duty to his country.

Harold W. Smith was ideal. He was retired from the CIA after an oddly brilliant career, and he was about to take on the role of a college professor. Countless university students didn't know how lucky they were to miss being his student.

Smith's ingrained dedication to his country would not allow him to refuse a request from the President. CURE was formed, using Folcroft Sanitarium as its cover. The President who founded the organization was gunned down in a motorcade.

CURE continued. Smith and Conrad MacCleary, Smith's friend from the CIA, were the sole employees of the secret organization. A large staff of data-gatherers and data processors worked in the sanitarium and around the world. They never knew they actually worked for CURE.

CURE channeled information in all directions, digging up evidence the police were not allowed to find, fouling organized crime systems, monitoring international intelligence agencies that the CIA couldn't tap into for one reason or another. CURE made a dent, but not a big one.

It became clear that CURE needed to do more than gather information—it needed an enforcement arm. It needed an assassin.

Harold W. Smith was still running the show. Conrad MacCleary? He was long gone. For decades Smith managed the agency alone. Smith still thought of Mark Howard as the new man.

Mark Howard was watching a news feed from one of the global news networks. They were interviewing Americans on the streets of an unnamed city.

"They took over a bunch of dogs?" asked a woman in a business pantsuit.

"Not the breed," answered the reporter. "There's a province of Canada that's named Newfoundland. It's been taken over in a bloody coup."

The woman was shocked. "Did they hurt any of the dogs?"

"Thank you," the reporter said, then walked to another figure on the city street. He asked an elderly man, obviously well-to-do, about the troubles up north in Newfoundland and Labrador.

"Newfoundland is up north?"

"It's a Canadian province."

"How come I've never heard of it?"

"I couldn't say, sir," the reporter replied. "Have you ever heard of Saskatchewan?"

"New kind of wheat bread, right? No carbohydrates, comes with a free pedometer baked into every loaf."

Finally the reporter found a black, blue-collar worker in his sixties, his face a mask of gray grizzled beard. "Of course I've heard of it, son. I can't understand it though. Makes no sense, even from a crazy man's way of lookin' at it. Why take over Newfoundland? What's in Newfoundland? It's like trying to take over the Falklands. What's the point?"

"I wish I knew the answer to that one," Howard said.

"I may have an idea." Smith was scanning a series of stacked on-screen windows one after another. "I think I've found the Proclamation of the Continuation of the British Empire."

Howard frowned. He had already looked for it, combing a hundred intelligence systems and online libraries. How had he missed it?

Smith looked up at him. "It was just posted," he explained. "It's a new message on alt.history.british.medieval."

"So where did it come from? Why couldn't I locate it?"

Smith regarded the screen like he would have looked at a bitter piece of fruit he had just been forced to spit out. "It came from many places and many times."

7

"Not today," Remo Williams said. "I have a headache."

"Liar!" Chiun spit.

"Okay, I made up the part about the headache. I'm just not in the mood for a history lesson," Remo said to Mark Howard. "I've had enough tall tales in the past couple of days."

"They were not tall tales," Chiun responded. "They were brief, accurate and compact with relevance—but it takes a wise man to see it."

They were in the office, in uncomfortable and ancient chairs that had served Harold Smith's office forever. With the chairs, an equally old couch and the two desks, the office was tight. Smith would return momentarily.

"When you moving back to the other office, Junior?" Remo asked.

Mark was tapping at his keyboard. "We work pretty well together in here."

"You wouldn't want some privacy?"

"Not really."

"You've got a girlfriend, you know."

Mark didn't look up. "I do know that, thanks, Remo. But I don't plan on having make-out sessions while working. So it's okay sharing an office with Dr. Smith."

"You could use some more space in here, if that's the plan long-term. There's nobody next door. Why not break out the wall?"

"We'll see."

"Hush," Chiun said.

"I could do it while we're waiting."

"You speak to hear yourself talk," Chiun admonished.

"Shutting up now."

Remo watched the tides batter the shore of Long Island Sound. He listened to Mark Howard tapping his keys and making small sounds when he found something of interest.

"Huh. You know what? I'm missing that idiot bird. He was rude, but at least he was interesting. Maybe I'll buy Smitty a big bird for Christmas. Bring a little life into this room."

"Emperor Smith has no desire for a big bird," Chiun said. It was his habit to refer to the CURE director as Emperor. Masters of Sinanju hired out their services only to state leaders with true power. Smith qualified easily—he wielded great influence around the globe, although almost no one was aware of it. Still, the title of "Director" was insufficient in Chiun's eyes.

"Feel like I'm waiting at the dentist's office," Remo complained, but even then he heard Smith's footsteps coming through the reception area.

"Remo," Smith said sourly. "Chiun."

The door opened again before it had closed. The late arrival was Sarah Slate, newest addition to the CURE staff, and the girlfriend of Mark Howard. In contrast to Smith, Sarah gave Remo a smile. She always gave him a smile, although they rubbed each other the wrong way. She placed her hand gently on the narrow shoulders of the ancient Korean man. It was the kind of intimate touch that Remo still couldn't get used to. Chiun just didn't take to people like he took to Sarah Slate.

Still, everybody seemed to take to Sarah. She was annoyingly likable. Remo had to admit he had some affection for her—above and beyond his appreciation for the fact that she had saved his life. Above and beyond the fact that she was as hot as a tamale and as cute as a button.

"How was the bird?"

"He is at home with his People, healthy and content," Chiun reported. "His leg gives him no more trouble."

"You've heard about the business in Newfoundland?" Smith asked when Sarah had departed.

"Yawn. I mean yes," Remo said. "Doesn't sound like a threat to U.S. security."

"The Newfoundland coup is no threat," Smith agreed. "The next coup attempt might be."

"Is there another one?"

"Not yet."

"Then call me."

"Sit down and listen," Chiun admonished. "The Emperor clearly has more to say."

"Thank you, Master Chiun," Smith said. "The man who occupies the capital building in Newfoundland is claiming his actions are legal, based on a document called the Proclamation of the Continuation of the British Empire."

"I must have slept that day in history class," Remo said. "I've never heard of it."

"You're not alone. Nobody heard of the proclamation until today, when it was posted on an Internet Usenet group. The proclamation uses all original, authentic source material, but combines them in unorthodox and creative ways. They've got several royal documents in here, dating from 1655 through the middle eighteenth century. They were mostly put in place to strengthen the authority of the British Crown by giving more incentive to its field agents. Essentially, it bestows salvage rights on colonies whose control has slipped from England's hand—either through negotiated treaty or revolt."

"Snore."

"It gives this authority only to the knights of the realm and former colonial governors. Theoretically, a man who has a knighthood is too honorable to abuse his power."

Remo shook his head. "Yeah, right. So they give some knight the authority to take back a piece of real estate that England stole from somebody else in the first place?"

"They then have the right of taxation and authority in the restored colony," Smith added.

"They're sanctioned despots," Mark Howard explained. "Remember, these rules were established when England was wrestling with all kinds of colonial problems—not the least of which was the developing crisis in North America."

"So what?" Remo said. "The 1700s were a long time ago—I know it because I saw it on TV."

"But this morning, Sir Regeddo Tulient staged a takeover of the Newfoundland government seat, called the Confederation Building, and used the proclamation as justification for it," Mark Howard said. "He claims his knighthood makes it his right and duty to restore the lost holdings of the British Empire."

Remo stared at Mark Howard. "Don't tell me people are buying into that load of bulldookey."

"Not exactly," Mark Howard said.

"But the situation is politically delicate," Harold W. Smith added.

Remo got to his feet. "Fine. I'll handle it delicately. Where should I mount his head?"

"Sit down," Chiun said.

"Tulient's mercenaries killed fewer than a dozen security staff—plus the former premier of Newfoundland and Labrador," Smith explained. "They hired back most of the staff at triple wages, paying U.S. dollars. They're promising business-as-usual in St. John's and throughout the provinces if the people accept the new leadership."

"So?" Remo demanded.

"So, we have a man who has received a high honor from the queen of England. We have hundreds of Canadian citizens. We have a relatively peaceful assumption of power, and we have a rationale that smells almost credible."

"To take out Tulient you would have to risk Canadian lives, humiliate a British knight and violate what some would consider a legal warrant."

Remo pantomimed a duck quacking. "Do you want us in Newfoundland or not?"

"Not," Smith said carefully, "as of yet."

"Can I go back to my room?"

"Uh. Hem. There's another matter I must bring up."

There was an awkward silence.

"Well?" he said.

"Be patient," Chiun said quietly.

"Why?"

"Can you not see that the Emperor wishes to discuss a matter of some embarrassment?"

"Embarrassing to him?"

"More likely you."

"It's not a problem of embarrassing someone," Smith said.

"Why me?" Remo demanded.

"The logical assumption is that it has to do with your hygiene," Chiun pointed out.

"There's nothing wrong with my hygiene," Remo told Smith.

"I didn't say there was," Smith said.

"Also likely, your alley-dweller attire," Chiun suggested. "Just a conjecture."

"It's the Technicolor kimonos that get people staring," Remo countered.

"Gawking rabble are of no consequence. The unprofessional image you present reflects badly on the Emperor."

Harold W. Smith could have launched into a lengthy argument with just about everything Chiun had just said. The old Master did attract attention in his brilliant Korean robes, and Smith preferred Remo's nondescript attire because, obviously, he didn't want any sort of attention whatsoever directed toward CURE activities.

There was a time when Smith enforced the anonymity of CURE to a harsh degree, but the truth was that such activities, performed by two such, well, personalities, could not stay invisible. In the past twenty years this became all the more difficult as the rest of the world closed in on Harold W. Smith in terms of his ability to collect and archive information from around the world.

Now his efforts were focused solidly on managing the inevitable exposure of CURE's activities. The real threat was not about the information being gathered, but about what information was gathered by whom—and how it was analyzed for patterns. The true risk to CURE was that someone might come to realize, from circumstantial evidence, that some sort of an extraordinary and covert force was at work on behalf of the United States.

It had happened before.

How close these investigators would get to learning any dangerous truths about CURE would be a testament to the spin doctoring of the intelligence by Smith and his assistant, Mark Howard.

On that note, he had an issue to address with the Master of Sinanju. Emeritus.

"Master Chiun, I'm afraid I must discuss this problem with you directly."

Chiun went blank. Before the ancient Korean could leap to a hundred conclusions, Smith pushed on. "There is a security issue caused by your mode of dress, as we have discussed in the past."

Chiun seethed—which was a good sign, actually, Smith considered. The old Master could have simply dismissed the subject and refused to discuss it. A delay tactic like that could stall the issue for weeks. On the other hand, he could rebel rancorously, lashing out at everyone around him and causing CURE's performance to suffer.

"Master Chiun, the Korean robes you wear are beautiful and fine," Smith said.

"Of course they are, Emperor." Chiun was stiff and formal. "The great assassins of Sinanju dress in attire befitting their station—recent draftees notwithstanding."

"Such finery is not necessary," Smith pointed out.

"It is," Chiun said, putting great weight into each word. "When one serves an Emperor, when one serves the leader of the world's most potent nation, when one is honored to hold the position of preeminent court appointee of such a ruler, then one must project the image of grace and cultivation that reflects best upon the Emperor."

Remo shifted in his chair, forcing his lips to stay shut.

Smith nodded. He was not an emperor and he did not see himself as the true leader of the United States, but he had long ago given up any serious hopes of convincing Chiun of these things. "And yet, your traditional robes, as fine as they are, compromise your abilities to serve your leader," Smith said carefully.

Chiun simmered. Remo stopped wriggling.

Smith knew what he was doing. Casting doubt on Chiun's effectiveness risked insulting the old Master, but it might breach his stubborn mind-set. "You are surely unique, Master Chiun," Smith said almost casually. "You're too special for most of the world. How can lesser men of any nation help but notice a personage such as yourself?"

Smith folded his hands and tried to remain neutral, inside and out. Had he laid it on thick enough? Had he laid it on too thick?

Chiun said just one word. "Unique."

"Yes."

"If I dressed in the styles of the teeming rabble, then I would not be subject to such insults?"

"I meant no insult."

"A Western double-breasted suit of machine-woven wool is common. Would this suffice?"

"Certainly."

"Golf shirts and pleated trousers and loafers of

leather. This is the garment of the casual business. Is this common enough?"

"That would be perfectly accept—"

"Shirts of the Hawaiian islanders are today often seen in any airport in the world, worn by all races of people who are not Hawaiian. Is such a garment common enough that it would pass muster? I use this only as an example."

Smith was trying to figure out where this was headed. "Hawaiian shirts are acceptably common."

"Perspiration garments?"

"Sweatshirts would be fine."

"Denim slacks? Even those that are obscenely low-cut in the front?"

Smith could see Remo biting his lips to keep them closed. "Jeans are common garments, of course."

"Turtleneck sweaters?" Chiun looked at Smith sharply. "What of them?"

Smith's mind was racing. Was Chiun about to trip him up? Why was the old Master talking about turtleneck sweaters, of all things? Mark Howard saw Smith's trepidation and came to the rescue.

"I'm not sure if they are in style," Howard pointed out. "I get this men's lifestyles magazine. I'm no fashion buff, you know, but I think it said turtlenecks are out."

"And yet, they are always about," Chiun said. "Such is the ignorance of the world that does buff fashionably. They rediscover the cut of dress that was discarded only five years before. There are always those who adjust too slowly, and thus, one sees them as commonplace at all times."

Smith said somberly, "Master Chiun, I would have no objections to you wearing turtleneck sweaters, regardless of the current fashion."

"Pah! They are hideous!"

Smith gave a rehearsed, helpless looking gesture. "There must be some middle ground that we can reach."

Chiun rested a baleful glare on the window behind Smith. "I shall carefully consider what we have discussed today, Emperor."

Chiun folded his hands and adopted a pleasant expression that said he was waiting for the next topic of conversation. As if prompted by the old Master, Smith and Howard were both alerted by small sounds from their computers and began concentrating intensely on the displays.

"Well, I can see you're busy guys," Remo said. Watching Cybernerd Senior and his young intern play with their computers was almost as bad as trying to work a computer himself. "We'll be going."

Smith didn't look up. "To Ayounde."

"What's Ayounde?"

"Please hurry. We just might have time to avert another crisis."

"In Ayounde?" Remo asked, as he was heading for the door.

"Come, simpleton!" Chiun held Remo's elbow suddenly, and Remo yelped.

8

When they were on the Africa-bound airplane, Remo received a brief lecture on Ayounde. He wasn't listening. He was still sore at the old Master.

"Master Chan-Su Hom worked for the sultans of Ayounde on three occasions," Chiun said. "This is something you should know."

"I know about Master Chan-Su Hom. I've read everything in the scrolls about him," Remo said. "I don't remember any mention of him working for Ayounde. I remember him working for the Sultanate of Bueni in the armpit of Africa."

"Bueni was its name once."

Remo thought he'd made a pretty incisive connection, but Chiun dismissed it without further comment. That made Remo more sore.

"The sultans in those days used gold with extravagance in their own homes but not for purchasing their own security," Chiun said. "Chan-Su Hom describes a palace with gold-gilt chairs, gold eating utensils and gold oil lanterns. But when the sultan hired Master Hom, he wanted to bargain in the basement. He paid Master Hom for the assassination of just one man, when he knew that three men plotted against him."

Chiun looked purposefully at Remo. Remo was listening. They were in an aircraft for the next eight hours and it wasn't as if he had anywhere else to go. He might as well show interest, although he knew the history of Master Chan-Su Hom.

Chiun continued. "The man that Master Hom assassinated for the sultan was the sultan's own brother, who plotted fiercely to overthrow him and take his riches and wives. His companions in the plot were two of the sultan's uncles. Of course, the two uncles continued their plot once the brother was dead. So Master Hom was again hired by the sultan, but for the assassination of just one of the uncles. The sultan's desire to hold on to his gold was so strong that he could not bear to spend more than was necessary—and not even that."

"But he had to eventually," Remo said. "Didn't Master Hom go back again?"

Chiun's nodded. "The sultan perceived his folly early enough. He again summoned Master Hom. Hom had been expecting more employment in the sultanate, by the sultan or his usurper, and was quick to respond. The sultan was not pleased when Chan-Su Hom announced his fee was increased."

"A little told-you-so toll?" Remo asked.

"An inconvenience premium. So Chan-Su Hom came

and left three times when he could have easily performed all three assassinations on his first visit."

"But it wasn't inconvenient. You just told me Master Su Hom was in the vicinity."

"But the sultan was not told that."

Remo considered it. "The way we get shuttled all over the planet doing Smith's tricks, we should get all kinds of inconvenience fees."

"It was the beginning of the end for the sultanate. Its power decreased. The sultans of Ayounde never learned the lesson of gold. Gold is not for gilding chairs. It is for increasing one's power."

"We have gilt chairs," Remo said, picturing at least one ornate golden throne in the house in the Village of Sinanju, which was the ancestral home of the Masters in what was now North Korea. It was Remo's house now, according to tradition. "I mean, I have a gilt chair."

"How is your elbow?" Chiun asked.

Remo scowled. "Still hurts. What did you do that for, Chiun?"

But Chiun said nothing, his eyes fixed out the window of the aircraft, where the wing flexed in the rush of air. Chiun didn't trust aircraft wings. Aircraft wings, he knew, could come off at any moment.

AYOUNDE'S ROYAL FAMILY lost control of the nation and the palace was sacked, although the dynasty continued as just one of many warlord territories. The former ruling family fought the slave traders and the pirates of the eighteenth century. They also fought the Europeans who wanted to help protect them from the pirates and slave traders—and from their own paganism. The warlords were demolished and scattered, and Ayounde was colonized. Half the country became a British protectorate in 1888, and the family that ruled the nation was related distantly to the sultan's lineage of previous centuries. The other half of the nation became a French territory. The French claimed they had purchased their joint of land legally from a former warlord who was its rightful proprietor. The British weren't willing to fight the French over the claim. Ayounde wasn't worth much to either of them.

It wasn't until 1964 that the British finally granted British Ayounde her independence. The French followed suit, and the nation of Ayounde became reunited and independent. New oil reserves were discovered in Ayounde in the late 1960s, and the government was stable enough to make use of the resource. The country prospered, instituted a gradual process of democratization and became one of the most livable nations in Africa— which wasn't known for having livable nations. This annoyed the British, who remembered that Ayounde had been theirs. The oil profits should be going to Britain. By rights. But there was nothing to be done about it now.

Until Sir Michele Rilli got a call to perform his duty as a member of an Order of the Green Garter of England.

The cargo ship *Giancarlo* eased up to the cargo dock without fanfare. The Ayounde customs agent was the only individual in the entire nation who knew about the surprise visit by the one and only Sir Michele Rilli. The agent was sworn to secrecy.

"So wonderful to meet with you, Sir Rilli!" He pumped Rilli's hand energetically. "I have watched your performances time and again on the television."

"Yes, I'm sure you have."

"The Monaco GP last year was a real nail-biter, sir! But we knew you would be victorious in the end. My good woman and I, we knew you would win even if all our friends and neighbors hooted and rooted for the Cobbler driver."

Sir Michele Rilli bristled at the mention of Kenneth Cobbler. Cobbler had been nipping at Rilli's heels throughout the entire racing season last year. The Australian Grand Prix. The Malaysian Grand Prix. Race after race, Rilli won by the skin of his teeth, Cobbler sticking like glue to his derriere.

Then, a disaster in Spain. A bent rim. A two-minute setback to change the tire. Cobbler used it to his advantage to pass Michele Rilli on the final lap and take the checkered flag.

More races followed. Monaco. Canada. The United States. The famous French Grand Prix race. Rilli won them all, but the season was not a sweep. He did not *own* it. Throughout the history of great car racing, they would not talk of "The year that Michele Rilli won them all." They would call it "The year that Michele Rilli lost in Spain."

"The purpose of this visit?" the customs man asked.

Rilli looked at him, startled, but the customs agent was speaking with the captain of the *Giancarlo*. Just regular customs-agent questions. Nothing to worry about. The captain described his cargo of foodstuffs and small retail goods, and the cars.

"Automobiles?" the customs man asked. "They are not on the manifest. Am I not seeing them on the manifest?" He was quite worried.

"They are Sir Rilli's automobiles," the captain added.

"Captain, you do not have them on the manifest. This means you have not secured the permits for the importation of automobiles, and this is a serious problem. I cannot allow you to off-load these vehicles. Why are you bringing in vehicles that are not properly permitted?"

The customs man was suspicious. Rilli knew it was time to turn on his French charm.

"I shall explain this to you," Rilli said, turning on his Parisian accent. "The secret is bigger than you were led to believe."

That only made the customs man more suspicious, but that was fine because his relief would be increased when Rilli told him the secret, and this would propel him into greater carelessness.

"You see, we are planning to stage the first Ayounde Grand Prix."

The customs man gasped.

"This is our secret," Rilli snapped. "You can be trusted with my secret?"

"Oh, of course, Sir Rilli!" the customs man gushed. He was a brown-skinned African with cheeks that bulked like shiny dark apples when he smiled.

"It shall be a demonstration only, this time," Rilli snarled, "but we shall make such a spectacle of it that next year, it will be an official grand prix race."

The customs man was tearing up in his excitement and joy. Rilli was not surprised. He was London-born and raised, but he was a Frenchman by blood, and he knew how to turn on the famous French charisma. It made men into agreeable puppy dogs who did what he required, and the women—it positively melted the women.

"These cars, they will not stay here in Ayounde, for this is my personal collection of race cars," Rilli pointed out. "These are the cars that won so many races for me last year."

"Yes, all but Spain!"

"Yes. Spain."

"I watched every single one of them on the satellite!"

"I am happy for you. Getting a manifest for these cars and the required licenses—this was impossible and unnecessary. Firstly, the cars are not for staying in Ayounde. Nextly, getting such permits would have upset the beans, and the news of this race would have been all over the world. The beauty of this demonstration is in its surprise. This is obvious to you. *Oui?*"

"*Oui!*" the customs man replied, his pronunciation more natural than Rilli's. French was commonly spoken in Ayounde.

Still, the customs man was under his spell and would do whatever Rilli asked. And it wasn't such a big deal, allowing entry to a few race cars for a short time. The promotional stunt would help the country and certainly couldn't do any harm. Right?

"So, my friend, what say you?" Sir Michele Rilli asked. "Will you be a part of the new Ayounde Grand Prix spectacle?"

"Of course, Sir Rilli!" The customs man was about to faint from excitement.

Such a bunch of goody-goody types in Ayounde, Rilli thought. He wished he was getting one of the tougher African nations. Truth be told, any African nation other than Ayounde would be rougher and tougher.

Everybody here was just so repulsively *pleasant*.

It would feel good to subjugate them, give them a little something to suffer over. Wipe some of those ugly smiles right off their faces.

9

"So we have a potential bad guy who was born in England, but he acts and talks like he's from France," Remo asked. "Why again?"

"Many respect the French arrogance and see it as strength of character," Chiun said.

"Not all French people are arrogant," Remo said.

"This is true. Those French who lack self-esteem are merely rude."

"Some are nice. I'm sure there are nice French people, Chiun. But if this race-car driver wants to be French so bad, why did the queen of England make him a knight?"

"The queen was compelled to take this action so as to reclaim him for England," Smith had explained on the phone as they were en route. "Rilli had an extremely successful season last year, and his popularity wasn't spilling over on England the way it might have. Being knighted reminded the world that Rilli was from England."

Now Rilli was going to take advantage of his knighthood. Maybe. Smith and Mark Howard had been on the watch for unusual behavior by any persons knighted by the queen of England. Rilli's clandestine travel to the former British colony of Ayounde—by freighter—qualified as suspicious.

As Remo and Chiun were making quick time through the sparse Ayounde airport terminal, Remo veered off course to intercept a hustling ASN broadcast crew, conspicuous in their brand-new AllSportsNetwork jerseys. The network was resurrected from the recently humiliated Extreme Sports Network. The former executives of ESN were on trial with fraud charges pending against them in more than seventy countries worldwide; ASN had been assembled from the liquidated assets—including the human assets.

"What's up, you guys?"

"Like you don't know," said a frumpy woman in overalls, dragging a wheeled luggage cart burdened with video equipment. "You a driver?"

"I have a driver's license," Remo said.

"Are you a *grand prix* driver?" she added.

"No."

"If you're not on a car crew, what are you doing here?"

"I asked you first. Shouldn't you people be in Hoboken, shooting a high-school soccer match?"

"It's that jerk Michele Rilli," a pudgy crewman gasped as he huffed along with a large equipment case in each hand.

Remo gave the man his full attention. "Let me give

you a hand." He slipped the cases out of the man's hands faster than the man could see, but he was happy for the relief. Remo strolled along with him.

"He's staging a sort of surprise grand prix demonstration. Wants to launch a real grand prix here next year. Wants it to be early in the year, the first grand prix of the season."

Remo considered that. "Why make the demonstration a surprise?" he asked.

"Generates more excitement among the locals," the pudgy one explained, rolling his shoulders. "How do you carry those things so easy?"

Remo was toting the heavy cases as if they were filled with lacy lingerie, not steel camera and light mounts. "But he won't get the coverage he wants, right, by making it a surprise? I mean, you guys will be here but none of the big networks will come, will they? No offense."

"Ha!" The woman in the overalls laughed. "When Michele Rilli calls, they'll come. He's huge."

Remo nodded and placed the cases back in the hands of the pudgy man, who wasn't expecting them and felt his shoulders get yanked out of their sockets.

"Makes sense to me, Little Father," Remo said as he returned to Chiun, standing impatiently still and silent in the middle of the terminal. "I think this really is just a big PR stunt."

"You are usually wrong," Chiun pointed out.

"I'm sometimes right," Remo added.

CALLING IN A FEW FAVORS, the customs officer managed to have the wharf cleared within sight of the French cargo ship as it off-loaded its herd of grand prix racers.

"I cannot contain my excitement at seeing this famous collection of cars, sir." Getting no answer, the customs officer turned and found himself alone. Sir Rilli was hustling back up the ramp and shouting orders.

Men began emerging from the deckhouse in racing gear, and the officer grew concerned when he saw that they were wearing heavy, padded race suits of a type most unsuitable for the high temperatures of the Ayounde capital city of Ayounde. More men streamed out behind them. The customs officer blinked and looked again. Certainly they were not toting grand prix car maintenance tools of any kinds; those could only be automatic rifles.

"Sir Rilli, what is the meaning of the guns, sir?" The customs officer was running up the ramp. "Why was I not informed that there were guns aboard, sir?"

"Because it is none of your business," Rilli replied. He was relieved that now he could drop the charade of French friendliness and fall back on his more comfortable French obstinance. Most people did not realize that the French could be downright contrary when they set their minds to it. This was the side of the French personality that the tourists never saw.

But the customs agent was given the rare privilege

of seeing just how ornery a British-born Frenchman by blood could be.

"This is inexcusable, sir! I will require you to keep those men on the vessel. I am afraid a more thorough inspection will now be needed."

"Uh, well, now yuh become quite the inspector," Rilli snarled in a French-Cockney accent that would have shattered a sparkling-wine glass. "You are unfit to work for the next governor of this colony!"

The inspector was stopped short by this confusing statement. "Pardon?"

"No pardon!" Rilli cried, and backhanded the unwitting inspector. The sucker slap sent the inspector reeling off balance on the steep ramp while Rilli danced in a circle and shook his smarting hand. "Ow! Ow! Ow!"

"Are you hurt, Governor Rilli?" asked a worried assistant.

"Oui! Oui! Oui!"

Just as the customs inspector was about to regain his balance, one of the silent gunmen placed his foot on the ramp and gave it a quick, soundless shove. The inspector yelped. Rill turned just in time to see him vanish. There was a thud. Rilli stepped to the rail and found the man flattened on the wharf, limbs akimbo.

"Did I do that?" he asked.

"Yes, of course, Governor," said his assistant, trying to wrap gauze around Rilli's hurt hand.

"Auspicious start to the takeover, innit, killing a guy?" He was back at full-strength Cockney.

"Indeed, Governor." The assistant was mummifying the bruised knuckles in bandages.

"Forget that!" Rilli shook his hand until the gauze unfurled. "Let's begin. Deploy!" He marched down the ramp, yanking his car keys out of his pocket, and hit the master unlock button on his remote. The cargo containers chirped electronically, and their locking bolts shot open with hundreds of angry metallic snaps. The walls on the front and sides fell flat, while the back wall stayed up and held in place the top of the container.

Revealed inside each container was a very dangerous racing car, its engine coming to life as the crates opened. The cars looked at first glance to be the latest, state-of-the-art models, like the ones Rilli drove to victory time and again the previous season. In Bahrain and San Marino. In Hungary and Italy. In Belgium and China and Japan and Brazil and in every other bleeding grand prix race of the season last year except bleeding Spain.

These cars had a few extras not to be found on the average twenty-first-century grand prix machine. Offensive hardware.

"Let's ride," he called excitedly, and because it sounded like a good line. He jumped into the McGaren-Yhuihobi Special and stepped on the gas pedal. The machine rumbled like a waking carnivore.

The gasoline-powered McGaren-Yhuihobi Special was the prototype of the Grand Prix-Type Offensive Attack Race Car, designed for more reliability, better street performance and greater flexibility in offensive maneuvers. Still, they had the aggressive power and handling of a true grand prix racer.

Assembly of a full two dozen such vehicles, with their special accessories and custom cargo containers, hadn't been cheap. But then, that's why professional racing had sponsors.

BERNIE SAWARD WAS practically crooning on the telephone. "It's happening, Mr. Hammerstone. Michele Rilli's promotions coordinator just called me from his offices in Paris. Sir Rilli is on the ground—he's in Africa!"

"Africa?" Hammerstone repeated groggily. He'd been dozing in his desk chair in his spacious top-floor office. "What the hell for in Africa?"

"Ayounde. They actually have a consuming economy in Ayounde. Doesn't matter—what matters is that the surprise grand prix is about to begin."

Bernie Saward was meeting the members of the board of directors at the door of the conference hall, beaming and greeting each one of them like the happy bride just after the ceremony. The directors were slow to respond—it was three o'clock in the morning in Connecticut. None of them wanted to miss the big Ayounde Grand Prix—with their corporate logos plastered on the cowlings of half the cars in the event.

The large plasma screen at one end of the boardroom table was showing CNN, but it was muted. CNN was running a segment on the latest film box-office results.

"Check it out," sang Bernie Saward, and he clicked the sound on as a pair of big oblong shapes appeared on the television, transforming each into the broad grins of two happy youngsters holding their gigantic soft-serve ice-cream cones.

"Mine's dipped in pure milk chocolate!" exclaimed the girl.

"Mine's sprinkled with sprinkles!" cried the boy.

"Thanks, Milkie Queen!" they shouted together, and the camera pulled back as the animated, well-endowed Milkie Queen waved back to her ecstatic young customers from the walk-up window at a neighborhood Milkie Queen stand.

"Good work, Bernie," Saward said. "How did you get us on the same night as the Ayounde Grand Prix?"

"Easy, Mr. Saward. I bought time on every news network on every overnight this week. Cut us some great bargains, too, I don't mind saying. And about an hour from now, our viewership is gonna go through the roof."

There was a murmur of excitement. "You're sure this is going to happen?" asked the ever morose vice president of accounting.

"It *is* happening, within the hour," Saward assured him.

"You sure it'll get coverage?" asked the guest director from an Oklahoma cattle conglomerate.

"With Michele Rilli's name behind it, it will get huge coverage."

The cattleman's doubt reflected on his face. "I'm trusting you on that. Never heard of this Mr. Michele."

"He's the biggest star in the world of grand prix racing," Saward said impatiently.

"Which don't hold a candle to NASCAR," the cattle executive grumbled.

"Outside the U.S., people care about grand prix," Saward said in a firm voice to settle the argument. "Milkie Queen must penetrate Europe if she's going to keep growing."

"And Milkie Queen Must Enlarge, gentlemen. Remember our mantra." He thrust a hand at the banner that hung like some Roman drapery over the wall, above the screen. "Milkie Queen Must Enlarge."

The swathe of fine silk was handwoven and hand-dyed, using natural pigments derived from creatures that should have been on the endangered list. The color was milky yellow, a color belonging to human illness. The handmade embroidery used a variety of rare threads. The fringe was silk spun with gold filament. Every detail of the banner was intended to increase its cost. Only by making the object outrageously expensive would it have an impact on the men whom it was designed to impact. Their logic went this way: we invested hundreds of thousands of dollars into it; we had better pay attention to it, or the money was wasted.

Oddly, the high-priced message was designed to focus their attention on increasing profits.

The banner was necessary, because these were men who had failed before. The banner was their penance and their punishment.

Shareholder Profit Is The Only Purpose was one of the smaller messages stitched in the rising and falling folds of the banner.

Dividends Or Termination was another.

At one time this board of directors was satisfied to keep the chain of soft-serve restaurants floating along without appreciable growth. There was a little profit made; there were a few stores opened every year. The product line might go unchanged for three or fours years at a stretch.

For years Milkie Queen was the target of critics in every facet of the food-service business. "Management without ambition," the financial journals reported. "Goin' Nowhere Fast, Not Carin' Much" was the title of mockumentary on the company. The company executives seemed not to care. Since they were the majority shareholders, their attitude festered at every level of the Milkie Queen management structure.

In the early years of the twenty-first century, Milkie Queen was briefly held as an example of a "civil" corporation, in which profits could be made without resorting to ruthless tactics.

The backlash was immediate and vicious. "A scandal on league with the Enron fiasco," spouted critics from other retail giants and the financial media—all of whom depended on ruthless tactics to keep their companies functional and reporting on them interesting enough to be readable.

"They're trying to bring back hippie culture," decried an op-ed piece that was reprinted in a thousand newspapers. "They're lazy and proud of it. The Age of Aquarius school of management didn't work in the late 1990s, and it won't work today!"

Seething with contempt, the big business lobbies paid millions to quietly purchase an obscure amendment to the anticorruption rules being put in place by the Federal Trade Commission. They timed the law to go into effect the week before the death of Farris Milkie Jr., CEO of Milkie Queen and son of the dairy farmer who started the business. The rule forced the sale of one percent of Farris Milkie's stock.

The result was catastrophic. With fifty-one percent now owned by nonfamily, the company experienced a traumatic shift in culture.

No more Mr. Nice Firm. No more Our Company Is Okay, Your Company Is Okay. Milkie Queen became a backstabbing, soulless greed machine with one overriding purpose: to make profits for shareholders.

"Now they're one of us!" proclaimed the financial journals ecstatically.

Now, Milkie Queen's directors had to slash costs and payrolls and absolutely had to grow. Fast. Which meant growth outside the United States. Which meant Europe.

"You sure they're gone watch an exhibition race that hasn't been promoted ahead of time?" asked Director Farris Milkie III, who had become fantastically wealthy in the last year even as he began experiencing depression and anxiety attacks.

Burt Latch, treasurer, shrugged it off. "They'll watch it. Think of it not as a promotional sporting event but as a news item. That's how it will play—on every news channel, over and over. We'll be front and center for every broadcast."

"What if something goes wrong?" Milkie persisted. "They haven't planned for this. What if some locals get hurt?"

"Won't matter," Latch stated. "It's Africa. Nobody cares much about Africans."

"Burt, you're black!" Milkie exclaimed.

"Hey, I do care," Latch assured him. "But nobody else would."

Milkie sucked on his steroid inhaler. "What if something big goes really really wrong?" he whined.

"It won't."

10

Shund Beila, prime minister of Ayounde, raised his hands. "Who among you can confirm the identity of the man in the leading car?"

His hastily assembled cabinet of ministers all began talking over one another again.

"Enough. Fudende, what's your assessment?"

Minister of Internal Security Antoine Fudende was attempting to get his arms into his uniform jacket, but every time he stuck an arm in, it was pierced by one of the medal pins. There were countless medals on the jacket and he couldn't find the open pin. He helplessly sat down with one arm in the jacket, another arm not. "My people say it is the genuine Michele Rilli in the car, Mr. Prime Minister. For one thing, the cost and resources that went into staging this demonstration must have come from someone very wealthy and with very strong ties to grand prix racing."

"Or one of a hundred wealthy, insane individuals known to us in Europe, Australia and Latin America," added the minister of foreign security.

"Also, the coverage of the event by the media is tremendous. We estimate there are more video news production crews inside Ayounde at this moment that there has ever been."

"Ever?" the minister of foreign security demanded. "I know for a fact that your media-activity records only date back to the 1950s."

"Since the 1950s, then," Fudende stormed.

"Enough. Fudende, how are we preparing for this 'spectacle'?" the prime minister asked.

"All our troops are standing by. None is deployed." Fudende looked nervous, but no one was alarmed by this lack of readiness. Even the exterior security minister nodded with his eyes.

"My honor guard?" the prime minister asked.

"They're in full dress and ready for any call to duty."

The prime minister sighed. "We should arrest him and put him in jail."

The ministers murmured in alarm.

"That would be disastrous," said the minister of tourism gently. "He's a star in every corner of the world except the States. The networks claim the demonstration is intended to bring a grand prix into our country. To arrest him would be to shoot ourselves in the foot."

"I know that!" The prime minister was scowling. "So how should we respond to this reckless display?"

The minister of internal security felt a rush of indecision. There was the warning from the United States government to consider. The Americans claimed that

Rilli was trying to stage a coup in Ayounde. They said that such a coup had already occurred in a place called Newfoundland, which sounded like a blatant fabrication. Surely not...

He actually opened his mouth to voice the alarm. The know-it-all minister of foreign security looked at him expectantly, his broad mouth already showing his amusement at whatever bit of foolishness Fudende had to say next.

Fudende said nothing.

"THE ENTIRE CABINET of ministers are moving all together," Chiun announced. He listened to another stream of Ayounde patois from the radio announcer. Chiun never seemed to run up against a human language that he couldn't understand. "The prime minister is among them."

"To safety, I assume?" Remo cranked the wheel and sent the stolen Chevrolet taxicab tearing around a near empty corner in the city of Ayounde.

"To National Square in the center of the city," Chiun said. "The prime minister's honor guard is clearing the way and the national police are being asked to keep the public safely away from the race route."

"It's like they want to be conquered," Remo griped.

Fruit stands were untended. Electronics shops were standing unlocked and empty. Even would-be looters were on their way to the grand prix route as the stragglers streamed toward the city center.

"They sure didn't take Smitty seriously. They're actually getting themselves all bunched together so Rilli can send them to heaven without exerting himself."

"You must transport us to National Square in time to prevent it," Chiun said.

Remo already heard the sound of the excited crowd, still several city blocks ahead of them. The timbre of the crowd told him there were more human beings than he had expected. "Depends how close we park."

"We will not be close. We will be on the opposite end of the square from the national pavilion."

Remo glared at him. "If you knew that, why didn't you say anything?"

"You are the driver," Chiun sniffed. "It would have done no good. We are too late to approach in this vehicle."

As if by magic, the city with the auras of a ghost town turned into an African version of Carnival, with blasting music and intense, happy crowds. Remo hit the brakes.

"We hoof it."

"You have hooves. I have feet."

Remo slithered through the densely packed population of the city, moving as if through the reeds in the swamp shallows, and by unspoken agreement he followed in the wake of a figure that moved with even less notice. Chiun, the ancient Master of Sinanju Emeritus, was brilliant in his kimono colors but remained unseen. Even Remo couldn't help but admire the stealth of the old Master. He was tiny, light skinned, dressed in expensive silks in primary yellows with red-and-green bands of flashing gold stitch work. Logic said he would have contrasted sharply with the tall, dark-skinned African peoples in drab earth tones and occasional tribal colors. Instead, Chiun was a sprite, glimpsed peripherally or not at all.

As Remo followed Chiun, he found the people excited and distracted by the coming demonstration. They were poor by his standards, but then, he was born and raised in America. The Western world didn't know how good it had it.

The Ayounde people were positively flush with riches by the standards of Africa, where nation upon nation suffered from malnutrition, generations of civil war and the persistent lack of recognition by the rest of the world.

But Ayounde was making strides of some sort. Somehow, they had gotten past the tribal conflicts and stifled the power grabbers—the cause of endless misery in one African nation after another. Not as many starving kids in Ayounde. Not as much rampant disease. Those were the things that mattered, weren't they?

And now some idiot race-car driver was going to try to subvert the nation, making it ripe for fresh destabilization.

That ticked Remo off big-time.

He hoped he was going to be in time to do something about it.

But a moment later, he knew he wasn't.

THE CARS STREAMED into National Square from every direction, and Remo went into the air, hopping atop a bronze statue along the roadside and finding himself sitting high over the happy crowds. Finally, he had the lay of the land, but his spirits sunk. They were still more than a mile from National Square, with a sea of Ayoundis packing the street ahead of him and the square itself. Six streets converged on vast National Square, and parade routes opened on all of them as the race cars rumbled toward the square.

"Chiun!" Remo called, spotting the flicker of the old Master, who seemed to float from the ground and land with all the weight of a bird atop a vendor's canopy of mottled scarlet. Chiun assessed the situation at a glance.

"I go this way," Chiun snapped. His voice was a squeak that was easy to distinguish from the cacophony. Chiun slipped from the canopy and slithered toward the next intersecting street.

Remo bounded into the open parade route, which filled quickly in the path of the racers. Remo put on his own best speed, but the racers were moving dangerously fast. It was a miracle none of them had hit a spectator. He was on the rear racer in seconds and gave the tire a snap-kick that blew it open.

As the rear end swerved abruptly into the mass of spectators, Remo was leaping over the vehicle and delivering another kick that exploded the other rear tire, and its forward momentum dragged the rear end back to center. As Remo left it behind, the racer's rear chassis ground noisily on the pavement and shuddered to a stop.

It took just seconds, but Remo knew it was too slow.

There were a lot of cars to kill and not much time for the killing. When he reached the second car, he bashed his fist on its rear end, tearing off the spoiler like a paper towel and crushing the back end of the car as if a wrecking ball had dropped on it. The tires exploded, the body panels withered and the mechanics inside the rear end became scrap metal—and then Remo realized his grave error.

He felt the pressure wave coming, an explosion, a killing force. Weapons inside the car. Remo hit the deck with inhuman speed and lashed out powerfully at the crushed end of the car.

As it exploded, the car's rear jumped skyward and the starburst of ugly orange fire and black shrapnel flew above the heads of the Ayoundis—mostly. The car stood on its oddly intact nose a moment. The driver dripped out of the cockpit in chunks and splashes. Then the car collapsed slowly onto its belly once more.

Remo was on his feet. The crowd was screaming. People were bloodied. One man was flat on his back with a gash in his head. Amazingly few casualties, Remo thought in the small corner of his brain that was still capable of being rational.

Most of his brain had stopped being rational many, many jiffies ago. Most of it was screaming.

Remo ran like something white-hot that is propelled from a volcanic crack in the earth. When he caught up to the next car, he hit the part in the middle—the soft, human part. That stopped the car just as well, and nothing exploded into the crowds except for a few flecks of brain matter. Remo kept moving. Fast. Still screaming, silently.

Idiot! Idiot! How many people had he wounded? How many would die because of him?

He came upon the front car as it was about to turn into the mile-wide parade wing within National Square. Remo slithered up to the side of the car as it slowed to forty miles per hour, hopping over it and batting at the helmeted driver—just hard enough to turn everything inside to jelly. The car missed the turn and hit the decorative stone wall, grinding along the wall until it stopped.

Chiun had done as well or better than Remo at neutralizing another avenue of race cars, but there were four more attack fronts coming, pulling into National Square even now. The people were cheering them, but now the awareness of trouble was spreading. The race cars slowed abruptly as they entered the makeshift track around National Square. The national police were getting the message and moving quickly into new positions.

National Podium, the great central dais that stood out in the open at the north end of the square, was getting the message late. Remo could see them now, the ministers in their perfect suits and medal-festooned military uniforms. Even a mile away Remo recognized the prime minister from the photo Smitty provided. The prime minister was said to be a pretty smart guy, but right now he looked as dull-witted as the rest of them, squinting at the smoke and the wreckage of the cars. Now the honor guard was showing signs of alarm.

But they were standing on National Podium with crowds on all sides of them. They had no easy way to escape. But also, the attackers had no easy way in.

Or so he assumed.

Idiot! he thought. Why didn't he ever think the worst of people? People always did the worst thing you could imagine them doing. At the first signs of trouble, the race-car drivers escalated their attack timetable. They veered off the parade route—directly into the crowd of onlookers.

There was a traveling tide of horror as arms of flame protruded from the nose of each racer into the people, who fled from the cars, some of them burning. Remo could see clear plastic canopies sliding into position over the tops of the driver cockpits. They were in attack mode. He scooted among the crowd, but even he was having trouble finding room to maneuver as the concern turned to panic. He moved up onto the light posts, clinging and leaping onto the high-tension lines that stretched between them with banners bearing patriotic and advertising messages. Remo moved hand over hand, fast, as the sea of humanity became a shocked swell just inches below his feet.

He could hear the individual screams, but he could hear, too, the ugly sound of a population in terror. The swell pushed relentlessly. People began to go down in the crush. Many of them would never get up.

No matter if Remo had saved ten or twenty lives by diverting the explosion on the packed street—the true death toll was going to come from the riot of panic that gripped the tens of thousands of Ayoundis.

He found himself in the open, hard on the heels of an attacking column of race cars. What kind of morons was he dealing with here, attacking in frigging race cars? He hit the ground and ran fast, catching the front racer and leaping onto it. The driver inside showed surprise when the white man suddenly perched on the cowling of the racer. The racer veered hard right and left, and somehow the man with the thick wrists stayed where he was, as if his scuffed Italian shoes were glued to the Milkie Queen logo.

"This will get you off!" shouted the driver inside his cockpit, and he stabbed at the fire button on his flame thrower. One of those Italian shoes was just inches from the nozzle....

Remo felt the mechanical movement inside the car as the discharge valve snapped open and the high-pressure tanks pushed out a powerful stream of flammable liquid. He grabbed the nozzle and gave it a quick twist, just as the igniter snapped. The torrent of flame drenched the car from front to rear and the tires burst open, bringing the car to a halt.

Remo stepped off and caught a glimpse of the driver, gazing in horror at the plastic shield just an inch above his head. It would have protected him from defensive gunfire, but now it was melting in the intense heat and in seconds it would start to drip on him. Remo wondered how good his helmet and driving suit would be at protecting him.

Not much, he decided, when the screaming started.

Already the Master of Sinanju was moving like a shadow around the fire tongue from the next car. His training taught Remo long ago that one might step aside from any projectile, be it rock or bullet or slow-moving flamethrower. The driver discerned the failure of the flame and quickly turned to more conventional firearms, tattering the square with machine-gun fire. Remo dodged the fusillade. A bullet, after all, was just a fast rock.

But he was painfully aware that the good people of Ayounde didn't know how to dodge bullets. He put a halt to the gunfire by leaping like a feather into the air, then falling like a boulder onto the protruding muzzle of the weapon. The canopy collapsed under him, crushing vital components, but Remo kicked out the tires for good measure. He delivered an identical kick to the plastic cover over the driver.

The plastic didn't budge. It didn't shatter, or even crack.

The infuriated driver laughed heartily at Remo. "You couldn't get me with a bleedin' sledgehammer!" he taunted.

"But I can get you with this finger," Remo replied, and he used it to tap the plastic in a few places. Even over the sounds of confusion he could hear and feel how the plastic resonated with each tap, until his brain had identified a weak spot in the plastic. Then he tapped that spot quickly, creating a destructive vibration. The plastic shattered.

"Son of a—"

That was as far as the driver got. Remo palmed his head by the helmet and withdrew him from the cockpit, stretching him out and dragging him into the jagged shards of leftover plastic. He moved the driver in a circle, gashing his throat open completely all the way around.

Remo spotted the smoking ruins of another column of cars and glimpsed the rapid flash of Chiun heading toward the podium. Remo was already on his way—and it was already too late. Another column of cars was already reaching the podium, reaching it from the side opposite himself and Chiun. A pair of cars was making widening circles around the podium, driving back the crowds and cutting off the officials on the podium.

Remo heard another sound above the whine of the racers. A helicopter was coming. That couldn't be good news.

Remo came upon a flame-throwing car so quickly the driver never saw him. He leaped, landed and took the front wheel of the racer in both hands, bringing it to a sudden halt. The other front wheel tried to move but shuddered on the pavement as the rear end flew up. The driver wore a shocked look. The racer landed upside down, flamethrower still spurting and creating a pool of flaming liquid under the car.

The second flame-throwing racer came straight at him, revving up, spurting flame, and Remo ran to meet it. It looked like a suicidal game of chicken. Remo was feeling a great deal of satisfaction from the fact that the crowds had fled. He had lots of room to work with. He skirted the line of flame and walked onto the cowling of the grand prix racer, grabbing the flamethrower nozzle and making a quick adjustment.

The driver yanked the car into a series of quick swerves, but the g-forces didn't dislodge the attacker. The man simply jogged over the top of the car, perfectly balanced, which was impossible. Right? The driver pulled the car into a hard U-turn and found the stranger running toward the podium faster than was humanly possible. But the race car was faster than that. It had to be. The driver accelerated and jabbed the flamethrower. He'd barbecue the intruder yet.

The driver noticed too late that the flame nozzle was now pointed straight up, and the column of flame that flew skyward became a mushroom. Burning incendiary liquid rained down.

The driver forgot the man he was trying to kill and focused all his concentration on attempting to outrun the fountain of flame coming from his own car.

AYOUNDE PRIME MINISTER Shund Beila couldn't quite believe what he was seeing. His people were being herded out of the square at gunpoint. The attackers were using race cars, of all things, and the race cars were turning out to be extraordinarily effective.

"Where's the emergency-response units?" Beila demanded.

"Assembling, Prime Minster." Minister of Internal Security Antoine Fudende looked in every direction, except into Beila's eyes.

"Assembling? What's that supposed to mean? Why are they deploying now?"

"They were, uh, dispersed," Fudende reported. "So it seems."

"So it seems? You're supposed to know!"

"They were, against orders, not in a state of readiness. Watching the race, Prime Minister."

The prime minister stared at him. Then turned back to the spectacle. The grand prix racers had cleared a path through the crowds. The PM's own honor guard engaged the cars, and the ministers saw the sparks of ricocheting gunfire. The cars deflected everything the honor guard had to send them.

Beila had already seen the racers use gunfire, but they didn't return fire on the honor guard. Instead, they waited until they were in range to use their flamethrowers and let loose with streams of flame. The soldiers in the honor guard—all brave, proved fighters—died writhing and screaming.

Beila began to pray silently. The minister of finance leaned over the railing of the large podium and was sick over the edge.

"Oh, shit, there's a video crew! They shot they whole thing!" exclaimed the minister of tourism. "We're not going to have vacationers in this country for ten years!"

Beila wanted to belt him, but he was pulled away by another development. More columns of attacking racers were now visible—and they were being defeated.

But Beila couldn't see who was defeating them.

"I thought I just saw a little old man in a dress disable that car," said one of the executive assistants.

Beila saw him, too. He was little. He was in a colorful robe. He was light skinned. He disabled a heavily armed grand prix racer with a flying kung fu kick that flattened the cockpit and crushed the driver.

Beila didn't have time to think about how impossible that was. The brave old soul was going to be killed before his eyes. Two grand prix racers roared down on the old man with their flamethrowers spewing fire.

The old man was trapped. He seemed to see his doom and he raised his arms to either side, as if in a gesture of penitence to whatever god he worshiped. The twin tongues of flame swept over his tiny body.

Or did they? The old man seemed to shimmer out of existence for a moment, as if he had soared up and over the tongues of flame at the moment they would have engulfed him—but not before his hands slid over the front end of the racers.

Beila was amazed when the front tires flattened where the old man had stroked them with his fingers, and the two racers veered violently into each other, slowing and bathing each other in flaming liquid.

And the old man was still standing there, as if he had never moved. His brilliant Oriental-looking robes were not even singed.

A blast drew Beila's attention back to his honor guard, just as a knot of them were engulfed in a billow of white-hot flame. The internal security minister screeched and fell to the ground with a tiny hole smoking from his arm. Inside was a tiny burning speck, like an impossibly hot burrowing worm. The internal security minister went quickly into mute shock.

Beila had never felt so helpless. All around him were horrific dramas. He didn't know what might happen next. He saw a young white man now, gliding like a ghost toward the pavilion, unarmed, but behind him was a spinning grand prix racer that was trying to outrun a fountain of flame coming from its own flamethrower. Beila instinctively knew that the young man had somehow accomplished this; it was no stranger than what the old Asian man had accomplished a few seconds ago. The grand prix racer might actually have survived if he had not been so frugal with the use of his flamethrower. He was still ten seconds away from exhausting its tank of incendiary liquid when he turned the wheel a little too tightly and skidded the tires just slightly. It slowed the grand prix racer just enough to allow the fountain to drench the vehicle. The tires melted to mush and the car wobbled to a stop, covering itself with fire.

Beila was so engrossed in the scene he failed to notice the helicopter.

REMO HEARD IT coming but he wasn't prepared for it. The helicopter that soared from beyond the rooftops and soared over National Square was a long, gangly-looking bird with a pair of huge and powerful rotors. This wasn't any sort of military chopper. It was a piece of construction equipment. He'd seen them carrying air conditioners to the tops of skyscrapers—that kind of thing.

He hadn't expected to see it here, at the scene of a coup d'état. There had to be a reason. It was dangling a set of three steel claws at least six feet long and held in an open position as if about to grab something.

But what?

Couldn't be good, whatever it was. He ran for the pavilion, and the helicopter sped up to beat him there. The helicopter won, pulling up hard as it came over the pavilion and its dangling hooks clanged against the pavilion roof. Remo hadn't been paying attention before, but now he observed that the pavilion was constructed of wrought iron and polished brass.

The ministers fell flat when the claws slammed into the structure. As a few men scrambled down the steps on hands and knees, they were met with a murderous wall of flame. One of them rolled down the steps, a writhing fireball, but the other man pulled back slapping at his burning suit jacket sleeve.

The helicopter whined and strained, and it yanked the pavilion off the ground. It was nothing but a welded iron cage that shed its roof shingles and wooden floor as it became airborne. Remo forced himself to run faster, to get to it in time, and yet he knew he would never make it. He looked around for Chiun, hoping the old Master had somehow managed to be close enough to do some good.

Chiun was not. He appeared at Remo's side as they

came to the place where the pavilion had once been. Now it was a hundred feet overhead, swinging wildly from the helicopter claw. As they watched, something in the structure of the cage snapped and the iron bars collapsed in upon themselves. More wooden floor pieces fluttered across National Square, along with a spattering of blood, before the helicopter disappeared over the rooftops.

The surviving grand prix racers were in retreat.

Remo made an ugly sound, and he went after them, not caring if Chiun joined him or not.

11

Raw video feeds are broadcast via satellite around the world, from production teams in the field to news organizations that turn the raw video into news segments.

"That's an encrypted feed, mate! You can't send that for any poor sap with a dish to be picking up!" The field producer couldn't argue anymore. He was throwing up again.

"Guess what will happen if you don't send it?" Remo asked.

The field producer swallowed, hard. He wished like hell he had never agreed to videotape this exclusive footage for the killer in the T-shirt.

The man had come to him after the violence in National Square, claiming he could give the man exclusive access to the remains of four of the grand prix racers who were involved in the takeover.

He was a freelance video producer with experience in some nasty situations. He had seen dead bodies. He had never witnessed a freaky nightmare like this before.

When he reached the place, he found four demolished grand prix racers and four very dead racers. Standing guard over them was an ancient Asian man in happy-day colors—but the old man was not happy. He was very old and very displeased. Although he looked frail, he wasn't frail. Somehow, the videographer could see he was exceedingly strong.

But the old man was nothing compared to the younger one. The one with wrists like steel girders.

"You killed them?" He took one look at the bodies and tried not to take another.

"First I talked to them. They didn't know anything. They were just scum, hired for some dirty work."

The videotaping required him to look at the remains again, and that was what started the vomiting. He broadcast the footage back to his contact at one of the big networks stateside.

"Let me use your phone," Remo said. The videographer tried to hand it to him. "No. You dial. Call the U.S. Ask for Hershey, Pennsylvania, information, for WUNT radio."

"I'm from Pennsylvania. I never heard of WUNT."

The killer didn't say anything. The cameraman was sorry he'd said anything. The old man seemed to be in some sort of his own never-never land and wasn't aware of anything going on around him. The cameraman dialed without further back talk and asked for information in Hershey, Pennsylvania.

"There is no WUNT radio here in Hershey," said the pleasant information operator.

"Just look," snapped the cameraman.

"Yes, sir." The nice operator became cold and officious in a hurry. "Well, what do you know. Here's the number."

"Connect me directly," the cameraman said. "Please."

When the phone started ringing, he handed it to the killer.

Remo heard the phone ringing and an obnoxious man answered with, "WUNT Radio, Home Of Today's Hottest Hits."

"I want to hear 'Sugar Sugar' by the Archies and I want it dedicated to my girlfriend, Edith."

"This is a joke, right? We don't play no music that ain't new, dude."

"Get me Smitty. 'Cause I'm not in the mood to argue with a young punk. Even if it is a computer-simulated young punk."

"*You* called *me,* dude."

The banter feature was a feature of the computer system put in place by Harold W. Smith and Mark Howard to allow the CURE field operatives to contact the home base. It involved some sort of a voice verification system.

Once upon a time it had been very easy to call CURE. Because of Remo's notoriously poor recall when it came to phone numbers, Smith had concocted a system that allowed Remo to phone home by holding down the number 1 on any phone, almost anywhere in the world.

But Remo had himself forced Smith to abandon that system. Part of his recent labor action. His methods—

Smith called them "extortionary actions"—were successful, but now Remo was once again forced to use more complicated methods to contact his employer. The latest strategy was to have Remo phone a nonexistent business, at which point the voice verification would identify him and patch him through to CURE. Nonmatches would end up talking to the computer-simulated person and the nonexistent place of business.

Remo was always amazed at the accuracy of the human voices on the other end—so much so he was starting to doubt they were, in fact, computer simulations. They even made natural breathing sounds. But he rarely had the patience to chitchat with the role-playing computers.

"Listen, dude," Remo growled, "give me Smitty or I call an honest-to-God radio station and talk to them."

"Hello, Remo, I am happy you called," Smitty replied. The CURE director never sounded happy about anything, but there was a note of relief in his sour voice.

"Glad I could make your day," Remo replied. "This place has gone to hell. We were too late to stop it. I think you can write off the ministers of Ayounde."

"No, they're alive," Smith said tersely. "There's a news conference going on right now. Michele Rilli himself is speaking."

"Oh, Rilli? I'd been hoping he was one of the drivers we snuffed in the square. Where is he?"

"It does not matter where he is now," Smith replied. His voice sounded hard, as if he were girding for battle. "He has most of the surviving ministers with him, including Prime Minister Beila."

"Yeah? And?" Remo had a bad feeling about this.

"Sir Rilli is invoking British colonial law, just like in Newfoundland, and he's named himself governor of Ayounde, based on his legal rights from the Proclamation of the Continuation of the British Empire. The independence treaty of 1964 was declared null and void, again claiming validation from the proclamation."

"Uh-huh. Why all the disclaimers, Smitty? You're setting me up for something."

"I am not. I am giving you the information you need."

"And me not taking notes. Now hit me with the bad news."

Remo could hear Smith tighten his mouth. He had actually learned to hear Smith get more sour. One of the Sinanju benefits. "British law is invoked. So far, the British haven't come up with a response to the crisis, so they're failing to deny the legitimacy of the takeovers."

"*Failing to deny* is pure politico-speak. You saying the Brits might actually be supporting the takeover of the colonies they gave independence to?"

"I'm saying they have failed to deny the legitimacy of those takeovers. British law therefore holds in the colonies, and we're not going to test our relationship with the British by deconstructing the colonies."

Remo huffed. "That was one of the filthiest bits of claptrap ever to come out of your sour little mouth."

"Regardless, your work there is done. We see signs

of a coup attempt about to occur in Jamaica. I'd like you to head for Kingston."

"The government of Ayounde is still held hostage," Remo reminded him.

"CURE will cease activities in Ayounde."

"You're pulling us out on a technicality?"

"On a political reality."

"You talk like a two-bit whore from the Senate floor. I'm gonna wash your mouth out with Zest."

"Just accept it, Remo."

Remo hung up the phone. Since he didn't know how to hang up these new mobile phones with their tiny buttons, he pushed his finger through the middle and watched the color display go dim.

"Oh. Sorry." He handed it back to the videographer with a bunch of bills. "Will this pay for it?"

"Mate, that'll buy me fifty phones." The videographer was nervously expecting some sort of a trap. He wouldn't touch the stack of U.S. hundreds.

The tiny old Asian went from statue to hawk in a flash, slipping in and snatching the cash from the younger man's hand. A trio of hundreds fluttered at the videographer's feet. "More than sufficient," the Asian squeaked, and the wad of bills vanished, like a magic trick.

The videographer took the bills without complaint. The pair of lunatics walked away from the scene of death and violence without a backward glance.

The videographer wondered who was going to clean

up this mess. He decided he had best not be around for it, and he left, too. But he went in the opposite direction.

Amazingly, he spotted the pair of lunatics at the airport. While he was struggling to deal with the chaos and get a flight out of the country, the old Asian and the younger man with the thick wrists were already boarding a chartered Airbus—alone. The gleaming, sleek aircraft was one of the immensely expensive luxury craft.

"They're the only ones going anywhere," said the ticket agent in accented English. "All the scheduled flights are running hours late. The security's searching everything. Nobody knows what the situation is."

The videographer nodded thoughtfully. "Where they headed?" he asked, nodding at the chartered plane, a white virgin visible through the terminal windows.

"How should I know, sir?"

The videographer prompted her with a twenty-pound note and got the information in a whisper. "They're going to Jamaica! Believe it? From this mess over to Jamaica, with all-you-can-eat-and-drink buffets! If those boys be friends of yours, now's the time to ask a favor."

The videographer considered that, but at that moment the younger one turned, looked directly at him across the vast terminal and spoke in a voice that was somehow as clear as crystal. "Don't even think of it, bucko."

"Hey," said the ticket agent in a quiet voice, "how did he do that, sir?"

"Do what? I didn't hear a bloody thing." The videographer ran for a pay phone.

12

Remo didn't want to go back to Jamaica. He'd had enough of all things Caribbean. He also didn't like waiting around for things to happen. "I especially don't like standing around waiting for things to happen in Jamaica."

"This you have stated ceaselessly." Chiun was impatient, too, but better at hiding it. They were on foot and they had been strolling the gardens and neighborhoods in the vicinity of Jamaica House, where the prime minister was ensconced, apparently taking the warnings of a possible coup attempt more seriously than his compatriots in Africa.

Hope Road was busier than normal, with a few extra Kingston police on the beat, a few extra Jamaican military folks visible. These were ostensibly the "precautionary measures" the government was taking in light of recent troubles around the world. There were also plainclothes commandos, Jamaican and U.S., roaming the Hope road vicinity, to be on hand should the expected attack come. Some bumbled; others were so good Remo couldn't be sure if they were undercover or real tourists.

Still, he had little confidence in their ability to halt whatever was coming. "What'll it be this time, Little Father? Will they attack with dreadlocks? Will they hurl coconuts?"

"There will be no more taking of governments off their guard," Chiun mused as they strolled by the Bob Marley Museum. "The next strikes will use conventional Western methods of brutality."

"Booms and thunder-sticks?"

"Perhaps people-killing booms that spare the buildings."

"How encouraging."

The hundredth street peddler approached them with a cart of brightly colored souvenirs. "You need a cap, mon, to keep off the fierce sun of Jamaica."

"Can I have my money back now, Little Father?"

"You would purchase some of these cheap trinkets?"

"I would use the edge of the bill to slit his eyeballs open."

"That is worse! You need no weapon! Simply slit them!"

The vendor attempted to push a baseball cap with nylon dreadlocks into Remo's hands. "Just twenty dollars, mon—" he exclaimed, overplaying his accent and his friendliness.

"Twenty dollars for what?" Remo asked.

The vendor's hands were empty. He stopped smiling,

looked on the ground, looked at his customers and shrugged. He grabbed another dreadlocks cap from his cart and presented it to Remo.

Then it was gone. The merchant seemed to sense that it had flown up into the sky, but he couldn't say for sure that he had actually seen it.

"You do that, mon?"

"Do what?" Remo asked.

"You some kind of magic man?"

"Who knows? We all have a little magic inside us, don't we?"

The merchant never took his eyes off Remo as he reached for a dreadlocks cap and held it out in front of him, but nothing happened.

"No, thanks. I don't get sunburn."

The vendor nodded at him and took his eyes off the cap in his hands for a second. Just a second. And it was gone. The young, tall American had not moved, and the little Asian grandpa hadn't moved, although there had been that sense of movement again, like something in fast motion. Or something spiritual.

"Hoodoo?" the merchant whispered.

"Spread the word," the American whispered fiercely.

At least they were bothered by no more street vendors as they wandered Hope Road. By the time they were back at the museum, their peddler friend had discovered his dreadlocks caps perched atop the Bob Marley Museum, the dreads dangling over the side. One of the Marleys were knocking them off for him. He snatched them and ran when he saw Remo and Chiun.

"You shall be feared forever among the trinket-peddlers of Kingston," Chiun commented.

"Better than being Qetzeel the Destroyer," Remo snapped.

Chiun looked at him. Remo looked at Chiun. "Sorry, Little Father. Didn't mean to sound like an asshole. Guess I'm a little bitter about the scene in Brazil."

Chiun nodded, but he showed a trace of rare confusion. "Why, my son?"

"Not again, Chiun."

"Humor this old man. Why does this disturb you so, to be the fulfillment of the myth of those peoples? What part of it was disagreeable to you?"

Remo thought about that. "I'm not sure. I don't like being thought of as the channeler for somebody else."

"But that is what is."

It was strange, walking the streets of Kingston on a hot summer afternoon and thinking about the thing that was Shiva, the Hindu god who was called the Destroyer.

There was a weight in the name, or nickname or whatever it was. Somehow Harold W. Smith had come up with the code name Destroyer when Remo was first brought into CURE, years ago. That was before he was a Master, before Chiun had come to the belief that Remo Williams was, in fact, the earthly avatar of the genuine god Shiva.

Remo would not believe the outlandish notion at

first, or for a long time afterward, but now he believed that there was something that came through him, and it did use the name Shiva. It called itself the Destroyer. Remo had learned to retain his awareness when this thing called Shiva came into him. He had learned to summon it and control it—sometimes, and just barely—at will.

But he didn't like it. He didn't understand it.

"It's not me. It lessens who I am."

"It is who you are," Chiun chided mildly.

"Cut the crap, Chiun," Remo said, feeling hostile. "You get to be in your body all by yourself. Me, the mind that is me, Remo, doesn't. I have to share it with this supernatural creep who is not me. Do you get that?"

"I get that, and yet I get not the fighting of that. It is not a choice you have to make, Remo Williams, so you must choose instead to make the most of it."

"Yeah, so I've heard. And I do that. I make the best of it. But sometimes I think it's getting crammed down my throat, like the scene in Brazil. I'm already Shiva. Why do I have to be Qetzeel, too?"

"They are the same," Chiun answered.

"Yeah. Probably." Remo was dissatisfied by all these answers—and dissatisfied more by knowing that there were no better answers. "Man, I wish this business would get started. I feel like going Shiva on these British knights."

They were facing Jamaica House again. The afternoon was at its hottest, and even the die-hard tourists were abandoning their sightseeing until later. The guards around the home of the prime minister and King's House, the government offices, were looking droopy.

"Now would be the ideal time to hit 'em," Remo observed.

"But not the ideal time for a walking tour of Kingston's fabulous Hope Road," Chiun added, as a tour bus pulled up, bearing the freshly painted billboard, Walking Tours Of Kingston's Fabulous Hope Road!

It was an old school bus, painted sky-blue and allowed to rust for twenty years. Lately, however, the sign was added and the windows, inexplicable, changed to black mirror windows.

"Let's catch that bus," Remo suggested.

THEN CAME THE SECOND bus. And the third. Remo stopped counting at six.

"First we keep the prime minister from getting whacked or napped," Remo said. "Then we'll worry about the rest of them."

They moved down Hope Road as the bus pulled to a stop at the unloading zone. The driver of the bus pressed his fingers into his eye sockets—for a moment he thought he had seen human beings shimmering in the haze of heat coming off the asphalt.

The doors of the bus were removed from their hinges noisily.

"Hi."

"Mother of gawd!"

"You here for the King's House tour? I'm Remo Lee, and I'll be leading the tour."

The passengers were stunned for all of three seconds. Then they began muttering among themselves in Spanish and Haitian Creole.

"All men on this tour?" Remo asked.

"Who are you?" the driver demanded. Remo sensed the man was suitably outraged and fearful to be sincere. He dragged the driver out of the seat and onto the sidewalk in a flash. "Get out of sight or you're gonna get killed."

"Wha'? Wha' 'bout dem passengers?"

"Dem haffa getta beatin'," Remo shoved the large Jamaican driver, slamming him through the front doors of a gift shop, where he dropped out of sight, and then he was on the bus.

There was a rattle of machine-gun fire that took out the front windows and Remo lunged for the gunner, pushing the gun into his stomach and into the seat behind him. Then he went down the row snatching weapons and tapping heads. "Guns are not allowed on my bus. No cigarettes, no alcohol, no pornography. Give me that, mister!" He snatched a length of cable from a dark-skinned man in a pink golf shirt, looped it around the man's neck and pulled it taut. The man's head bounced on the aisle and rolled toward the rear. A group of four in the rear came to their senses and dived for the rear emergency exit. As soon as they went out, they came flying back inside, bouncing off the ceiling and crumpling onto the seats, lifeless and limp.

"Okay, I think we can all see that there is going to be no government takeovers by this bunch of ill-mannered boys today. If I get some honest answers out of you hoodlums, I'll go easy on you later. First question—who's the boss?"

There was a chorus of answers. Even the ones in English were too accented to understand.

"Little help?" Remo asked. Chiun was now standing in the rear entrance.

"Have I not assisted enough? I count four assassinated by me, and just two for you, who are the Reigning Master."

"I mean translating, Chiun. What the hell are they saying?"

"Muffa Muh Mutha," repeated one of the attackers. "That is the name."

"Muffa Muh Mutha?"

"He is star of reggae from Brighton in England."

Remo understood. "*Sir* Muffa Muh Mutha?"

"Yes, mon."

"I see. Is he a part of today's activities?"

"Yes, mon."

Remo smiled. "I see!"

SIR MUFFA MUH MUTHA didn't take the news well. "Get everybody back to the Mutha-rev," he ordered. "I'll personally make the move on the PM."

"That's not safe thinking, Sir Mutha." Sissy Muh was his chief of security and general of his army. She was also his foremost lay at the moment—a smart woman and quite adorably beautiful. She wore her glossy black hair braided down to the small of her back, like an elegant Egyptian princess. Like Muffa, she was from the streets of Brighton, where she grew up being unexceptional in every way, until she dropped out of school and started looking for a cause.

For the young man named Reginald Parkins, the cause became music. Using a personal computer and illegally downloaded music files, he learned to splice together bits of sound, thus creating something entirely original and new. He took on a new name to go with the career—nobody would take Reginald Parkins seriously, but Muffa Muh Mutha sounded like reggae and American street combined.

No matter what anyone said, he was an artist who created music that was new and fresh.

Skirting and dodging copyright-infringement lawsuits around the world, Muffa became a star of the British reggae scene. Jamaica was another story. His first visit, he had been heckled the moment he was off the plane. His concert sold well—but it turned out the tickets had been sold to vehement Muffa-haters. He was booed offstage before he finished performing his first track, "I Knifed the Constable."

"Thief! Thief! Thief!" the crowd chanted.

"I'm no thief. I wrote the damn song," he snarled to

an entertainment reporter later on. Being from the British press, the reporter sided with Muffa.

"They claim that a similar song was performed by another reggae star some time ago," the reporter said.

"Maybe it was—how should I know?" Muffa said. "Let's face it, there are hundreds of thousands of songs that have been done throughout the years and I can't know them all, right? But I didn't steal my songs. The music is my own creation."

The reporter steered around the subject of the borrowed music samples. It was widely known that one hundred percent of the music used by Muffa was electronically appropriated and altered enough to make it legally "new." Until Muffa fell out of favor, the subject was out-of-bounds.

Muffa, amazingly, stayed in favor for almost eighteen months. Even more amazingly, he was given a knighthood.

Filling A Quota? asked a prominent British newspaper, which implied that the reggae star had simply been the only potential black candidate in the year's crop of potential knights. Was Muffa Knighted Because He's Black? the paper wondered.

Cicilia Garen took a different course in life, joining radical groups without finding a cause worth fighting for. She gained an education in street fighting and changed her name to Sissy Gard. When she was paired up with Muffa, she changed her name to Sissy Muh. Muffa was flattered.

She was trying to take the measure of this man. The

man who hired her for the job wanted to know if Muffa had the guts to do what needed doing. "He was humiliated in Jamaica," she reported. "He'll do it for the sake of vengeance."

"Oh, very good!" replied her employer, who sounded like one of those wealthy snits with old British titles.

The British snit had come through with mercenaries and equipment, enough for eight Jamaican tour buses. Within minutes of the start of the battle, the first report of casualties had come in. Strike Force A was gone.

"I don't know wha' tah tell ya. One American guy goes charging into the bus before ya guys even starts comin' out," reported the shopkeeper who was being paid to watch the situation in front of Jamaica House. "He drags out the driver and goes in, and the windshield goes flyin' all over from guns. Then, whatchoo know? The American guy comes out again. Everybody be dead on the bus."

"There were twenty-two men on that bus!"

"Now theh be twenty-two corpses."

"He must be wrong," Sissy said.

"Maybe. I'm not taking a chance. The PM's gotta go, Sis, or this all's for nothin'." Muffa looked grim. "I want all them to come to the PM's house and we'll take it together for sure."

"But that means we'll get none of the other targets. It won't be enough to take just the PM, Muffa."

"We'll take the rest. We'll just take the PM first. Then we start goin' door tah door."

Muffa cut her off when she tried to press her point,

and Sissy felt a dismal sense of failure. There was a reason the attacks were planned the way they were. Hit the Jamaican government targets quick and all at once. Don't give them time to muster a defense.

Sir Muffa Muh Mutha's bus began moving toward the city center and Hope Road, where it would converge with all of Muffa's attack buses.

"It will work, Sis," Muffa assured her. "We'll have a human shield. Once we have the PM, we can strike at them and they won't strike back."

Sissy Muh smiled. "Sounds lovely." But in her heart she had serious doubts.

THE FIRST OF THE BUSES halted on squeaking brakes before the cordon around Jamaica House, then quickly swerved in a half circle. The side windows dropped open and gunfire exploded from inside, mowing down security soldiers as they ran for cover.

Remo sprinted alongside the bus and slapped at the guns, bending and breaking them. Some of the hands holding them broke, too. A man in a body armor leaped from the door and opened fire, his rounds peppering the side of the bus until Remo turned and ran back to him, removing the gun from his grasp before the man fell dead with a finger-sized hole in his skull.

Another bus screeched to halt nearby, and something large protruded from the emergency exit. Behind him, Remo heard the frantic snaps of windows being closed and the thumps of men diving for cover inside.

Something big whumped out of the barrel from the second bus. Remo watched a bulbous, gray, round object arc through the air and hurtle down on him. He stepped aside, using the front of his own bus for cover from the blast, which rocked the vehicle from side to side. When he looked again, his bus was blackened but undamaged.

They were lining up for a second shot when Remo jumped onto the hood, looked back over his shoulder in what appeared to be abject panic and scrambled onto the roof.

They were laughing at him in the second bus. He could hear it all the way over here, even over the whoof of the second round.

The slow-moving projectile was going to come down right on top of Remo Williams. He wondered if he had enough time to do what needed doing.

He thrust his stiffened fingers into the metal of the roof of the bus and used his entire body to pull. The roof was rusting old metal on the outside, hardened blast-proof composite underneath, but it wasn't designed to be tear-proof. Remo felt it come up in his hands and he dragged it back hard, peeling it away and exposing the interior through the ragged gash. The mercenaries inside had just enough time to figure out what was happening when the flying grenade deposited itself directly inside. Remo felt the bus lurch under his feet.

He laughed boisterously. "You're right," he called to the second bus. "Very funny." He pushed the roof sloppily back in place to hold in the billowing black smoke. That ought to asphyxiate any survivors.

There were angry, disbelieving shouts from the other bus, and the occupants triggered their weapon at Remo again, but something went wrong. As the grenade launcher was firing, the emergency door on the bus slammed shut, pushing the launcher inside. The grenade fired and detonated instantly. Fire and smoke shot from the open windows, and more explosions followed as the heat reached the ammunition.

Chiun stood holding the emergency door closed with one hand as smoke whistled from the seams. "Sir Mutha assembled a cultimultural assortment of rabble, but few Reagans," he pointed out.

"Huh?"

"To what does your 'huh' refer?"

"Never mind. Look who's coming to dinner."

More buses were converging on Jamaica House, flanked by jogging ranks of soldiers in dark urban fighting uniforms, and their faces were of all colors. The troops and buses quickly formed a half circle and began filling the streets with gunfire. The Jamaicans guarding the prime minister's residence took dangerous chances to return the gunfire, and were shot down for their risk-taking at every chance.

Remo drifted into the open space, drawing the gunfire to him, then running directly at the runners, doing a quick series of sidesteps to avoid the hail of bullets. Chiun was alongside him, and together they landed in the midst of the gunners. The direct approach in a fire-fight was always so disconcerting to the gunners that they usually had trouble responding in the most logical manner: by ceasing their gunfire. Attempting to follow the impossible movements of the Masters, they inevitably ended up shooting their comrades.

Five of the attackers toppled before the gunfire halted and the soldiers attacked man-to-Master.

Remo slithered through the mayhem, kicking rib cages to splinters, snapping arm bones, opening skulls. One of the gunners placed the barrel of a handgun within inches of his head and triggered the weapon. The fighter was perplexed to see that the American had transformed into a Colombian mercenary named Dinito—the gunner's own brother—but there was no time to stop the blast of the bullet. Dinito sprayed all over Hope Road.

"My brother!"

"You'll see him soon enough. But first, where's Sir Mutha?"

Remo held the gun, and the Colombian couldn't make it move. It was as if the thing were locked in place.

He kicked savagely at Remo's shin to shatter it, but the shin seemed to have a life of its own. It was never where the Colombian thought it was.

Then Remo grabbed him by the elbow and applied pressure. The Colombian howled like a coyote.

"Sir Mutha. Yes, you know where he is, or no you don't."

"I don't."

"Fine." Remo pushed the gun into the Colombian's face and just kept on pushing. The gun didn't break. The face did.

"This is getting us nowhere," Remo complained as the last of the attackers collapsed at his feet. "We don't get paid by the scalp. We need to locate the man in charge."

Chiun nodded at the wave of reinforcements coming their way and looking wary.

Twenty jogging troops half encircled the Masters of Sinanju.

"Hands up," ordered a black man with a dangerous scowl.

"You are Haitian, not Jamaican," Chiun observed. "Do none of this country's people feel compelled to battle alongside Sir Mutha?"

"You can ask him when you see him."

"Will we see him soon?" Chiun gave Remo a cocky look.

"In about thirty seconds. Now put your fuckin' 'ands in the air."

"Is he in the bus in back?" Chiun asked.

"Yes. Now put you 'ands fuckin' up."

Chiun cocked his head. "Whatever you are telling me to do, it sounds lewd and impossible. I decline."

Remo wanted to get out of there soonest. He glanced at the ground, and Chiun gave him an imperceptible nod.

"Kneecap that old fuck!" snarled the Haitian, but as

the gunfire rang out, the victim vanished. One second they had their prisoners backed up against a burned bus, the next they had nobody.

REMO AND CHIUN went to ground and came up on the other side of the bus before the Haitian had figured out they were gone. "Thanks for getting what we needed out of that guy, Little Father."

"It was no great skill to do so. All you had to do was think to do it."

"Yeah, well, I didn't."

It took them seconds to come upon the rearmost bus, which had a number of visible differences. Welded-on steel plating, extrathick glass for added blast resistance. It was also guarded, but the guards never even got the chance to deny admittance to the Masters of Sinanju. Remo gave them each a blow to the chest that flattened their hearts as if their chests were compressed by a toppled snack machine. The door wasn't a standard bus door, but a locked steel vault door.

The weak spot was in the bolt, which possessed a minuscule structural defect in the cast-alloy housing. Remo found the defect and gave the housing a few fingertip taps. The defect was transformed by the perfect vibration into a crack in the metal. The housing fell apart.

"Sir Mutha? You home?"

Chiun heard a tiny creak of metal above and chose not to follow Remo into the bus. He placed his fingers against the plating and pushed the bus down, which effectively lifted the old master up. His sandals were noiseless when he touched the roof, and he padded to the round porthole without creating so much as a squeak.

The porthole was apparently a complicated affair in the opening. Chiun folded his legs beneath him to await the port opening. Finally, the wheel ceased turning and the mechanism clicked. The port opened six inches, and a pudgy black face looked into the face of Chiun, the ancient Master of Sinanju.

Chiun smiled his warmest smile. "Good afternoon, Sir Mutha." He closed the porthole lid, which made a deep musical note against the head of the famous pop star.

SIR MUFFA MUH MUTHA felt the blackness almost claim him, but he somehow managed to hold on to consciousness. He pushed himself off the floor of the War Room, the electronics hub from which his war was coordinated.

When he was sitting upright, he saw the same old Chinaman, smiling at him in exactly the same way.

"Good afternoon, Sir Mutha."

"Who are you devils?" shrieked Sissy Muh. "Who are you?" She cut savagely at the arm of the younger white man, who was holding her off the ground by her long French braids. Sissy wasn't short, and the white man wasn't extratall; still, he managed to keep his arms out of the reach of Sissy's mean-looking hunting knife.

"Come on, let me cut you!"

"No, thanks, sweetheart." The white man pinched

the blade with two fingers and flicked it out of Sissy's grasp. It buried itself in the plastic interior walls—ten feet away.

"Devil!" She kicked and clawed but she contacted nothing but air, every time, until she was as furious and wild as a hooked eel landed in a rowboat.

The white man sighed and snatched at Sissy's neck as if he were flicking a switch. Sissy stopped, as if she had been turned off, and she slumped into one of the console chairs.

"Did you kill 'er?" Mutha asked.

"Naw, she's still alive and kicking on the inside. See?"

Sir Mutha observed that his security chief's eyes were flickering around the room like a wild animal's, but her body was absolutely limp.

"You paralyzed her!"

"Not permanently. The peace and quiet is nice, though, isn't it? And now to restore some peace and quiet to Kingston town. Would you call off your coup, Sir Mutha, please?"

Sir Muffa Muh Mutha careened to his feet, overtaken by the urge to self-defend. Joining his hands into a club, he walloped the little Chinaman with all his body weight, but the Chinaman was gone. Sir Mutha felt himself carom off the plastic wall and descend onto his knighted backside once more.

And the Chinaman was right back where he had been, and he was giving Sir Mutha the same Chinaman smile.

"Sissy's right—you be devils! Demons!"

"Not I, Sir Mutha," the Chinaman said cheerily. "He is another story."

"Don't go there," the white man said. "Time to call off the dogs, you Mutha."

"Never!"

Never lasted for all of ten seconds. By then, Mutha had endured all the earlobe pinching a human being could ever expect to endure. The agony was unbearable.

"Fall back. Retreat. This is Mother. I'm calling off the holiday. Repeat. I am calling off the holiday."

"Get them out of Jamaica," Remo added. "And tell them not to come back."

Sir Mutha urged his soldiers to evacuate, then Remo sat the British pop star down for a chat.

"Even you are not a Reagan," Chiun pointed out. He was still smiling, and the smile had Sir Mutha's flesh crawling.

"Iya, dunno…a what?"

"A Reagan. You are not. She is not, although she has one long hair thong, at least."

Sir Mutha couldn't make sense of it. "As in reggae music?" Remo asked, seeing the light. "Don't think they call them Reagans, Chiun. Some are Rastafarians. Some are just Jamaicans. This mutha, I have no idea. What are you?"

"I'm an artist."

"'Course you are. You go right on believing it. Me, I like to pretend I'm master of my own destiny. Now, here's the important question. Who put you up to this?"

"Nobody. I'm my own man."

"Your turn, bad cop." Remo nodded at Chiun, who intensified his smile and took Sir Mutha by the elbow again. Seconds later, Mutha was begging them to let him speak.

"Even I'm getting creeped out by you looking so happy," Remo said. "Now, Mutha, spill it."

Mutha stopped screaming from the agony. "Okay! I'll talk! What was the question?"

"Who put you up to it?" Remo asked impatiently.

"I don't know."

"Somebody is behind this. Somebody got you on board. Who is that somebody?"

"Oh. Easy. It was Sissy."

"Convenient scapegoat, her being right here with us."

"No, it was her, really. She's my go-between with the Royals. That's what she always called them. The Royals."

Remo nodded. "You hush now." He turned to Sissy Muh and adjusted her spine with a touch.

"Now, young lady," was as far as Remo got.

When she had her voice back she began screeching at them. "You don't scare me, freaks!"

Remo shrugged. "I can be bad cop, too. See?" He touched her on the elbow. She stopped screaming and started singing.

REMO THOUGHT that any self-respecting revolutionary with his or her own mobile command center ought to have a telephone. Chiun pointed out that there were various devices that could be used to communicate with the outside world. Sissy was eager to help them place their call.

"To a delicatessen?"

"Not just a delicatessen—Oppheim's is *the* delicatessen in all of Sioux City." Herschel Oppheim himself— or the computer-generated equivalent of an Iowan deli owner—was on the line now.

"Yeah, we're the best. Now what do you want?"

"What's good today, Mr. Oppheim?"

"It's all good. You name it, it's good. Now name it, bud."

"My mouth's watering for corn beef on rye," Remo said. "Extra, extra mustard. Chiun?"

"Fah!"

"Let's have the usual for my dad. Pastrami on white bread. Pile it on high."

"Pile what high?" Mark Howard asked.

"I think you know. Where's Smitty?"

"He's monitoring another situation. He asked me to get your report."

Remo heard the hesitancy in the voice of the young assistant director of CURE. Remo was almost starting to like Mark, and he had come to respect the man's capabilities. But Mark Howard wasn't a good liar, even when it was a lie of omission.

Remo played along for the time being. "We managed to stop the recolonization of Jamaica," he said.

"We've heard," Howard said. "The Jamaicans are arresting mercenaries all over the island."

"Quite a rainbow coalition," Remo said. "He got Colombians, Haitians, Americans, you name it. But no Jamaicans. You wouldn't believe this guy. Says his name is Mutha."

"That would be Sir Muffa Muh Mutha," Mark Howard said. "He was at the top of our list of possible ringleaders of the Jamaican coup attempt. Did he survive?"

"Oh, sure, he's here with me now. Funny thing is, Jamaicans hate this guy, from what he says. I guess he's some sort of hack reggae imitator who steals everybody else's good bits and repackages them as his own. Says he was run out of the country when he tried to stage a show. Now he's back to take over the place and exact a little revenge."

Howard sounded impatient. "Yes, but what about the organizers? Who put him up to it? Who organized it?"

Remo reported the interrogation of Sissy Muh, who was the real brains behind the operation. It was she who recruited mercenaries from throughout the Americas, who purchased intelligence, who equipped the forces. Her instructions and her funding always came anonymously. "She calls them the Royals. Says her contact has an accent like a rich British type."

"Have you questioned her thoroughly?" Howard asked, sounding impatient.

"Yeah. Thoroughly," Remo replied, feeling a little annoyed. "We also thoroughly stopped the takeover of the government of Jamaica. Isn't that a good thing? Didn't we buy you some time?"

"Yes. Well, not really." Mark Howard was flustered. "Another former colony is being taken over even as we speak."

Remo looked at Chiun. Both of them heard the strange discomfort in Mark Howard's voice.

"Which former colony?" Remo asked pleasantly.

"Nowhere near you. You'd never get there in time. It'll be over within the hour."

Remo asked again, slowly, "Junior, *which former colony?*"

13

How he loved this blessed land. Oscar Dowzall had devoted his adult life to the service of the green hills, the shining seashores, the powerful industries and the wonderful people of his beloved New Jersey.

New Jersey had loved him in return. He started out as a representative in the New Jersey state house, was appointed secretary of state and eventually ran for governor. He was put in the governor's mansion by a landslide vote.

For seven glorious years he reigned supreme. He was a great leader because he adored the people and the land he led. He accomplished many victories and made a mark on history.

All of it swirled away in one afternoon. The conniving bitch he had married stabbed him in the back. She found out about his indiscretions. A truly loyal politician's wife would have kept it to herself. Not his wife. First she screamed at him for a week. She said he humiliated her. "If you're going to go screw around, couldn't you at least find somebody attractive?" She thrust the photo of Sabrina in his face. "This one is built like a bodybuilder."

"He's a construction worker and a very sweet man."

"But he's a man," his wife harped. "Why'd you marry me if you're into cross-dressing men?"

"Men who are into cross-dressing men aren't the kind of men who get elected to high office," Dowzall explained, very reasonably, he thought.

"So you used me."

"Well, yes."

That set her off again, wailing like a siren. He tried being reasonable. She had a pretty nice life as the first lady of New Jersey, didn't she? Wasn't that good enough? Apparently it wasn't. She just kept screaming, and come morning she filed for divorce. The divorce papers got the newspapers on the trail of the nature of his indiscretions, and pretty soon he was outed in front of the entire damn state—Dowzall's Dirty Deeds.

The backlash was intense—especially when Greg "Sabrina" Uddersholf and Derek "Jasmine" Gorey sold video recordings of their private sessions with Dowzall to a maker of porno DVDs. They were distributing "The Governor Begs for His Just Deserts" within a matter of days. The morning radio stations were playing outtakes.

It saddened Oscar Dowzall. He had sort of expected his wife to turn on him, but he never thought he would be stabbed in the back by Sabrina and Jasmine. It shook his faith in mankind.

In a twinkling, Dowzall was a pariah. Even his own party distanced itself from Governor Oscar Dowzall.

"What's the problem?" Dowzall demanded. "There are other gay politicians."

The state party chairman chuckled grimly. "It's not that you're gay. It's that you cheated on your wife with a pair of cross-dressing masochists and had yourself filmed being tied up and dominated. I don't know how to start calculating your lapses in good judgment."

"Homophobe!" Dowzall shot back.

WHATEVER. HE WAS OUT of office so fast they had to Fedex him the clothes and toiletries he left in the governor's mansion. Far from enjoying the easy lifestyle of a retired politicians, with classy dinner parties and wealthy peers, he was outcast and snubbed. He tried getting speaking engagements, but the only ones who would have him were the fringe groups. He found himself taking two thousand dollars to deliver a half hour of commiseration at the monthly gathering of New Jersey Cross-dressers in Crisis. He felt like a cheap, depraved whore—but not in a good way.

One thing they couldn't take away from him—his knighthood. He'd worked hard for it, and it was going to be his salvation.

One of his guiding principles as governor had been his insistence that New Jersey was just as good, with just as much to offer, as New York. New Jersey loved him for his tenacity in this regard. He had argued with reporters, with heads of foreign nations, and even with famous late-night talk-show hosts who were known for constantly making fun of New Jersey.

Jersey had everything New York had, only better. All the advantages, more benefits. New York was just bigger, that's all. That's why everybody thought of New York first and New Jersey second.

"Or not at all," the gap-toothed talk-show host replied. He got a big laugh for that one. Jerk.

"The point is, we're as good as New York City," Dowzall had insisted.

"The point is, New York is a city and New Jersey is a state. You can't compare them." The talk-show host thought this was all a big joke. "It's like New York is the apple and New Jersey, I dunno, a cigarette butt."

Another big laugh. What an asshole.

Such ridicule only spurred on Governor Dowzall. He demanded equal treatment for New Jersey, in all forms. He lobbied the federal government for highway-improvement dollars on par with New York—although it had fewer miles of federal highway. He publicly berated the executives of Kartoons for Kids channel for their *School-Toons* program, "Fifty States in Fifty Minutes," which actually devoted just thirty-nine seconds to New Jersey and a whopping one minute, eight seconds to New York.

When the mayor of New York City was honored by the British government with a knighthood—simply because he stayed cool and collected in a time of crisis—

Dowzall was ticked off. Just because he was on the television a lot, just because he was the mayor of New York City, he got a knighthood. Dowzall did a lot of public speaking himself during that time of crisis, and none of the damn TV stations bothered to pay attention—even the Newark stations!

Then came the crisis Dowzall was waiting for. The Jersey City water-main break was "the worst crisis that the brave people of New Jersey have ever faced, but we will face it together," Governor Dowzall said, face slack with drained emotion as he spoke to the reporters from the streets of Jersey City.

He spoke on the network news, his suit pants soaked with sewage water. "It is the courage and fortitude of these brave people that enables them to pull together, especially when in the face of calamity and devastation."

He spoke from the serving line at the emergency housing shelter. "Someday we will prosper again. Today, we can only mourn, but we mourn together, as a united people."

Even back then, when he was New Jersey's golden boy who could do no wrong, there were a few in the state who thought he was laying it on a little thick. "It's just some flooding, Oscar," his lieutenant governor said. "It's a big mess, that's all. It's not a catastrophe."

Dowzall shook his head sadly. "People are dying, Mel."

"What people?" the lieutenant governor asked. "You mean the old bag lady who was bobbing down Kensington Avenue? Oscar, she'd been dead since February.

The water just floated her out of wherever she'd been stashed all that time."

"Think of the loss, Mel."

Mel was thinking that the loss would be covered by insurance agencies and disaster assistance. He conceded that the governor's high profile during the flood secured federal disaster funding in record time.

The real dividends came later. Dowzall sent video tapes and press clippings of his performance during the disaster to the queen of England—under the name of a citizens appreciation group that didn't exist. Despite assurances by the British that "one does not lobby for knighthood," knighthood happened. Just like the mayor of New York City, Dowzall officially became one of the members of the Order of the Garnet Corset. He was Sir Oscar Dowzall.

"Uh, no, I'm afraid you can't call yourself Sir Dowzall," said the queen's royal secretary of nonroyal relations. "That's a privilege reserved for British citizens." They were at the small and somewhat hasty reception staged for the new knights. The queen wasn't in attendance. In fact, most of the Brits who were in the room seemed to be serving disgusting canapés. Dowzall was distinctly aware that he was among this year's crop of second-class knights.

"But I am a real knight, right?" he insisted.

"Oh, yes. Absolutely a genuine knight, so to speak."

"That's all I care about," Dowzall said agreeably.

"I know," said the queen's royal secretary of nonroyal

relations, who found relating with nonroyals to be thoroughly repulsive.

The knighthood added luster to his star as governor, but when his downfall came, it was just a trinket of honor for him to cling to. It didn't do much for him once his political career was ended.

Or so he thought.

A phone call woke him up one afternoon. The man on the line sounded like an American trying to imitate a snobby British accent. In fact, it was an authentic British snob on the line.

"Hold on. I can't hear a thing you're saying."

He muted the TV, which was playing *The Governor Begs for His Just Deserts*. Dowzall had to admit, it was pretty good as far as homemade sadomasochist transgender gay porn went.

"My God, was that someone tortured?"

"Just TV. Who is this?" Dowzall asked, intrigued by the accent.

"I'm not going to tell you that. I will tell you I am a member of a political organization in the United Kingdom. We are proponents of a return of the British Empire. We would like you to join us, Governor Dowzall."

"What? Why?"

"You are a knight of England. With knighthood comes a series of responsibilities. One of which is to protect Her Majesty's interests against traitors and foreign aggressors."

"I'm not following you." Truth was, Dowzall was

convinced he had a prankster on the line. "You sayin' I owe you money?"

"No, not at all, Governor Dowzall."

"Hey, buddy, have you read the papers this year? I'm not governor anymore."

"How would you like to be again?"

"Huh. A British guy is gonna get me reelected governor of New Jersey? How much is it gonna cost me?"

The man on the other end made a breathing sound that was the equivalent of a manly, snobby British chortle. "It is I who will provide you with the funding you need."

"Now you're talking," Dowzall said. "I'm listening."

"Then listen carefully to what I am about to ask you. To what do you owe your highest allegiance? To the United States, whose political system stripped you of your rightful place? Or to the land called New Jersey, legally and in perpetuity a colony of the British Empire?"

"Is this a trick question?"

That was how it started. Every step of the way, Dowzall was quite sure this was going to turn out to be some elaborate prank pulled at the expense of the poor, disgraced former governor.

But the prank became too elaborate to be a prank any longer. He was assigned a persona strategist—an old, slightly daft retiree from MI-6. The man was prone to daydreaming, and he looked like a stock British scientist from a 1940s jungle movie, but he was a superb strategist. Commander Alfred H. Denharding left the intelligence agency in some sort of disgrace involving a lost disk of vital data.

"Those bastards claimed it came from a source in Baghdad, they did. Said I misplaced the only intelligence on actual hiding places of Iraqi weapons of mass destruction." Commander Denharding blew forcefully into his bushy mustache. "They were about to use me as their whipping boy. They wanted me to take all the blame for the mess down there! Then I found the bleedin' disk stuck under the floor mats in my Ford. You know what was on there? Office supplies inventory for the whole MI-6! Paper clips! Notepads!"

"But they fired you anyway?" Dowzall asked.

"Couldn't stop the process then. I was already officially discredited. Once it's official you can't take it back, you know. Not in intelligence circles. They wanted me to take a job in organization supply. They said, 'You're so bleedin' good with ballpoint pens, you can just be in charge of ballpoint pens for the whole agency.' I told them to bugger themselves with their ballpoint pens and retired. With a bonus, mind you, and full benefits. They had to keep me hushed up, see."

"I see."

One thing Denharding didn't have intelligence about was who was putting the whole thing together. "I talked to him on the phone maybe eight or ten times, and he never said a name. I call him Duke Earl. He talks like somebody from an old family. Not many of them have money anymore, but Duke Earl has cash, I'll tell you that."

Dowzall believed it when the equipment started arriving. Weapons. A fleet of armored vehicles. Electronics. The hardware was followed by the arrival of the humanware. Trained soldiers. Skilled programmers. Media-relations professionals of the highest caliber. All of them were outcasts, however, of one kind or another, brought into the Recolonization of New Jersey Alliance to give themselves another chance at achieving a level of greatness in their lives.

All of them, Commander Denharding included, were in it for themselves, but every one of them had something to prove: that they could make themselves look good again.

Dowzall understood that no matter how far you had fallen, no matter how heinous your disgrace, you could change the world's perception of you with a few simple strokes of promotion. If there was one lesson he had learned from politics, it was that the people would believe you if you could just get them to listen to your message often enough.

Forget facts, forget reality, forget common sense. The mentality of human beings was that they would listen to what you said, regardless of the words' validity, if you said those words often enough.

Dowzall began to believe that the mission was not a hoax, that it would truly happen, that it was meant to happen and he was meant to be the spearhead. He was fated to be the governor of recolonized New Jersey. Everything else that had come before was leading up to it. He would have more power than he ever had as the elected governor of the state of New Jersey. Most importantly, his post would be permanent.

Governor for life.

No matter how many more of his videotapes got into circulation.

He watched the news snippets about the takeover in Newfoundland. He heard about the successful recolonization of Ayounde. Newfoundland didn't have much to offer the British Empire in terms of resources, as far as Dowzall knew. He wasn't even sure where Newfoundland was. He had a feeling it was one of those sections of the Arctic Circle that didn't even have land—it was just a big sheet of ice that sometimes melted and refroze, like the North Pole.

But Ayounde would be a valuable addition to the empire. Ayounde had oil, and its population was amazingly stable and non-self-destructive by African standards. Ayounde would enrich the empire.

But they wouldn't hold a candle to New Jersey, with all kinds of industry, a big stretch of North Atlantic seacoast, and a skilled population of blue-collar and white-collar professionals. New Jersey was going to be the jewel in Britannia's North American crown.

And it was going to happen today.

14

"Morning, Charlie." The governor gave Charlie Fagen a hurried smile.

Fagen looked worried, and he looked at the electronic device in his hand. "Governor, I already got you checked in this morning."

"Oh." The governor was stripping off his trench coat to go through the metal detector. He was clearly in a big hurry. "You know, I was in, then I left for a quick meeting down the street. I bet they didn't scan me out properly."

Fagen punched his thumb on the keys, looking for some answer on the electronic display. "That never happened before," he muttered.

"Well? What are you supposed to do about that?" The governor, the former lieutenant governor of New Jersey, was a friendly enough guy, but right at that moment he was clearly in a big hurry. The undercover state trooper who was always nearby was also getting uneasy by the unexpected delay. He was edging in close, just in case this small problem was in fact a setup of some kind. That was not too likely, seeing as this was the governor's office and security was awfully good. The governor's impatience and the trooper's suspicion quickly got Charlie Fagen all squirrelly.

"I guess we got to have some sort of a meetin' to figure out the flaws in the system. You go on through, Governor."

"Thanks, Charlie."

The governor passed through the metal detector without making it buzz. The trooper had his special pass, allowing him to be armed.

Charlie Fagen hoped he hadn't made a mistake. But how could it be a mistake letting the governor into the offices of the governor? He'd recognized the man with his own two eyes. Right?

Something bothered him, though. What was it?

He wasn't the smartest man alive, but Chief of Security Charles Fagen did have a near-photographic memory, short-term. He replayed in his head his encounter with the governor. Was there something wrong with that picture?

Had the trooper looked suspicious? How could that be? They were always suspicious looking because they were always suspicious of you. And there was a new guy every few months.

Something wrong with the governor, then? Had he been under duress? No. Just in a hurry. Man like that you expect will be in a hurry sometimes. He had walked through the metal detector like he had a meeting to get to right away.

Oh. Wait. The metal detector. With its color-coded

height markings. The governor's head had blotted out the purple mark at five feet nine inches. But every other time before, he had reached just halfway into the orange mark, at five feet eight inches.

He was either wearing lifts in his shoes, or that wasn't the governor at all.

Fagen snatched the hot-line phone to security central, but then everything went black. Charlie Fagen collapsed, and someone else replaced the hot-line phone in its cradle.

"Got something to say about that?" The man with the gun pointed it at the security pair who monitored the metal detectors. They were ashen faced, having just witnessed the long-distance electrocution of Charlie Fagen. Their screens were blank. When Charlie fried, their electronics fried, too.

Exactly as he was trained to do, the operator on the left pushed the hidden alarm button with his left foot.

"The alarm is out of order," said the man with the strange firearm. "But you should have known better than to try something behind my back. Now I get to shoot you."

The operator tried to protest. The gunner, who was in an identical uniform, shot him. The evil-looking prongs slammed into the operator's chest, pierced his shirt and imbedded in his flesh. The thin cable that connected to the gun had to have carried a hell of a current, because the operator began doing a spastic dance that ended when he flopped to the floor.

"Want to know what I think about nonlethal weaponry?" asked the man in the security guard uniform. "What I think is, why bother? So I juiced up the system a little. Now this nonlethal stun-gun thingy is lethal as dropping a toaster into the bathwater. Don't believe me? Give him a feel. I bet there's no pulse pulsing."

"I believe you," said the last operator, who was thinking that the attacker had fired both his prongs. It was a two-barrel device. He should make a run for it....

"I can see it in your eyes." The killer laughed. "You think I shot my wad." With that, he depressed a lever where the cocking mechanism would have been on a conventional handgun, and with a whir the cables were withdrawn onto hidden spindles. The needle-tipped prongs were lodged in the firing position on the wide barrel of the gun. "Better think twice."

"What do you want me to do?" the operator pleaded.

"Just do your job. Look. He's Charlie. I think the two of you can handle it."

The man who ambled down the hall looked, sure enough, like Charlie Fagen—poor, dead Charlie Fagen. A little heavier, his skin a little lighter, his dirty blond hair a little too carefully put together. Still, nobody was going to notice.

"You think you can work well together?" the gunner asked.

"Yes, sir."

"Good."

"That's fine," said the fake Charlie Fagen, with just the same weird Alabama-tinged accent Charlie used to speak. The fake Charlie even smiled the same way. The metal detector operator was an intern, without much experience, but he knew professionals when he saw them.

Whatever they were planning to do, it looked as if they would succeed.

The operator considered playing hero when state officials began arriving by the dozen. He could have jumped up and shouted that they were walking into a trap. The problem was, the man with the electrocution gun was inside the secure area now, sitting on a bench, reading *The New York Times*. If he warned them, he would die. First he would jerk around for a long time with those forks in his body.

Well, what good would it do, anyway?

He played his part perfectly. He pretended to study the dead monitor. He nodded at the secretary of state and the new lieutenant governor and the various state senators and representatives that he recognized.

Had to have been thirty or forty men and women who passed through by him and entered the suite of offices from which the State of New Jersey was governed.

"Are you going to kill them all?" he asked mournfully when they were alone again.

The gunman looked up from the comics. "Don't I wish."

THE LARGE MEETING ROOM was never designed to hold so many people. As soon as he walked through the doors, Senator Baskin knew something was very wrong.

By the time he turned to leave again, the doors were being closed. The New Jersey state troopers, charged with the personal safety of the governor, removed their personal weapons and stood guard at the doors.

"Open it," Baskin demanded, and felt room go silent around him.

The guard said nothing. Baskin reached around him and put his hand on the doorknob, but then he felt the muzzle of the weapon against his temple.

Senator Baskin let go of the doorknob. The worry among the New Jersey officials became fear. One of the young representatives lost his cool.

"What's going on? Tell me what's going on! You can't keep us prisoners! Are you going to kill us? Talk to me!"

The trooper didn't say a word, but he swung his weapon in a long arc that brought the base of the hand grip into the representative's head. The young man bounced off the wall and sprawled on his face, motionless.

The trooper looked around questioningly. The room was silent until the governor entered through his private entrance, hands cuffed in front of him, feet in shackles, mouth covered in gray tape. He was followed by a look-alike governor, who steered him with little nudges on the shoulder.

"Hello," said the fake governor. "Thanks for coming. I see Lansing lost his cool."

"What's the meaning of this?" demanded Lieutenant Governor Ortega, just eight months on the job. "Release Hermani."

"All will be explained when the governor arrives," said the fake governor.

"Another imitator?" Ortega snapped.

"No. The real deal. The true governor of the colony of New Jersey."

There was a sudden hiss of quiet talk among the captives. Lieutenant Governor Ortega gritted his teeth with suppressed anger when he understood what was happening.

The recolonization attacks. They had succeeded in Africa. They succeeded in one of the northern territories called Newfoundland. "You're crazy," Ortega seethed. "You might be able to push over some Third World countries, but there's no way you're going to overthrow part of the United States of America!"

"Just watch me do it, Alfonzo."

All eyes turned. The former governor of New Jersey, Oscar Dowzall, strode in via the governor's private entrance, wearing a mask of perfect confidence.

"You're a lunatic, Dowzall," Ortega said with bitter amusement. "A stunt like this will never work here. This is America."

"This is Her Majesty's New Jersey Colony. It has been occupied illegally."

"It's been independent since 1766!" Ortega cried.

"There's no statute of limitations on the theft of the properties of the British Empire. Although it was occupied and exploited for almost two and a half centuries by the United States government, it never ceased to be, legally, a colony belonging to the Crown."

More murmurs. Ortega snorted. "That's just stupid."

Dowzall shrugged. "I'll let you know something just as stupid. You are all criminals. You have served the occupying United States government, allowing this aggressive nation to further exploit and control this territory. As you are all citizens of New Jersey, you are worse than criminals. You are traitors."

More consternation. "What? Then so are you, Dowzall!"

"Yes. I was. But I repented, and I made an oath to never again commit such acts against Her Majesty. I promised never again to give aid to the enemy."

"The U.S. is your enemy?" Ortega was getting exasperated.

"This has always been, legally, a British colony. As a knight of England, under the provisions and obligations put forth by the Proclamation of the Continuation of the British Empire of 1655, 1702, 1709 and 1742, I'm reestablishing British control. As the new governor, I'm prepared to offer every person in this room full amnesty in return for your sworn allegiance."

"You must be kidding," Ortega said.

"You'll even get to keep your jobs. Every one of you will be needed to help me make the transition. It's going to be a big job, scrapping the old government, bringing in British rule. Who's with me?"

Ortega shook his head. "You're a freak, Dowzall.

You belong in some sort of a mental home for homos."

Dowzall sighed. This was going to be the unpleasant part of the job—but a necessary one. "Mr. Ortega, does this mean you decline to be a part of my team?"

"Of course I decline!"

Mr. Ortega's head jerked sideways as his brains spattered the wall and ceiling. The state trooper at the door had attached some sort of a suppresser on his weapon, as big as a can of soda, and they hadn't heard more than a loud cough.

"Talk it over."

The wide-eyed governor, the smirking fake governor and the self-appointed colonial governor retired to the governor's office. One of the troopers dragged out the lieutenant governor and stowed him somewhere.

A discussion among the entire group was out of the question. The troopers were still there, watching them wordlessly. A small knot of senior officials gathered in a back corner and had hasty words together. When Dowzall reappeared after ten minutes, he folded his arms and waited.

"Can we discuss this with you privately, Mr. Dowzall?" asked Senator Mercer, strolling causally toward him.

"No."

"Will you at least sit and answer our questions?"

"No."

Mercer, a former Navy SEAL, had hoped for a better advantage when he made his attack, but he made the attack anyway. He lunged for Dowzall. He'd get the son of a bitch in a headlock and threaten to snap his neck.

But he never touched the colonial governor of New Jersey. The bullets slammed into his side and dropped him hard. Dowzall knew about Mercer's military career and his Special Forces successes, and he'd warned his bodyguards to keep a close eye on the man.

Dowzall shrugged at the quickly dying state senator. "Poor choice, Mercer. Anybody else want to take a shot?"

Nobody else did. Mercer died. Dowzall smiled. "So, who's with me?"

Everybody else was with him.

15

With very few exceptions, every high-level state official was present at the ceremonies.

It was billed as a free concert by New Jersey's favorite rocker. Bruits Sprigstern had been off the touring circuit for two years, but out of the blue he announced a free show in front of the state capitol building—and it would be that very day. The stage was being constructed. Apparently, the State of New Jersey had given its go-ahead for the show.

The stage was built on the steps of the capitol building, and the plaza became crowded with fans. Governor Hermani, looking boyish and exuberant, did quick news spots asking New Jersey employers in the vicinity of the capitol to let their staff off to attend the show.

The crowd rocked and rolled. Bruits was going back to his roots, performing the fast, upbeat street anthems. Rock critics calls these songs his "Great" period, from 1978 through March 1981. He ignored all the morose, unpleasant material from his "Suck" period, from March 1981 to the present. When he performed "Made To Move Fast," he drew out the jam for an extra four minutes and the crowd was cheering for more. To the side of the stage was a special set of VIP bleachers. The people there looked quite official.

"All right, Jersey!" Bruits bellowed. His mike was turned down, the levels were cranked to their stops, and his speech was garbled beyond recognition. They did understand the word "Jersey" and cheered wildly.

"New Jersey's a colony again!"

They heard "New Jersey" and began to chant. Some chanted "Jersey." Some chanted "Bruits."

Jersey City TV was provided a direct sound feed. They understood the words, even if the crowd did not. "Uh," the soundman asked the video technician, "what did he just say?"

"The British Empire is back!" Bruits pumped his fist in the air.

"Did he say 'British Empire'?" asked the soundman.

"I think he said 'Bruits something something is back,'" said the reporter, a pretty, pale blonde who had put on headphones.

"I don't think so."

"The sun is never gonna set on this party! Are you with me?"

The crowd heard the word "party" and they could tell from his tone of voice that Bruits was asking them a question. Twenty thousand of them answered, "Yeah!"

Bruits belted, "Hail Britannia!"

Nobody understood a word of that, but still they answered, "Yeah!"

"Weird," the pale blond reporter observed.

"Yeah," said the soundman.

"You gonna swear allegiance to Her Majesty the queen? Raise your fists and say yeah!"

They heard the "yeah!" part and they answered, "Yeah!"

"You swear?"

"Yeah!"

"You're the greatest!"

"Yeah!"

"You're all a part of the colony of New Jersey!"

Yes! They understood some of that! He said New Jersey! And that's where they were! New Jersey! The crowd went wild. "Yeah!"

"Get the cameras going *now*," the mousy blonde said. She was on the air in eight seconds.

"...reporting from the Bruits Sprigstern concert in front of the capitol building in Jersey City, where Bruits Sprigstern has apparently repatriated twenty thousand fans to what he is calling the British colony of New Jersey."

By the time the local station had rerun the minutes-old tape of Bruits's odd message to the fans, the concert was paused for a message from the governor of the colony of New Jersey.

"I believe the man we're seeing on stage is Oscar Dowzall, the former governor and current star of several extreme gay pornographic videos. Governor

Dowzall was also knighted by the queen of England during his last term as governor. Bruits Sprigstern also holds an honorary title. I believe we're looking at a takeover attempt in New Jersey, just as occurred in one of the small African nations and as was attempted hours ago on the Caribbean island of Jamaica. There are even reports of just such an attempt in a rumored territory of Newfoundland, and now Dowzall is starting to speak. Let's go live."

The concert volume was adjusted. The volume went up. The levels went down. The multimillion-dollar sound system had been broadcasting voice messages like a high-school public-address horn; now it sounded as clear and rich as the sound system in a well-equipped Pontiac. Every word spoken by Dowzall was like he was talking to you in your own living room.

"Thank you, all of you, for what you have done. I am gratified that you have shown such enthusiasm and eagerness. Thanks to my special guests. We have most of the New Jersey government sitting right here. Please welcome them!"

Cheers. How cool that politicians were watching a rock and roll show.

"Hey, who's minding the store, anyway?" Dowzall asked. If anybody understood the pilfered quip they didn't think it was funny—except for Bruits Sprigstern, who laughed into his microphone like Ed McMahon. Dowzall laughed with Bruits, then addressed the people. "And thanks for welcoming me back—you people are the best!"

Twenty thousand fans still didn't have any clue what he was talking about, but they knew he was being flattering. They cheered.

"I said, New Jersey is the best!"

"Yeah!" the crowd responded.

"Let's make it official!"

"Yeah!"

Dowzall handed the mike back to Sprigstern and, of all things, a horse was led onstage, with a gleaming silver breastplate and silver blinders and wild peacock feathers standing from its mane guard.

"We're gonna raise the flag," Sprigstern shouted. "You helped us do it. I knew you'd come through for me. The people from New Jersey are the best people in the world! Way to go, New Jersey Colony!"

Bruits's infectious enthusiasm got the crowd chanting, "New Jersey, New Jersey," and most of them were wondering what this was all about, but most of them were too embarrassed to turn to ask the people around them; everybody else, after all, seemed to understand what was going.

A wheeled set of stairs was positioned alongside the horse, and Dowzall stepped up and gingerly swung one leg over the back of the horse. The handler gave him the ceremonial reins—keeping a set of reins for himself—and a stagehand gave Dowzall a gleaming chrome helmet.

He held it under one arm, waved to the crowd, then put the helmet over his head. It was custom made for him by an armor maker he had met at the Annual

Newark Renaissance Festival. Across the nose bridge was an evil-looking gash of an opening, fitted with darkened glass. When his head was fully inside the helmet, the top of his head pressed together a pair of contacts, and a rhythmic bar of light began to travel back and forth across the eyepiece. Annoying from the inside, and probably not authentic, Dowzall knew, and yet it made him look quite intimidating and frightening. He had been very afraid of the Cylons from the original *Battlestar Galactica* television show and they had the same back-and-forth eye thingy.

The stagehand put his chrome lance into his hand.

Now all he had to do was stand there, while the official transfer of power happened.

Bruits Sprigstern and the band was jamming on "God Save the Queen," filled with so many extraneous guitar fills and saxophone improvisations that it was unrecognizable.

All eyes turned to the opposite side of the stage, where the capitol building flagpoles stood. They were empty, and the concrete circle was surrounded by a stony-faced ring of state troopers.

"Under normal circumstances, we should be seeing the Stars and Stripes flying there, alongside the flag of the state of New Jersey," reported the mousy blond woman. "Both are conspicuously absent today."

Two state troopers in dress uniform, walking in a stiff, military gait, entered the ring of guards and ceremonially unfolded a banner between them. They attached it to the flag line. The Sprigstern band had now completely lost the tune and was simply jamming messily, but they raised it to a fever pitch as the flag was raised.

The crowd cheered. Most of them were too far away to notice anything was wrong—they could see a brownish banner with stuff in the middle. Those who could see the flag thought maybe it was just a new design—the plows on the shield were gone, replaced with a more colorful red, white and blue square. Maybe that's what this was all about—a redesigned state flag.

"It's the New Jersey flag, all right," the blonde reported. "But now there's a Union Jack in the middle."

COLONIAL GOVERNOR Oscar Dowzall held a press conference, right there, on the capitol steps, as the concert was dismantled. "I have the full support of almost every senior member of the former state government. I intend to retain these skilled people in their positions—although there may be small adjustments to accommodate British law."

"What of Governor Hermani and Lieutenant Governor Ortega?" asked one of the reporters, playing it cool. None of them were sure how to handle this.

"I have no idea where they are at the moment," Dowzall replied without hesitation. It was true. He didn't know. "They, along with New Jersey State Senator Mercer, declined to be a part of the colony of New Jersey. As far as I am concerned, that makes them traitors in this land. They'd best get back into U.S. territory. My authority does not extend into Maryland, for example."

"What about New York?"

"What about it?" Dowzall said, wrinkling his nose.

"New York was a former colony, was it not?"

Dowzall seemed to be considering this fact for the first time. "I suppose it was."

"Does this mean the British Empire will attempt to retake New York?"

Dowzall was amused. "New Jersey has so much to offer. Ayounde has rich resources and even Newfoundland must have something to offer—but New York? Why would Her Majesty even want it back?"

16

By evening, the mobs filled Times Square, ire rising. The people of New York had been one-upped by New Jersey. It had never happened before, and the citizens of the Big Apple weren't enjoying the experience. Riot police were quietly dispersing the people in small groups and keeping new arrivals from joining in the demonstration. They were in a race against time—whittle down the mob before the mob worked itself up enough to take action.

"I know how they feel," Remo Williams said.

"You're not from New York," pointed out Mark Howard.

"But I'm mad enough to start breaking things."

Remo wasn't looking at Mark Howard. He was looking at Harold W. Smith.

"You shall not engage in foolish vandalism against the Emperor," Chiun chastised Remo.

"If I engage in vandalism it will be violent and destructive and widespread," Remo said. "But not foolish."

"All vandalism is foolish."

"Are you laying the blame on me for the action in

New Jersey, Remo?" Smith's cup was brimming with his own bitter brew this evening.

"What do you think? We had an agreement. You broke it, Smitty."

"Remo!" Chiun snapped. "Take care how you speak to Smith the Generous."

"I broke no part of our agreement, Remo," Smith answered, daring Remo to contradict him.

Remo did. "You signed a piece of paper that promised that I got to have some say in prioritizing what I did. You remember that, old man?"

"Remo, do not be insulting," Chiun warned.

"I remember. I haven't violated one letter of that agreement."

Remo was momentarily speechless. "What? You sent me to freaking Jamaica!"

"I did."

"Without bothering to tell me about freaking New Jersey."

"You're correct."

"You omitted the most important facts, on purpose. That's wrong."

Harold Smith sat back in his chair, but was as stiff as a plank. "You mean to say that, in addition to prioritizing your missions, you want to evaluate the urgency of the missions? I am obligated to give you a list of all possible crises?"

"Yes. How else can I figure out what's the most important?"

Smith nodded tersely. "So what would you have had me do, Remo? Read off a list of all pending crises, then detail each of them so you can choose the mission you feel is in the best interests of this country?"

"All you'd have had to say is, 'The British are coming to New Jersey' and I would have been on it," Remo said. "Come to think of it, New Jersey is in our country and Jamaica ain't. I don't see how anybody could say that us going to Jamaica was the best thing to do."

"So," Smith said, "regardless of the lack of potential damage to U.S. stability, you would have put that theater of the crisis above all the others? People would have been dying in droves in the streets of Jamaica. Just a few were killed in New Jersey, but New Jersey was still more important?"

"You're twisting the truth and you're dodging the point. You broke our contract by failing to give me all the facts."

"I don't agree. I know I did the right thing, however, if my actions led you to keep Sir Mutha from perpetrating genocide in Jamaica."

Remo folded his arms on his chest and glowered. Mark Howard tried not to look at him. Remo Williams, sometimes goof, could also be the human embodiment of death. He was the most skilled assassin on Earth, and sometimes you could read it in his eyes. Sometimes he was the manifestation of something terrifying.

Harold W. Smith could ignore it, somehow. He looked at Remo and waited.

"So? What do we do about New Jersey?"

"We do nothing."

"What you mean to say is…?"

"What I mean is, we do nothing. Right now we're in a holding pattern. This is a politically delicate situation."

"Bulldookey."

"Consider the complications, Remo," Smith said. "First of all, there's the legality of the actions by the British."

"There's no legality to it at all," Remo said. "We declared our independence. We showed them the door. This was a while back, but they've got no claim over New Jersey."

"Of course not. Still, the President is waiting for the British parliament to officially denounce the Proclamation of the Continuation of the British Empire. They've been slow in doing so, in part because of a groundswell of support for the movement. It's a politically dicey situation for parliament—and here."

"You can't go offing British knights, Remo," said Mark Howard.

"If the knights have done bad things, why not?"

"Because it is a slap in the face of the queen of England," said Chiun evenly.

"She shouldn't have knighted these no-goodniks in the first place," Remo said. "Just because they're a part of the Royal Order of The Green Hankie they can't have immunity. It doesn't work that way."

"But the United Kingdom is our closest ally," Smith

pointed out. "We can spare a day or two for England to figure out its response to the crisis before we start taking up arms against the British."

"There is also the problem of support within New Jersey," Howard added. "Colonial Governor Dowzall seems to have the backing of most senior state officials. They're working for him."

"Under threat of death," Remo reminded him.

"Probably. Even the manner in which he made the transition public helped garner support for the recolonization. Even if the concert-goers didn't know what they were agreeing to, they all did take an oath of loyalty to the new governor and the queen."

"Stupid games," Remo responded. "Cheap tricks. That's no way to pick leaders."

"But more sensible than how this nation normally chooses leaders," Chiun pointed out.

"Some of the support for this movement is genuine," Mark added.

"In Ayounde, maybe they want to be colonized," Remo said. "Not in New Jersey."

"Yes, in New Jersey," Smith said. "There's a fairly vocal movement backing colonial rule."

"Truly?" Chiun asked.

"Former anarchists, mostly. They want the U.S. to keep its hands off the new governor. They want to give colonial rule a try."

"You don't mean to tell me the President is going to listen to a few nuts?" Remo demanded.

"Of course not. The President is also not going to send any sort of armed forces against Americans. And he's not going to send in Special Forces to remove the colonial government until our closest international ally, the United Kingdom, has come to terms with this crisis internally. We're staying out of New Jersey for the same reason."

"You're all mad as hatters," Remo stated. "And you're on my shit-list, Smitty. You violated our contract."

"I've already explained that I didn't. As far as I'm concerned, that settles it. I'm not going to discuss it further."

Remo stood and held up his fingers. "One, it is not settled. Two, you will discuss it further. Three, when it is settled, I will make sure it is of the utmost concern to you."

"Remo, you are far too loose with your tongue," Chiun snapped.

"Emperor Smith-for-Brains is far too loose with the truth."

"You will not accuse the Emperor of telling lies!"

Remo shook his head. "I did and I do. Smith, you lied to me. Understand?"

"I did not."

"I believe you did. Do you understand that much?"

Smith's thin lips came together in a craggy line. "Yes."

"Call me when you're ready to own up."

17

Sir James Wylings was exhausted—and never happier.

For years he used his influence and power to accumulate trust, to collect favors and to stockpile influence among the politically powerful in the United Kingdom. He played a little, enough to keep himself sharp, but he knew not to extend himself too far.

One time only had he enacted a great scheme. That was in the 1990s, when he deemed it was necessary to procure a knighthood for himself. Already he had his long-term strategy mapped out. Already he had begun assembling pieces of old British law that would become his Proclamation of the Continuation of the British Empire. Only a British knight could be a credible leader of the Knights of the Proclamation—and a knight with some seniority, too. Not that it made any difference in reality. All was perception and politics.

But Wylings knew, even as a relatively young man, that he would need well-established knighthood to come across as a legitimate commander of the Knights of the Proclamation. So he got himself knighted.

It had to be accomplished through an act of bravery and selflessness. It had to be an act that sold well. It had to be, of all things, an admirable act that earned him enrollment in the honorary orders.

It took him a long while to figure out what would be the right thing to do, and then he came up with the idea of saving a bunch of starving refugees. Wylings owned shipping companies. He could just ship in some food to some starving refugees, right, and save them from miserable death.

But that wasn't as easy as it sounded. It turned out there were already various organizations busying themselves with just such an endeavor. They didn't even want Wylings's gifts of food, because they already had their own food-shipping systems in place. "What we could really use is cash donations," they told him.

Cash? Nobody was knighted for writing a check to the Red Cross! He needed something better.

What he needed was a group of refugees who weren't being serviced already by the world's food-services charities. Even the best of them were afraid to go into war zones. Trouble was, Wylings was afraid to go into a war zone, too.

So what he really needed was a war zone that only looked like one. Everybody else would be scared to go in; he would know it was truly safe and could bravely and personally lead in his cargo of food for the pathetic, dying natives.

That's when he hired Jeremy Southeby.

Jeremy Southeby was a kindred spirit in many ways—a throwback to the days of the British Empire. He lived a life that shouldn't have been livable any longer, adventuring and hunting and traveling through Africa and Asia. He lived for the thrill of cheating death and evading foreign law.

His favorite undertaking was ivory hunting, starting with the tracking of the biggest elephants in Africa. He would pursue them on foot, just as they did in the old days, bringing them down with nothing more than a high-powered rifle.

"You chase 'em down, mile after mile, hopin' not to be tracked yourself by the preservationist," Southeby related. "They're using helicopters these days. They know how to spot a dying beast from the air. You have to hope they're not around to get to the prize first."

The truly successful hunt came when the elephant finally dropped from exhaustion. Southeby would catch up to them, preferably while they were still alive, and cut out the great heart of the beast. "When you sink your teeth into that great mass of muscle, that's when you're a real man. That's when you're a hunter!"

He would personally cut the tusks from the pachyderm and pack them out of the interior, assisted only by a small knot of trusted Africans who had hunted with him for years.

But Southeby's hunt for thrills didn't stop there. This ended just the first part of the thrilling epic.

Southeby would smuggle the ivory, one way or another, onto his private sailboat, an old family yacht. The once luxurious appointments were now shabby, but Southeby had installed diesel engines, as well as radar, sonar and other electronics to allow him to sail it almost anywhere in the world—and infiltrate marine monitoring from Morocco to Mongolia. On board was another bunch of compatriots, just as hard-bitten and loyal as his African guides.

They would take the cargo of ivory and sail it across the Indian Ocean, usually through the Pacific to Japan, where they would again need to sneak the cargo past the increasingly vigilant Japanese anti-smuggling enforcement.

"They're getting tougher. All over, they're getting tougher. Harder to get around them all the time," Southeby would say. "It's a shame when I get boarded and I have to dump a cargo." Dumping the cargo meant activating a trapdoor in the bottom of the hull. The illegal cargo was always stored in a watertight bulkhead, so the doors could be opened remotely, removing the incriminating evidence. "But that doesn't happen too often," Southeby claimed.

Sometimes it would be rhino tusks, or whatever other ephemera was in high demand in Japanese aphrodisiacs these days. Sometimes, Southeby hinted broadly, it would be living, human cargo that he would transport, often from Southeast Asia, taking them to exclusive island resorts at undisclosed locations in the South Pacific.

"Now that's a cargo you really hate to jettison."

Southeby grinned, telling the tale to Wylings at the club and drinking gin. "The others cargoes you might have a chance of coming back for to salvage, when the coast is clear. But of course, if you dump the pretty girlies, there'd be no point'n comin' back for 'em."

It made Wylings shiver to think of it—and he believed every word. He'd known Southeby for thirty years and had yet to catch the man in a contradiction. His weren't fairy tales but true exploits. Amazingly, it was all done for the sake of the adventure. Southeby was a millionaire who didn't need his smuggling income. In fact, every cent of the blood money was hidden away, Southeby conceded, for rainy-day use.

Southeby was just the kind of man to engineer Wylings's feat of heroism.

"Sure, mate, I can pull it off for you," Southeby said. "Sounds new and exciting."

Wylings offered to pay Southeby handsomely for his expertise. "Whatever, Wylie. I'll take a few pounds." Southeby was clearly, again, not motivated by greed.

Southeby found the right locale. The ideal collection of African villages ravaged by drought and completely dependent on food aid—and completely isolated from the outside world.

Southeby and his African mates hired a few extra helping hands. They were Unthu tribe, from a hundred miles to the northeast, and the type of renegades who would not notify any loved ones of their upcoming trip. They'd never be missed. They were ostensibly to serve as trackers, to help Southeby find a local sort of small, rare ape.

The trackers' guns were taken while they slept, then used to massacre them in the light of day. That was step one.

Step two, arrive on the scene shortly after the humanitarian airdrop came. Take the Fernis at gunpoint, with the food packs, to the site of the Unthu killings. Shoot the Fernis with the Unthu weapons and bury the food packs.

Step three, sit back with a bottle of lager and let the situation ripen.

Step four. English Gentleman James Wylings, traveling into a dangerous and isolated corner of Africa to photograph an endangered subspecies of small ape, stumbles upon a forgotten and starving collection of Fernis tribal villages. Without regard for the grave financial losses, he uses his satellite phone to reroute one of his own cargo ships, which happens to be transporting foodstuffs, as well as eleven thousand MP3 players made in Malaysia. Wylings's own private jet is used to airlift the supplies from the African coast to the isolated Fernis villages. Wylings's own equipment beams images of the starving children and villages with corpses lying where they had fallen.

The media picks up on the selfless act—somehow it becomes known that Wylings suffered personal monetary losses of hundreds of thousands of pounds by diverting his cargo ship and missing a delivery date of

MP3 players to Cape Town. When UN investigators arrived, Wylings himself led them to a place twenty miles from the village, where the rotting bodies explained how the monthly food shipment had gone missing.

"Wylings International, Ltd., is sending a team of doctors to service these people for the indefinite future," announced a tired-looking, but quite dignified, James Wylings in a press conference from the Fernis region. "I've also ordered one of our survey teams off the job in Australia so they can commence efforts at once to locate new subterranean water sources for the Fernis. We hope to have wells dug within the next week, and our engineers will design and build an irrigation infrastructure for these people. After these people have regained their vigor, Wylings personnel will remain here to insure these people are provided what they need to create new lives for themselves. Schools. Medical supplies. Most importantly—" and here Wylings paused to give a stern accusing look at the audience behind the camera "—will be a communications system. These people were starving for weeks and had no way to let their cries be heard by the outside world. This is an unforgivable oversight."

The oversight was clearly made by the humanitarian aid organization that had taken on the responsibility of feeding the starving Fernis. The organization tried to defend itself. "Every village in the Fernis region had short-wave radio, which we provided. It was a horrible happenstance that these radios became nonfunctional during these time of crisis."

Actually, sneaking in and sabotaging the radios in every village had been step 2-B. Southeby had done the work himself, all in a single night, creeping into the villages, finding the weather-protected radio huts and creatively disabling each in a unique way. "I felt like a ninja!" he exclaimed to Wylings later.

"Glad you enjoyed yourself."

"It wasn't just that, either. It was the thrill of the making things happen. You know what I mean, Wylie? I killed a bunch of these savages any other place at any other time and nobody notices. I kill the right bunch at the right time, and bam! Global interest! I have to tell you, mate, this has been great fun. I owe you a debt of gratitude. No more puny ivory runs for me. I'm going into the business of African geopolitics."

"Sound like great fun, Southeby," Wylings said. "I can't wait to hear about it at the club." But Wylings had just become extremely worried about Southeby. Southeby knew his secret. Southeby took chances. Southeby might get caught red-handed someday playing his games of geopolitics in the African interior, and there'd be no trapdoor to dump the evidence. Even Southeby couldn't be counted on to keep his mouth shut if he was interrogated by some African despot.

A few days later Wylings happened to be visiting the coast, prior to his return to England, and he joined Southeby on the old family yacht.

"I'm keen to see this bulkhead you go on about, Southeby."

Southeby was more than happy to show it off.

"There's a gear, see? Retracts the floor into the hull completely. I'll just open it partway." He had described it to Wylings ten times, how he could retract the door halfway and still go fishing or snorkeling. Wylings felt the floor move beneath his feet, sliding into the hull, until half the tiny space was open to the black seafloor beneath the old ship. He and Southeby could hardly stand in the little shelf that was left.

"So, why doesn't the room just fill up with water?"

"Air pressure, Wylie." Southeby grinned. "See that little vent? When I got to do an emergency dump, that vent is opened up. The air vents out and the water rushes in. Don't open it, you dolt!"

Wylings had already moved the lever. He knew it was used by human cargo to refresh their meager air supply during their days and weeks locked in the miserable, lightless box.

"Hell, Wylie, what'd you do that for?" The air was hissing through the vent and the water was soaking their shoes already. Southeby reached across and closed the vent, and Wylings stuck him with his tiny shiv.

"What the hell?" Southeby touched the wound and looked at the dollop of blood on his fingers. "What's got into you, Wylie?"

Those were his last words. The poison reached his nerves. It was fast-acting stuff and it took away his motor control, but it wouldn't kill him.

The water *would* kill him. Wylings didn't even have

to push him in. Southeby slumped into the ocean water and couldn't make his arms stroke, couldn't make his feet kick. They were doing their own thing. Southeby gave Wylings a last look from the dark water—not an accusation, but a question. They were mates. Why had he done it?

Southeby didn't sink like Wylings thought he would. He bobbed to the surface, facedown, in the small trap-door opening. Wylings let himself out in a hurry, the air rushing around him and rising the level of the water inside the cubicle, carrying Southeby into the cubicle for his crew to discover when they returned to the ship in a week or two.

BY THE TIME Southeby was discovered, Wylings had returned home a hero, although he modestly downplayed his feats in Africa. There were already rumors that he would receive royal recognition. He was on the short list for knighthood that season—just him and the British publisher who had originally come up with the concept of putting photos of topless women in the daily papers, thus gaining worldwide distinction for British journalism.

Wylings was given his audience with Her Majesty and got his ceremonial sword taps on each shoulder. He celebrated his new title, but he bided his time for ten more long years.

His first taste of his adventure showed him how risky it could be. Southeby was invaluable, but Wylings should have foreseen Southeby's inherent risk. He needed to think his plans through with greater care in the future.

He had all kinds of wild schemes brewing, all based on a single fervent conviction: England was the rightful ruler of the world.

The British Empire had been right and good. It should never have been allowed to disintegrate. England was the center of civilization, eminent in culture, superior in judgment. The world would have been better served in the past few hundred years if England had retained its grip on power.

The Russians would never have adopted communism, which meant they would have spent the twentieth century actually doing something productive. The Japanese would never have gone a-conquering across Asia, not with the English keeping a stern eye on them. The Germans—that problem would have been nipped in the bud in the time of the kaisers. Big War One and Big War Two would never have happened. The decades of violence in the Middle East would have been nothing more than a few tribal skirmishes. Africa would be more or less peaceful.

As for America, if she had remained under the control of the British, she would have served as the muscle to enforce England's wisdom.

And that was what America would be, some day. It would have to be skillfully done, but Wylings could foresee it happening. He would start retaking the colonies around the world—those that would benefit England the most, and those that would give England a new foothold in the lands that she had to someday conquer anew. The tide of support would help Wylings take back more and stronger territories, and with British rule would come a new and splendid peace.

The world was weary of war and violence. Once the people saw that the new British Empire could quell the violence, there would be whole nations clamoring to subjugate themselves.

One important point: the British Parliament was not equipped, or legally entitled, to rule a vast global empire. That required a single authority, as the proclamation spelled out in no uncertain terms. The rebirth of the empire was also the reemergence of the power base of British royalty.

Which begged the need for a powerful, benevolent and wise king of England.

18

Sir James Wylings came up with his crazy scheme years ago. Back then it was a pipe dream. These days it still bordered on the insane, and Wylings would be the first to admit it. But he was going to succeed. He had the strategy, he had the tools, he had the leverage to make it happen.

That's all his knights really were, after all—his tools. They'd help him get this project off the ground, with their petty ambitions and their celebrity status. Later on he could discard them like the disposable knights they were. When he was running things, England would once again return to the days when knighthood meant something more than pop music fame. For now, they had succeeded better than he had hoped—until Jamaica. In Jamaica, Sir Muffa Muh Mutha's coup attempt had gone down the drain with unexpected swiftness. Wylings still wasn't sure what had gone wrong there. Somebody had been on the ground on Hope Road ready to react the instant Jamaica House came under attack. Who was it? Some sort of special-forces unit? Whoever it was, they were few in number and skilled at keeping a low profile. Probably some American unit called in to assist the Jamaicans.

Sir Muffa Muh Mutha's death was no great loss. The man was an imbecile. He'd only been chosen for the coup because he had a bit of a score to settle with the Jamaicans. His chief strategist's loss was more painful. Sissy Muh was a mocha-skinned goddess. It took all Wylings's self-control to not succumb to her temptations—and he'd never even met her in person.

None of his recruits met him in person. None of them knew him for who he was. He would emerge into the public eye soon enough, when the time was right to wrest control….

"What's bothering you, Wylie?" It was Andrew Dolan. He and Wylings had been friends since boyhood. He was a member of parliament, and his sympathies lay on the same plane as Wylings. A good chap. It was just the two of them, in the bar of the club. The three-hundred-year-old club was a private establishment that was the second home to some forty-seven men of special character and breeding and status. Here, in the bar, Wylie laid out his plans to his best mates, Dolan and Sykes. Both sat in parliament. Both longed for the days of old when their forefathers were more than just bickering fools in an congress of bickering fools.

"Jamaica bothers me, Andy. Something strange about all that."

"Old man, you're too hard on yourself. You can't expect to succeed every single time."

The private, intimate bar was tended some of the time, but most hours it was to the members to fix their own drinks. It was a matter of privacy—this was where they discussed their business and their politics. The decisions made here impacted the UK and the world. It was more comfortable not to have a man standing there listening in, even if he was just a lackey drink mixer.

"It's not that we didn't succeed in Jamaica. It is the way in which we didn't succeed. Somehow our forces were trampled. They were wiped out. Sir Mutha and Sissy killed. Almost everybody killed."

Sykes was clenching his teeth around an ivory-inlaid pipe, but he removed it to laugh and knock the pipe on the ashtray. "Don't grieve for that trash, Wylie!"

Wylings wasn't feeling as jovial as his companions. "It's not grief. It's concern, to be perfectly up front about it. What kind of a tiger do we have by the tail? That's what I'm wondering."

Sykes laughed it off, but Dolan said, "What do you mean, Wylie? This is something we expected. What's worrying you now?"

Wylings went to the bar, a solid-oak affair hand-hewn in the late eighteenth century, and poured himself more Scotch, hand bottled in the 1970s. "The hell of it is, I don't know. Doesn't it strike you that Sir Mutha and his mercenaries were flattened a little too completely?"

Sykes and Dolan looked at each other. Wylings was

one of their own, a British gentleman who feared nothing and no one. He was also an extremely careful man, with a nose for avoiding trouble. When Wylings became worried, there was a reason to worry.

"Brings to mind what happened in Ayounde, doesn't it?"

"In Ayounde?" Dolan queried. "That was simply the Ayounde national police putting up a fight. Our boys put them to rights. We still took Ayounde."

"You heard the rumors out of Ayounde, gents. The people are saying it wasn't their own police at all, but a pair of white men."

Dolan chuffed haughtily. "A pair of unarmed white men, no less, Wylie. One of them as old as time, in a long Oriental shirt of some kind, another man in a T-shirt. There's no way a pair like that could have offed our boys in the grand prix racers. They were mounting flamethrowers, machine guns, you name it."

Dolan added, "Besides, we own Ayounde. Sir Michele Rilli has the place firmly under his thumb now, and nobody is going to do a damn thing to take him out of there. Sir Frenchie's one of the most popular celebrities in the world and he's known to be a favorite of the queen's."

Sir James Wylings nodded somberly. "One thing you don't know, lads. Sir Rilli himself reported back to me a few hours ago. It was the first time we could get a secure call since he took the government palace in Ayounde. He reported the same thing the people in the streets of Ayounde reported."

"What?" Dolan yapped. "You're joking."

"I'm not. He was watching it all from the pickup chopper. He saw those two. He said the same thing. One old man, looking small and dressed in bright colors, but moving fast. He says that old man stepped on one of the armored cars and brought it to a dead stop. The next thing he knows, the old codger smashes the cockpit shield with his bare hand, and when he pulls it away, there's blood all over the place. Later on he found out the man's skull had been squashed."

"Bare-handed?" Sykes laughed.

"The younger man was doing the same kind of thing. Running like the bleeding wind. They said he was dodging the flamethrowers and even dodging gunfire."

"Gunfire." Dolan seemed to swallow the word.

"Rilli thinks it was these two blokes who wiped out all the armored attack racers," Wylings said. "By hand."

"That's crazy," Sykes said, trying to be dismissive and sucking on his glass to get the last few drops of Scotch.

"Sir Rilli is convinced that these two men would have stopped the coup, just the two of them, if Rilli's chopper hadn't taken the ministers when it did. Stroke of luck, that, he calls it. Says if their plan had been different, and they hadn't been able to lift those hostages right off the ground, Rilli is convinced all of them, himself included, would have been wiped out by the assassins."

"Assassins," Dolan said.

"And that sounds awfully damn similar to what happened in Jamaica, lads," Wylings finished up.

"Wylie, listen to yourself," Sykes said. "You can't believe any of it. It's ludicrous!"

"Rilli's a pompous bore, but he's not stupid," Wylings said. "He saw what the Ayounde people saw. The mercenaries who survived gave Rilli similar accounts. Two men, no weapons, and one of them old as the hills and Chinese to boot."

"Korean," corrected Dolan.

When Wylings looked at Dolan, his chum was as white as a sheet. "Mother of Mary, Dolan, are you ill?"

"I'm not sick."

"You look like you've seen a ghost."

"Not a ghost. Something out of a fairy tale."

Sykes and Wylings looked at each other and Sykes said, "You sound mad. What are you talking about?"

"Sinanju." He shrugged. "Sinanju."

Sykes stood up straight, looked down his long square nose and declared, "Dolan, you *are* mad."

19

"You remember the stories of Sinanju?" Dolan asked. "Remember what old Gerold used to tell us about the Masters?"

"Of course I do! I remember when we used to play Sinanju in your gardens," Sykes answered hotly. "Gerold was definitely out of his mind."

Sir Gerold was Dolan's paternal great-grandfather, and indeed he had been as old as dirt when the three of them were boys who played vigorous games in the large, professionally maintained ground of Dolan Manor.

"Remember what prompted the old man to tell us about Sinanju?" Dolan asked.

Wylings was pouring them all a fresh round, a way of covering his new nervousness. He was not a nervous man, but his hands were visibly shaking. "It was the incident with the roses, right?"

"It was," Dolan said. "We sliced them to pieces, as I recall. We were pretending we were knights of old, fighting the invading French."

"Mongols," Sykes corrected.

That's right, Wylings thought. They had scrounged up some old practice swords from the attic storerooms and had a grand old romp in the garden that got out of hand. Dolan cut Sykes across the shoulder and actually drew blood, and Sykes flew into a rage, attacking Dolan with the old sword as if he meant to kill him. Dolan was backed into his great-grandfather's rose garden, where he sought cover behind a trellis of Dolan's Perfect Blush, a variety that Gerold had developed himself when he was a younger old man. Now he came charging into the garden after them with a vigor he hadn't shown in almost as long, and he disarmed Sykes with an angry flick of the wrist. He turned the sword on the boy and pressed it against his chest. Sykes went from mad rage to abject terror. He knew the old man was out of his mind. What was to stop him from killing him, right then and there?

"He cut me!" Sykes protested.

"What'd you expect? Little foolish boys who play with knives will cut themselves. That doesn't mean you have to ruin my roses. Who'd you think you were, anyway—Don Quixote? Fools!"

"We're trying to learn to be knights," young James Wylings protested to the old man. That was a worthy undertaking, wasn't it? he asked, demanding accreditation.

"What a waste of time. There's no need for knights in the world anymore. Flowers we can always use."

"We're going to be men of bravery," Wylings protested. "We're British, right? The toughest men in the world."

That seemed to take the wind out of the old man's sails. He silently disarmed the young men of their old weapons and started to walk away, seriously subdued, then he turned back. "No matter what, you'll never be the toughest men in the world. Remember this, lads, there will always be someone tougher than you are."

"That can't be true!" Wylings said, somehow stung by the implication. "Somebody in the world has to be the toughest!"

"But not you."

"Who, then?"

"Who? You really want to know who?"

Wylings certainly did. The fury that had enraged Sykes was forgotten, and the old man waved them along. They followed him to his private library, and there he told them the stories of the ancient Masters of Sinanju.

"They were fairy tales meant for eight-year-old boys," Sykes insisted, waving the already empty glass of Scotch from Wylings. "They weren't real!"

"Most of the stories were untrue," Dolan agreed. "In fact, I think all of them were exaggerated out of the realm of reality by the old man—but there was an element of truth to them, too. He heard the stories from his own father and swears that there are Dolans who actually had a meeting with a Master of Sinanju, in Buck Palace itself—with the king!"

"Come on," Sykes responded. "I was there when he said all that, Dol. It's the kind of thing you say to boys to fire up their imaginations."

"Maybe, but I talked to him about it later, when I was older. Must've been ten years back and the old bloke was on death's door. He tells me one day, out of the blue, he says remember the lesson he taught us that day. He wanted it to be the one great lesson he taught me before he checked out. 'There's always somebody tougher than you out there,' he says to me. I tried to tell him that wasn't so unless you count Orientals in fairy tales. That's when he tells me there really were Masters of Sinanju. 'There were and there are, to this day,' he says. 'And what I told you they could do, they could do. There's people known to me, to this family, who had run-ins with the Masters—but they didn't live to tell the tale.'"

"You're puttin' us on, Dol," Sykes said accusingly.

"I'm telling you the God's honest truth. And the old man tells me one more thing. There's two of them. The Master and his apprentice, and the apprentice was a bleeding Yank!"

Sykes was staring at Dolan, waiting for the punch line, but Dolan was as dead serious as they had ever seen him.

THEY LEFT IT at that—unresolved as to what to believe. Dolan had made his decision. He was convinced that this fairy-tale assassin actually existed, and that he and his American trainee had nearly crushed the Ayounde coup attempt—and had wiped out the veritable army of mercenaries that Wylings had placed in Jamaica.

Sykes scoffed sullenly at the idea. Even as a boy he resisted the idea that the most powerful person on Earth was an Oriental, of all things.

James Wylings was in the middle. He knew that not believing in the supremacy of the Masters of Sinanju because they were Korean and American was a poor reason not to believe. But there were many other reasons not to believe….

And there were many reasons to believe. Dolan's family had treated the old patriarch, Gerold, as if he was senile. They'd treated him that way for decades, and he wasn't crazy at all, just an eccentric individualist. Deciding that he was touched in the head made it easier to excuse his politically incorrect statements—and made it easier to remove him from the role of the decision-maker for the family.

But Wylings always thought the old man was perfectly sane, as sharp as a tack. He lived in the past, but he wasn't prone to fancy. Even when he told the fairy tales of the Masters of Sinanju he had seemed to be improvising about the plot, but not about the Masters themselves. The challenges were prone to change—what was a three-headed dragon one time would be a serpentine basilisk the next time the story was told. The Masters never changed. Gerold seemed to take them very seriously.

Were they true? Were they genuine, but something too dangerous to talk about? Did old Gerold work the Masters of Sinanju into his fairy-tale adventures just so he could talk about it in one way or another?

If only the old gent was still around to ask. What family did he refer to that had run-ins with the Sinanju Masters and had not survived to tell the tale? There was no way to even guess.

20

When Sykes and Dolan arrived at Wylings Manor, they found their old friend sunk in a chair in his private study, no drink in his hand. He was sunk so low, his face a mask of concern, it was as if a large and invisible weight were pushing down on him and he could barely tolerate it.

"Sit down. We have important matters to discuss."

They already understood that. They had been called in for a special meeting at Wylings's personal residence, and that never happened. They always talked at the club. On the off chance anyone was keeping an eye on their activities, they didn't want there to be any sort of pattern of activity that would hint that they were planning some sort of strategy, about anything.

Sykes and Dolan were supporters on the inside—power brokers in parliament. Wylings knew he could make his plan work only if he had governmental backing.

Right now, Sykes and Dolan were playing their games carefully. Parliament was trying to come up with a consensus on how to respond to the recolonization violence and the matter of the Proclamation of the Continuation of the British Empire. Sykes and Dolan were to keep a consensus from happening. Until parliament sent a clear message to the world that said the proclamation was illegal, then the actions in the colonies had to be considered legal under British law. Nobody wanted to offend the British—and notably the queen of England—until it became absolutely necessary.

"I have decided to ramp up the threat level, so to speak," Wylings announced without preamble. "I am going to assume that we are being hunted by the Masters of Sinanju."

Sykes sniggered. Even Dolan was surprised by it.

"Before you say anything insulting, let me explain further," Wylings said. "I did not say that I believe the Masters of Sinanju exist. They might. They might not. I am saying that I shall assume that they are hunting for us."

"Even if they don't exist," Sykes said tauntingly.

"Don't be an idiot!" Wylings snapped. It had been a long time since Wylings had said anything so harsh to his old chum. "Kindly let me finish speaking."

"All right, Wylie." Sykes sat and waited.

"Somebody is out there. They were in Ayounde and they were in Jamaica and they are against us. Maybe they are trying to find us or maybe just trying to stop our colonization efforts. Maybe it is not the Masters of Sinanju, but it is *someone* with extraordinary capabilities."

"Ridiculous," Sykes snapped.

"Maybe what we're talking about is something as

mundane as a special-forces team that's trained to operate at an uncanny level of efficacy and stealth," Wylings continued. "Maybe something more. Whatever it is, SAS or Sinanju, it's decimated our men when it could, and we need to defend against it. Which is why we must be prepared for it."

Sykes rolled his eyes to the ceiling. "Sinanju, indeed."

"Believe what you will, Sykes."

"And what do you believe, Wylie?" Dolan asked curiously.

Wylings nodded to himself, as if considering it anew, but he explained he had thought the matter over extensively in the past few hours.

"When the British Empire was pieced together out of the uncivilized world, there were always new dangers that the English hadn't counted on or had never heard of. Think of the other stories we know from our own families, like the wild yarns your old uncle brought back from India." Sykes made to speak, but Wylings held up his hand and cut him off. "Most of them just flights of fancy made up by savages to dazzle the other savages, naturally, but there must be some truth to some of those yarns. It's hard not to believe in some of them, and it's hard for me to disbelieve in the Masters of Sinanju. They're just human beings, after all, but they happen to be the world's most skilled assassins. What the witnesses saw in Ayounde and what Dolan's father told him about the Master taking an American trainee tells me that this is what we are up against."

Sykes was wavering, but he still made a face about it.

"And what we believe in is actually beside the point," Wylings continued. "I'm not going to take chances against whatever it is, lads. It's good at what it does and it might be stalking us this very minute."

"So what do we do about it?" Sykes asked, showing a little genuine concern for the first time.

"You do nothing about it, except what you're already doing," Wylings said. "I've got extra defensive measures ready to deploy, so to speak. I need you to keep the debate going in parliament. The world thinks England supports the recolonization and nobody wants to pick a fight with Great Britain. The one thing we cannot afford at this point is to get a declaration from parliament that says we're not sanctioned."

Sykes and Dolan looked at each other.

"Bad news on that front, Wylie," Sykes said.

21

Sir James Wylings sat alone in his private study after his old school chums had scampered off to parliament.

He was disappointed in Sykes and Dolan. They had performed their roles without ambition—and that failure dated back to their years at university, where they had failed to throw themselves into their careers as completely as they should have. They did well, but they were never driven in the way Wylings was driven.

If they had been truly ambitious they would have formed more solid relationships among the political elite of Great Britain, and they would have been better prepared to exploit those relationships when the time came. Oh, they had done well enough, sewing seeds of uncertainty among members of parliament about the legal basis of the recolonization movement. Parliament had been arguing the point for days, but Dolan and Sykes should have had the influence to stall a vote indefinitely.

Wylings didn't need to consider his next, drastic move. His plans for this eventuality had been set in stone a long time ago. Once the British officially came out against the recolonization efforts and declared that the colonizers were not acting with the authority of British law, then the reprisals would come. The Ayoundis would try to take back their country, even with the head of the nation and all his ministers held hostage. The Canadians would march their Mounties into Newfoundland and take back their precious province.

The American bastards wouldn't waste a moment before they flew choppers into New Jersey and decimated the capitol building, taking back New Jersey in a shocking, awe-inspiring onslaught of destruction.

Wylings was ready. He would make sure that there would be another reason for the world to keep its distance. He still had enough hours to make it happen in just the proper way. The news would break just after the news of the parliamentary vote.

Sir James Wylings was off to Ayounde.

He was met at the airport by his pilots. Wylings owned them. They knew how to keep their mouths shut.

The big jet lumbered down the runway and settled onto its route to Africa. The jet made this run each month. Air traffic treated it as a routine flight and never noticed that the jet was making unusually rapid progress en route to Sierre Leone.

Air traffic control in Africa landed the Wylings jet without delay and James Wylings debarked unseen, boarded a smaller, private jet and zipped away again. It took him twenty minutes to reach Ayounde, where he was granted landing permission without delay.

A taxi took him to the international bazaar. Wylings was relieved to see the street almost entirely deserted.

"Most of the stores not even bothering to open up again," his Ayounde driver told him. "Nobody coming to visit Ayounde yet. Ayounde people can't afford all this expensive things."

"Too bad," Wylings said, but he was delighted. He didn't want to have the blood of a lot of outsiders, especially Europeans, on his hands.

He used his pass code to enter a private door to a private flat above a shuttered shop selling one of the most expensive French designers. The rented flat was small, unfurnished and dusty, but it did have a loo, with a bathtub.

James Wylings drew himself a bath, then pulled a weapon of mass destruction out of his bulging trousers.

The small metal cylinder rested inside three sealed, flexible plastic capsules, the largest an inch in diameter and eight inches long. Inside each transparent capsule was a metal tube, as narrow as a drinking straw.

Wylings pulled on his rubber gloves and bent the capsule in his hands. The plastic should twist without breaking, but the cylinder would open up—eventually. He bent the plastic the other way, then back and forth. The crimp in the metal was getting easier. It had to give way sooner or later—

The metal broke, and a clear, viscous fluid leaked from the tube and seemed to fill the inside of the innermost plastic capsule. Sir James Wylings stood there looking at it, flooded with terror and fascination. He felt as if he had just summoned the Grim Reaper to the surface of the mortal world, which was more or less true.

The innermost capsule opened at one end and the viscous fluid began to seep into the second capsule.

"Christ!" Wylings released the capsule and it plopped into the bath water. He depressed the lever to open the drain, but he left the water running.

The bathtub in this flat had intentionally been plumbed incorrectly. The water didn't drain into the sewer; it was pumped directly into the water main from which it had come. The flat had been chosen for its proximity to the big pipe that channeled water to most of the residents of the capital city.

The plastic would be eaten away by what was inside, and then what was inside would drain into the water main and begin to spread. Soon enough…

A box of gasoline additive was resting on the loo, filmy with dust. A rolled-up piece of paper was sticking out of the top—actually a slow-burning fuse. A box of matches sat on the sink. Wylings had placed all the items here months ago.

There were some aspects of this operation that he had to handle personally. Some aspects that Sykes and Dolan didn't even know about.

Wylings lit the paper and got out of the flat in a hurry. The taxi driver was waiting for him and they started back to the airport.

"Forget something, sir?" the driver asked. "You weren't there long."

Wylings could see smoke coming over the tops of the buildings. The flat would be in flames already. Even if the contamination was traced back to the rented apartment, there would be no evidence left in the ashes.

But would there be enough time for the contents of the capsules to escape into the water main? Heat, after all, was the one thing that could kill them. But still, the water would protect them for minutes or longer. The contents would have escaped by then.

"Sir?"

"What?" he snapped. He had forgotten the driver. The man had asked him some sort of question.

"Forget something, sir? Need me to turn around?"

"Get me to the airport. I'm in a hurry. There's an extra ten pounds in it for you."

"Yes, sir." The cabdriver hit the gas. These days, he was getting maybe one or two fares a day. This strange British gentleman might be rude, but he was a godsend for the cabdriver. He could afford groceries.

The cabdriver didn't realize that he would be dead before he reached his neighborhood market. The man who ran his favorite shop would be dead, too. Everybody in his poor but friendly little neighborhood would be dead. Most of the people he knew would be dead.

The man in the back seat was their killer.

"I'm doing my best to get you there quickly, sir," the cabdriver said. He could sure use the extra ten pounds.

"Five more pounds if you shut up."

The driver happily shut up. He was an easygoing kind of guy, and he could tolerate a rude Englishman in silence—for free, let alone for fifteen pounds. He didn't know he would never get a chance to spend the fifteen pounds.

The cabdriver was hungry and thirsty. He'd celebrate his good fortune with lunch at the new Burger Triumph outlet, which was still in operation despite the recent coup d'état. He'd get their new Triple Triumph Megarific Meal. It came with an order of Trium-Phries and a large soda.

The bloke in the back seat was watching his telephone.

NOT MUCH FOR GADGETS, Wylings had bought the telephone for the great undertaking. There would be times when he needed to be in touch, no matter where in the world he was. Right now he was in the armpit of Africa and needed to see a legitimate news station. He got one, relayed to his phone via satellite from Gibraltar.

Breaking news on the BBC announced that parliament had taken an important vote. The prime minister had been on the scene and had scheduled a press conference within the next half hour, but unofficially the results were well-known. Great Britain had finally "come to its senses," as one of the fast-walking parliamentarians said. There would be a parliamentary condemnation of the recolonization movement and an official declaration that the Proclamation of the Continuation of the British Empire was not legal and never had been legal.

Even before the prime minister was allowed to make the announcement to the world, dissent was in the works.

There was his good man Sykes, Dolan at his side, orating for the news and taking just the right tone. "Of course a statement must be made to the world regarding the proclamation and retaking of British colonies," Sykes started out with—nicely worded so as to not actually commit to any instance against the proclamation or the colonizers. "But parliament has done everything wrong this time. Firstly, parliament has no authority to discard British law in such a sweeping fashion. It is especially ludicrous to believe that the lawmakers can go on record saying one of the laws of the land was never a law. That's patently absurd."

Well spoken, Sykes, Wylings thought.

"What's worse, parliament has delivered a stunning insult to the royal family. Parliament on this day has essentially given the aggressors of the world carte blanche to strike out at her duly appointed knights."

Interestingly aggressive stance, Wylings thought. Wildly overstated but most dramatic. Good work, Sykes! The man was a slower thinker, but a much more dynamic personality than Dolan.

But it was Dolan who delivered the truly delightful surprise. He stepped up beside Sykes and spoke in his ponderous, serious voice, which often lulled listeners to sleep—but on this occasion it had just the correct tone of morbidity. "For this reason, we have just this day formed a coalition of those within parliament and others within the British government who would like to go on record, and at this moment, to state that we do not wish to condone wholesale arrest and murder of British knights, as have our colleagues in parliament. We stand by the Crown. This debasement of the royal family was perpetrated in spite of our efforts and certainly not with our blessing."

Wylings almost laughed out loud at the extravagant claims coming out of Dolan's mouth, but delivered like a dirge. This speech would have impact. The cameras pulled back to show members of parliament crowding in behind Dolan and Sykes as the cameras pulled back—politicians rushing to be seen as supporters, not offenders of the Crown.

Wylings did laugh out loud at that moment.

The driver wanted to ask him what was so funny, but didn't say anything. He was in a pretty good mood himself, thinking about his fifteen extra pounds, and he didn't want to spoil it.

He dropped off the Englishman and was thrilled to get a fifty-pound note as payment in full. He wanted to thank the man, but the Brit was gone already, rushing down the sidewalk to the terminal for private aircraft. Maybe his fare had meant to give him a twenty instead of a fifty. Probably the man was too rich and too hurried to care. The cabdriver sang himself an old pop tune, but he changed the words around. "Hello, Yellow Gold Road."

He pulled into the shiny new Burger Triumph and

didn't have to wait in line. He ordered a Triple Triumph Megarific Meal.

"You would like to Terrifi-Size that?" asked the cute young cashier.

"What? What are you saying?"

"They make us say it like that," she explained, leaning over the register to speak confidentially. "It's their silly way of saying you wanna get an even bigger order of Trium-Phries and a even bigger cup of soft drink."

"Oh." The cabdriver was feeling self-indulgent. He was also very thirsty and the soda looked unbelievably good. He could count on one hand the number of times he had tasted a drink with ice in it. "Yes, please, missy. I'll take the terrifi-super-duper-giant whatever it is."

She giggled. "Okay, big spender."

"I'd even be willing to buy a terrifi-size for the terrific girly at the counter if she had a lunch break."

Oh, did she start giggling then. "Maybe later. I get off in a couple of hours."

He looked at the name badge on her shirt collar. "Couple of hours, then, Ms. Trainee."

Oh, you should have heard her giggle. "Actually, it's Maluuna," she said as she gave him his heavy bag of food and the obscenely huge soft drink.

He sat in his car feeling on top of the world and sipped the ice-cold drink, thinking he had never tasted anything better.

The tiny metallic bits that had come from the city water and mixed with the soda syrup were too small for him to feel in his mouth. They were too few in number to register on his taste buds. He was one of the first victims to ingest them, and they had yet to procreate in sufficient numbers.

In the Ayounde City water supply, the microscopic devices were fulfilling their reproductive function by pooling in the water conduits where the sediment settled in unused conduit junctions. They gathered metallic particles and worked them, speck by speck, into little copies of themselves. The copies created copies. By evening, a hundred thousand little robots had become a billion.

They were swept away by the millions, traveling up the plumbing and into the homes and restaurants of Ayounde City. They were consumed by the people. Once they sensed the first damaging attacks of stomach acids, they were triggered into performing their second function.

They fought back.

The cabdriver had a slight stomach ache as he waited for another fare that never came. He picked a deserted lot, parked and stretched out in the back seat for a restorative nap, and soon he was in agony, clutching his stomach.

He had consumed only a tiny number of the devices, so they had to work for some hours before they ate through his stomach lining and eventually out of his body. He saw the hole in his gut open up and then he died, thankfully.

A half mile down the road, Miss Maluuna was sitting on the bench in front of the Burger Triumph, getting a little irritated at the tardiness of her date. She sipped her soda—she got them for free, one soda a day. Well, she'd give him five more minutes and then, forget it.

22

The first time that Mark Howard had the pleasure of meeting the white Master of Sinanju, Remo Williams, he was pretty sure he was in the presence of some sort of assassin, and he was pretty sure the man had skills beyond the ordinary and he was pretty sure the oddly talented killer was about to assassinate Mark Howard. He was scared.

Now he felt that kind of scared again.

"Is it the stuff from Scotland?" Remo asked for the second time, and for the second time, Harold W. Smith said he didn't know.

"Find out." Remo said the words and he pointed with his finger. This was a man who could kill with his finger. He looked mad enough to kill Smith and Howard and just about anybody else who got in his way.

Remo was very, very angry.

"There is no way to know for sure," Smith replied.

"Figure out a way to know for sure."

"How am I supposed to do that, Remo?"

"Listen, Smitty, you figure out a way. Because if it

is the stuff from Scotland, the stuff that you wouldn't let me go back to make sure was gone, then I'm going to get really angry."

Angrier than this? Mark Howard thought.

"And I'm going to take it out on you. If you don't figure it out, I'll assume it is. Got it?"

"Calm down, Remo."

"Calm down?" Remo said, not loudly but barely in control. "You turn on the TV today, Smitty? You see what's happening?"

"I've seen it."

"People are dying."

"I've seen it."

"Lots of people. If it's the stuff from the burned-up castle in Scotland, then it is blood on my hands and yours."

"Not true," said Chiun, coming into the office in a hurry. Yet he appeared at Remo's side as if he had been standing there quietly for five minutes. "The blame lies not with you or with Emperor Smith."

"If it's the shit from the castle, the blame lies with both of us. I'll have to kill us both."

"Remo!" Chiun squeaked, but there was a strange lilt to his voice. "Such words are for fools and madmen."

"I'm pretty fucking mad."

"And yet you are mistaken."

"You don't know that. Smitty doesn't know that. Smitty didn't know what was left in the castle when he told us not to go back there. I didn't know that when I went along with him. What I should have done is say 'Go to hell, Emperor Smitty, I'm going back to Scotland to clean up the mess.'"

"Instead, you went to Sa Mangsang, to clean up a mess you were certain existed," Chiun exhorted. "This is the wise choice."

"Wise?" Chiun called him a lot of things, but wise was a new one and it took the wind out of his sails.

"It was wise to attend to the catastrophe at hand rather than the catastrophe that might come on the morrow," Chiun said. "From whence comes this anger?"

Remo fell into a chair carelessly. "Have you looked at the television? It's like Africa's 9/11. Only with commercials, because it's only Africa. Not nearly as important as Americans. And all the reporters are getting the hell out, because you know, they'll hang around to report on an American in distress but they're not going to risk their necks on some Africans."

"And the blame falls to me?" Smith asked.

Remo considered that. He couldn't come up with a way to blame Smith for that one. Come to think of it, why was he trying to blame Smith for that?

Remo sighed. "We're responsible. If this stuff came out of that pile of rocks in Scotland where they were brewing nanobots, then we let them get out. We should have stopped it from happening."

"And how would you have done so?" Chiun asked. "How would you have known if these things were spirited away from Loch Tweed Castle prior to our arrival?

Recall that when we arrived there were none of the re-searchers even left alive. There were only the local rab-ble, infected with the sickness caused by Sa Mangsang."

Remo glowered.

"What of secret chambers?" Chiun asked.

"What of them?" Remo asked. "We didn't find any. We didn't have a lot of time to look, either, before it got too hot to stick around."

"The explosives staged at the scene were put there as a safety precaution. They were designed to destroy everything in the lab," Smith explained. "Including the antechamber."

"If it worked right," Remo muttered. "If nobody screwed up and put a tube in the wrong cabinet. If all the bombs went boom exactly how they were supposed to."

"What if they had?" Smith asked. "The castle site was sterilized soon after the fire. I won't go into details. Suffice it to say, the very soil upon which Loch Tweed Castle sits was heated until it melted. Nothing could have survived that, Remo, and if it did, it's encased in a block of glass as big as a city block."

Remo nodded. "And before that? After the fire, be-fore the place was sterilized?"

"There was a window of opportunity. If someone knew something was there, knew it would not be con-sumed in the fire, knew it would be accessible after the fire, if they knew all those things and were prepared to go in and take it, then it could possibly have been taken. All those possibilities are unlikely."

"Are you forgetting that the place self-destructed when it wasn't supposed to, Smitty?" Remo said. "Somebody blew it up, on purpose. It wasn't the lab people who worked there. They were all dead. It wasn't the morons who killed the lab people, because Chiun and I killed them. It wasn't you, which leaves a very small number of people in the world who even know the place existed, if you were straight with me at the time. The President? The prime minister of England?"

"Not even them," Smith admitted.

"Who else could have done it?"

"Unknown."

"You're right, Remo, somebody could have somehow known of these weapons and triggered the self-destruct charges with you inside and come back to take an overlooked stash of nanobots," Mark Howard said. "What would you have had us do about it?"

"Anything is better than nothing, Junior."

"We dispatched the sterilization team to the site without Pentagon authorization so we could get it done faster," Mark Howard said. "You were dealing with the threat in the Pacific. That was more important at the time. And we don't know that this threat is caused by the nanobots."

Remo said nothing. He did know. There were no germs involved, according to the earliest reports, and the scientists who studied the cause, who were on the scene and dying on their feet, reported evidence of active, mechanical-looking organisms in the city water. They hadn't even managed to get off hard data before their own guts were opened up from the inside.

This had all come just after the incendiary announcements from London. Parliament had finally approved the official disapproval of the Proclamation of the Continuation of the British Empire and the recolonization movement, though the initiative was being undermined by some members of parliament even before the prime minister could make the authorized announcement to the world. Still, British law was now officially governing Ayounde, Newfoundland and New Jersey, and the United States, for one, had launched its gunships and ground troops minutes later.

Operation Attack To Take Jersey Back was short-lived. The President himself ordered the operation scuttled as reports started coming out of Ayounde. He reasoned that he wasn't giving in to terrorism if he gave in so quick that nobody really noticed.

Remo was feeling double-talked into exhaustion. "What's the situation now?" he asked resignedly. "In Ayounde? What about Sir Race Car Driver? He still governor?"

"He has announced that the contamination seems to have halted, but the country faces a new health crisis. The capital is littered with cadavers and there are not enough people to clean them up. Disease will begin to spread within twenty-four hours."

"The contamination is over?" Remo asked.

"A few health workers are already arriving on the

scene and they confirm it," Mark Howard said. "They've even taken water samples and found it clean."

"What?"

"They are trying to persuade other health organizations to come into Ayounde as quickly as possible, before a bad situation gets worse."

"How can it be over?" Remo demanded.

"How would you like to go to Ayounde and find out?" asked Harold W. Smith.

"No," Chiun said. "I think not."

"I'm on my way," Remo said. "What am I looking for?"

23

Sir Sheldon Jahn allowed the applause of thirty thousands Asians to carry him into the backstage area. He'd given them three encores. That was enough. Always leave them wanting more.

Sheldon knew show business. He'd been a superstar since the early 1970s, when he had more hit records than he could count. Now all his fans were grown up and had kids of their own and Sheldon was as popular as ever, even though he hadn't had a chart-topper in years.

Show business made him as rich as the queen, but he was bored with it all. The concert in Hong Kong was his last ever. He was quitting show business, and embarking on a new career, at age fifty-nine.

Tonight he would become a conqueror.

It made him giggle.

Strolling through the backstage area without pausing even to change his attire, he ignored the sumptuous catering and the bevy of Chinese cross-dressers brought in for his enjoyment.

"Ell, where're you going?" It was his manager,

Clarice. She was proportioned like an upside-down bowling pin and smoked Camels using a slender, ivory holder. The antique cigarette holder was worth thousands, but it made her look ridiculous.

"Out," Sheldon replied.

"Dressed like that?" She waved her cigarette holder at him. Sheldon was still in his sky-blue sequined suit. "Who cares?"

"But darling, you haven't eaten."

"I'm too excited to eat," he replied as he slipped out the rear doors and into the waiting limo.

"Excited about what?" Clarice demanded, but the door thumped shut and the limo pulled away. Sheldon sighed and stretched out in the seat. Let Clarice fret. She'd know soon enough.

When the phone bleeped, Sheldon snatched it up.

"You should be able to see your army, now, Sir Jahn," said the voice of the enigmatic duke.

"They're here," Sheldon replied, peering through the dark glass to make out the distinctive shapes of the Hummers that crowded in around the limo. "We're on our way!"

"Good. Keep it cool, Sir Jahn. No whooping."

"I'll try not to whoop," Jahn promised, but he felt like whooping already.

They muscled through the dense Hong Kong traffic for twenty minutes before arriving at a glass-and-concrete box as big as the stadium they just left, but quite somber. The perfunctory sign at the front entrance told them they were arriving at the Divisional Ministry of Financial Logistics. The Hummers stayed on the street when the limo pulled to the doors.

Sheldon Jahn came out of the back with a wide smile, and he waved at the pair of uniformed guards. "Good evening!"

The guards were stunned. There was no mistaking the celebrity in the sequins. "Mr. Sheldon Jahn!" one of them exclaimed.

"In the flesh! How are you gents?"

"We are fine, sir."

"Good. Glad to hear it. What in the world is this place? Some sort of an accounting ministry? How terribly dull! Is it dull?"

The guards didn't get a chance to answer.

"They should at least decorate the place a little. Maybe some sequins."

The guards laughed at the stupid joke.

"Anyway, I'm hear to see somebody. Mr.… Mr.—" he found a scrap of paper in his breast pocket "—Sui-wah. Mr. Sui-wah. Do I have the correct building?"

The senior guard nodded. "This is correct, Mr. Sheldon Jahn."

"Call me Sheldon."

The guard nodded seriously, privileged to be bestowed this rare gift of intimacy. "Yes, Mr. Ell. Mr. Sui-wah is within this building. But, I am ashamed to say, I think you cannot go to see him."

"Oh. Oh, dear me." Sheldon Jahn's face fell. "But I have a gift for—for his daughter." Sheldon began to weep.

The guards were mortified and deeply embarrassed. The senior guard grabbed the receiver and called upstairs, then hung up saying, "Please come with me, Ell."

They marched inside, the senior guard and pop star Sir Sheldon Jahn. The reception desk was more like a guard post, but the guards just gawked.

"Why does a place this boring need machine guns to guard it?" Sheldon asked on the elevator.

"There are some financial dealings that happen here in a secure manner," the guard explained.

"Say no more! That stuff puts me to sleep. I let my lawyers handle the money. How is Sui-wah's daughter?"

"Sir?"

"Last I heard, she was very ill. The treatments weren't working. They weren't expecting her, well, to recover."

The guard nodded seriously. He had heard nothing of this, but he was only the guard.

"She mailed me a letter, you see. She's my biggest fan in Hong Kong. But she couldn't come to the concert because she's too sick. It broke my heart. So I brought her this." He showed the guard the teddy bear. It wore sunglasses and pink sequins.

"That will comfort her very much, I am sure," the guard said.

The bear was X-rayed at the security station on the top floor, along with Sir Sheldon Jahn. The machines had problems with the sequins and he allowed the jacket to be searched by hand. "Shall I take my trousers off?"

"No! No. That is not necessary, Mr. Jahn."

He was led into the information labs. "Oh, my word, what an awful place!" Sheldon exclaimed. "Nothing but machines and more machines!"

The machines were banks of mainframe computers and data storage units. "It is one of the largest data-processing centers in all of Asia," the guard said with pride and a hint of defensiveness.

"It's cold!"

"The air-conditioning is necessary to keep the computers cool."

"Just awful."

A confused and official-looking Chinese man in a lab coat approached them. "I am Mr. Sui-wah."

"It is so good to meet you! Tell me, how is your daughter? Is she responding to the treatment?"

Mr. Sui-wah looked stricken.

"Oh, dear heavens," Sheldon gasped. "Don't tell me—"

"Mr. Jahn, I am afraid my daughter has perhaps told you an untruth. She is not sick."

Sheldon just stared.

"I am so sorry. I was not even aware that she was a great big fan of yourself and now I do not know what to say."

Sheldon sat down at a workstation. "Oh, goodness. I had this made special for her!" He thrust the bear at

Mr. Sui-wah, who didn't know what to do. Finally, he took it and stammered out further apologies, never noticing that the downcast pop star was actually peering at the open door behind him.

"Is there anything I can do to make this up to you?"

"No. No harm done, really," Sheldon said. "I just feel a little embarrassed." He looked at his watch. "I guess I'll just leave."

"May I at least offer you a cup of coffee or tea?" the mortified Mr. Sui-wah pleaded.

"Not necessary!" Sheldon Jahn laughed as the lights went out and the emergency lighting system sprang to life. Sheldon jumped to his feet and sprinted for the open door. Ten paces and he was inside.

"Mr. Jahn, no!" Mr. Sui-wah shouted. He and the guard were chasing after Sheldon, but they weren't anywhere near quick enough. The British superstar had lulled them into a state of total unpreparedness.

Sheldon slammed the door in their faces, then pushed against the red emergency button. The electronics threw the dead bolts with a thunk.

Sheldon ignored the pounding on the door, making himself at home behind the utilitarian desk belonging to Mr. Sui-wah. He found the buttons he wanted and pressed them in the correct sequence. It was as easy as playing "God Save the Queen" on a toy piano.

The power was restored to the building and the emergency lights in the office gave way to the flicker of the harsh fluorescent tubes from above. Sheldon had just six seconds during the changeover in the power supply to punch in the codes that would disable the building's electronic security. Six seconds was more than enough time.

"Ha!" he barked as he snapped out the commands and saw the confusion on the first floor. The guards were hitting every button on their controls to try to get their security system to function again.

They gave up when the Hummers screeched to a halt outside their door and the mercenaries burst in, triggering their weapons. The guards were well-armored, so the mercs all took head shots.

"Yuck." Sheldon found himself strangely fascinated by the sight of the exploding skulls.

The mercenaries ascended floor by floor, ordering the occupants to raise their hands. They didn't hesitate to cut down anyone who failed to comply.

But somehow that was just fine with Sheldon Jahn. He was a war protester from years back, but this was different. This was for a good cause, and it was okay.

In minutes, the band of mercenaries in camouflage had reached the top floor. With guards stationed on every floor, no one was going anywhere.

The leader of the mercenaries appeared in the screen from the security camera just outside the office. He had Mr. Sui-wah and the friendly guard on the floor with their hands behind their heads, and he waved to Sheldon. "All secure, Sir Jahn."

Sheldon laughed. He had control of the Hong Kong Department of Financial Logistics—and so he had control of Hong Kong. That meant he had a stranglehold on the People's Republic of China.

The Commies were soon calling.

"Hello?" he asked into the beeping, lighted dedicated phone line.

"Who is this?"

"Sir Sheldon Jahn, governor of Her Majesty's Hong Kong colony."

There was confusion on the other line. "You will surrender to the army of the People's Republic of China! Our forces will enter the building in fifteen minutes!"

"Better not. Big mistake. Bloody awful for you." Sheldon hung up. "Oh, please attack. Please attack. Please, please, please."

They PRC army attacked. Not eager to destroy their own valuable property, they sent the first wave of soldiers in firing light machine guns that rained noisily against the glass and dented the steel exterior panels.

"I warned them," Sheldon announced delightedly. He flipped the two cobalt-blue plastic switches and started counting in his head.

"Hello?" he said into the phone. "Sixty million pounds. Seventy million pounds."

"What have you done?" demanded a furious voice in heavily accented English.

"Turned off Beijing's access to the International Monetary Data Exchange. I estimate it's costing the People's Republic about ten million British pounds every three seconds. One hundred million pounds!"

"What?"

"One hundred ten! Electronic banking, stock trades, commodity transfers—thousands of transactions are not happening because I threw one little switch. How about attacking the building some more?"

"Surrender at once!"

"Not again."

"What? What does this mean, not again?"

"Britain surrendered its dignity when it agreed to the first Hong Kong handover treaty, and again when we actually did turn it over. I'm reclaiming the territory of Hong Kong for Her Majesty the queen."

"But! But! The United Kingdom signed an agreement with the Chinese to give back Hong Kong—"

"That agreement was illegal."

"Hong Kong belonged to China first!" cried the faceless official in Beijing.

"Hong Kong belongs to the British Empire, mate," Sheldon said seriously. "We fought for it. We took it. It's ours forever, and no treaty or law or war is going to take it away from us. Is that firmly understood?"

"You are mistaken—it was the English who illegally occupied China's territory."

"You're costing your country a hell of a lot of cash. One hundred fifty million pounds. Call me back when it reaches a billion."

"A billion pounds?' the Communist gasped.

Sheldon hung up and let the phone ring until his diamond-encrusted Rolex informed him that a total of five minutes had elapsed since the switch was flipped. He flipped it again and picked up the phone. "I did you Commies a favor."

"You did us no favor! You are illegally occupying our department and you shall be severely punished!"

Sheldon flipped the switch. "One billion ten million pounds. One billion twenty million pounds. One billion thirty million pounds. Say you're quite sorry and I'll turn you back on."

"I am sorry!" cried the bureaucrat.

"That wasn't so hard." He turned it back on. "Now I want the people's financial secretary on the line, along with the people's defense minister. Unless I'm talking to them both in ten minutes, I flip the switch again."

"I WILL NOT BE blackmailed," snapped the people's defense minister. "Give me that." He took the phone from one of his faceless drones. "Who is this?"

"This is Financial Secretary Kow."

"Kow, why are you groveling to these English terrorists?"

"The economic repercussions are grave, General Sou. He has most effectively isolated our electronic data transfer systems. I suggest you cooperate, as well. We have less than seven minutes."

General Sou made a laughing sound like a yelping dog. "I will not do it. I do not understand the ethic of the accountant class of peoples, but we in the military have some sense of honor." He sniffed. His staff nodded more vigorously in proportion to the increased visibility of the general's nostrils.

His nose dipped and his lackey's heads froze midbob when another phone rang—*the* phone.

The general dropped the phone to the financial secretary on the desk and snatched at the dedicated line to the leader of the People's Republic of China. "Good day, Premier."

"Patch in Kow."

The general didn't know what the phrase even meant. "Pardon me, Premier?"

"Patch in Secretary Kow for a conference call at once!"

Kow—that was the name of the number-cruncher he'd just been talking to. Had he hung up on him?

No, the phone was still on the table, but the general had no idea how to conference the call into the dedicated line. "Conference Secretary Kow into this call immediately."

In all the scrambling that ensued, the connection was somehow made. "Hello?" asked Secretary Kow.

"Brief me on the situation, Secretary Kow," the premier demanded, and Kow did, in just thirty seconds. "We now have less than four minutes to make the call, General Sou and myself."

"I have informed the secretary that we will not negotiate with economic terrorists," Sou stated.

"Premier, this man who claims to be Sheldon Jahn has penetrated our defenses expertly," the secretary said. "The economic benefits to the People's Republic suffer at a terrific pace when he interrupts the data transfer operations. Ten million pounds every three seconds is not an unreasonable estimate."

"It's absurd!" the general snapped.

"Not when you add up the lost trade, the lost banking transactions, the lost commodity trades and all the thousands of small business transactions that go through the wires every second," the financial secretary argued.

"How could a British pop star have the wherewithal to turn all of it off and on at will?" the premier demanded.

Secretary Kow had trouble getting his words out. "The Hong Kong backbones have all been routed through our offices for better monitoring, Premier."

"An extremely foolish strategy," General Sou judged.

"Under your orders, General Sou."

Sou felt cold. "You are mistaken," he responded, too quickly.

"One of my predecessors was removed for vigorously resisting your orders to create the data pipeline, General Sou."

"Incorrect!" Sou shot back. He vaguely recalled having a handful of number-crunchers dismissed a few years back when they submitted a formal report that spelled out flaws in the ministry's strategy to isolate possible data leaks. As if some accountant could tell him about security!

"No, I remember this myself," the premier added.

General Sou said, "Premier—!" But that was as far as he got.

"It is beside the point at this moment. We will deal with this crisis before we deal with the security failure."

General Sou couldn't let the accusation go unchallenged. "This is a finance department failure."

"Obviously, it is not," the premier said offhandedly. "And did I not say that the matter would wait for later."

A guilty verdict and a reprimand from the premier, in the presence of another official—what could be worse? Sou found out seconds later. "Secretary Kow, make the call and give the pop star what he wants. We'll begin damage control immediately afterward. General Sou, you will be on the call with Secretary Kow and you will say nothing unless asked specifically by Secretary Kow. Understood?"

"Yes, Premier." General Sou wished he were dead.

24

"Impressively timed," Sheldon Jahn sang. "You called back in nine minutes, forty-one seconds. I once wrote a multipart anthem that was exactly that long. It was called 'Take Me to the Conductor.' Should have been my 'Stairway to Heaven.' You know, of epic proportions, selling records year after year, played to death on FM radio. A standard to measure other epic songs of the era against."

"What are your demands and who are you?" asked Financial Secretary Kow.

"I'm Sir Sheldon Jahn, don't you know?"

"I know who you are pretending to be."

"Listen, Mr. Kow, I'm the real deal. I'm the one and only actual Sir Sheldon Jahn, pop star and knight of the United Kingdom. Anybody else, and this would be illegal."

The financial secretary said, "I don't understand."

"Thanks for asking. You see, I am one of Her Majesty's knights. Know what it means to be a British knight? It's a lot more than an honorary title, you know.

When I became a knight, I was shouldered with certain responsibilities. The security of the British Empire—past, present and future—rests on my shoulders. Do you understand?"

"Not at all."

"Then I'll elucidate. A knight's role is that of protectorate."

"You're a pop star!" The secretary was clearly losing patience.

"I'm a knight. I'm Sir Sheldon Jahn. That means I'm obligated to protect England."

"What does this have to do with China?"

Sir Jahn tsked. "I'll explain it just one more time. Hong Kong belongs to England."

"England occupied Hong Kong once upon a time—it never belonged to England!"

"Once a territory comes under the authority of the Crown, it is always under the authority of the Crown. Any agreement treaty, trade or purchase that would allow the territorial authority to be lost is illegal and nonbinding. By the authority vested in me as a knighted servant of the Crown, I have the legal right to resume control of any former colony, in the name of the Crown. That's what I have done. Hong Kong belongs to me. Governor Sheldon Jahn."

"But that doesn't even make sense!" the Chinese official blurted. "It certainly defies all legal precedent. Your claims are preposterous!"

"Sorry you think so. The fact is, I'm in charge and

you can't do anything about it. Let's discuss our future cooperative efforts, shall we? I need to meet with my staff. Would you be so good as to let them know who's the new boss around here?"

"IT'S INGENIOUS," Harold W. Smith said.

"It is?" Remo asked.

"It is," Mark Howard said. "Sheldon Jahn has gone to the true seat of power in Hong Kong, and it's a seat of power that almost nobody knew about."

"It is an office of accountants?" Chiun mused, stroking his beard. Remo knew he was only seeming to look wise. The telltale wrinkles of confusion were in the corners of his eyes. It made Remo feel better to know he wasn't the only one who didn't get it.

"I don't get it," he announced.

"Of course you do not," Chiun said. "The ways of the bureaucratic world are a mystery to you."

"And that's how I like it. I don't need to know what's going on. I couldn't care less about any of this."

"Since they took control of the island, the PRC has assembled a system of electronic data pipelines from throughout the island that funnel data to the Hong Kong Ministry of Finance, specifically to the Financial Logistics Department headquarters. This gives them a central point at which to access all the systems dedicated to financial transactions."

Remo nodded. "Doesn't seem too smart, even for Communists."

"Their compulsion to monitor and control their domain overrode their need to keep their systems distributed."

"They've even done what they could to hinder the use of direct-satellite transmission," Mark added. "Some satellite feeds go through the monitoring system before being transmitted to the satellites. Jahn's got control of those now, too."

"So why don't they just start sending everything through satellite now?" Remo asked. "Then Sheldon will be sitting there with nothing to control."

"Not as easy as flipping a switch to reroute the call," Howard said. "The Chinese designed the system to make it difficult to sidestep. Even if the data feeds could be redirected, there's the satellite transmission capacity to handle it. The real problem is that you're talking about all kinds of data, Internet and proprietary data protocols, most of it encrypted. It would take years, and cost billions, to change it all to satellite."

Smith made a sour, discouraged face. "And Jahn won't let them do it. He's created a financial disaster already with his manipulations of the financial data channels. He'll shut everything down again if he discovers any efforts to bypass his stranglehold."

Remo made a face himself. He didn't understand all this stuff. It didn't make sense to him that electronics had to go one way and couldn't go another way. It was just electricity, right? Why *couldn't* they all just flip a switch and start going into space instead of through the phone wires? "I guess they're just going to have to bite the bullet and make the switch, then deal with the lost income after they're up and running again."

Smith and Howard gave him the same look the other orphans gave him when he stood up in class and answered that Henry Ford flew the first airplane at Kitty Hawk.

"Okay, Remo is dumb."

"You don't understand the scope of the losses, Remo," Mark said, trying not to sound too condescending. "The Hong Kong economy has been devastated already. It will take them years to recover from the damage they've already sustained. The economy of China has suffered a serious blow. The world economy is affected. If the data pipeline went down for an extended period, every business in Hong Kong would go bankrupt, and probably the PRC, and the world economy would probably be pushed into global recession."

Remo shrugged. "That would be bad, all right. Can I go to Hong Kong now, before I say something even dumber?"

Smith pursed his lips, which gave them wrinkles like the lips of old movie starlets in too much pancake makeup. "Yes," he decided. "Remember, please, that discretion is the word."

Remo shrugged. "It is *a* word."

"We shall remain invisible," Chiun stated formally as he rose to his feet. "As always."

25

"I've had enough death to last me a lifetime," Remo said. He sounded bitter. He felt bitter. All those people who had been cheering in the streets of the capital city were now lying dead in those same streets. They were dead in their cars, and in the parks and everywhere people ought to be alive.

The Marines in the helicopter that air-lifted them into Ayounde from Sierre Leone had been wearing big suits that made them look like the marshmallow man who got toasted all over New York City in some old movie. They had been worried about Remo and Chiun going in without suits. They asked Remo time and again to change his mind. He ignored them. The old man, they thought, couldn't even understand what they were even saying.

They smelled the dead from sixty miles outside the city, and by the time they touched down it was an overpowering stench. This was equatorial Africa. In twenty-four hours the decay was well under way; Remo didn't want to think what this place would be like in a week.

"It's too quiet," Remo said. "Makes my flesh crawl."

"It disturbs me, as well," Chiun remarked. "But there is death and there is death."

"Don't start."

They walked. The place shouldn't be far from the park where they had been deposited. They found the Ayounde National University and let themselves inside the building that called itself the College of Natural Sciences.

The research labs had air-conditioning. The corpses here smelled less.

Remo's skin adjusted itself to the temperature of his environment, just like that of other people only more so, so the machine-cooled air wasn't more comfortable to him, or to Chiun. Still, the place felt more like a human environment. It made the presence of so many dead people even more unnerving.

"This is not the work of a proper Master," Chiun said.

"You go find some survivors to kill, then," Remo said, and jerked a thumb over his shoulder.

"Somebody got up on the wrong side of the mat this morning."

Remo halted. "Yeah, that's it, exactly, Chiun. I'm just having a bad day. Has nothing to do with this, or the hundreds of others like him." He thrust an open hand at some particularly gruesome remains against a hallway wall. "Her. Whatever he or she used to be. Why the hell did you say that?"

Chiun looked impassive. "Making conversation."

"You don't make conversation. You were trying to provoke me."

"You are mistaken."

Remo gave up. "Here. Ready?"

Chiun nodded. The lab door was locked from the inside. Remo applied a little extra wrist and the knob spun easily, metal bolts shearing off inside, and they stepped into a tiny research lab that was as cold as a meat freezer.

Remo shut the door, then he and Chiun stood inside and exhaled slowly, as if they were underwater, without breathing in. They allowed themselves to become cold.

CHIUN THOUGHT THIS WAS A curious sensation, and he even felt a little foolish for doing it—but he didn't dare to tamper with the unnatural horror that threatened them. He understood what they were up against, and he knew that it was probably in the room with them.

So he allowed himself to become cold. Being a skilled Master of Sinanju, he could control his body to acclimate it to his environment. He had walked under the blazing desert sun without discomfort. He had traveled above the Arctic Circle with only a windbreaker to protect him from the cold. He did this by adjusting the natural functions of his human body, but adjusted them to a greater degree than most human beings could ever believe possible.

Now, in a kind of perversion of this skill, he was purposely lowering the temperature of his skin. They could not allow their body temperature to melt, and thus free, any of the microscopic devices that they suspected were here.

Before, in Scotland, Chiun had encountered the things. One of them had looked at him, and the feeling of it was more unnatural than the feel of any demonic presence.

On the table in the tiny lab was a beaker of water, cloudy and frozen solid, and a binocular microscope was beside it. Sitting on a stool was a researcher, also frozen. His stomach was open and the blood had made scarlet icicles.

Chiun nodded at the puddle. Remo understood. Whatever had chewed its way from inside the lab technician was in the blood, which puddled on the floor and froze to a shiny surface.

WHEN REMO FELT his skin had become as cold as he could make it without killing his own dermal layer, he stepped over the frozen puddle of blood. The lab technician was still holding the phone to his ear. "I'll take it." Remo extracted the phone from the man's hand. "Hello?"

"Remo?" asked Mark Howard.

"Yeah. Now what?"

"Dr. Alcieni had identified the city water source as the contaminant carrier and was trying to make an identification of the pestilence when he died. He called a fellow microbiologist in Flagstaff, a man he knew was a specialist in infectious diseases, and he was on the phone with him until he died, working until the last minute."

Remo gave the corpse another glance. Dr. Alcieni could be just another corpse with a crater in his stomach the size of a kumquat. He wondered if anybody would every really recognize the man's heroism. Remo felt very, very cold.

"He told Dr. Palamas in Flagstaff that he had set the air-conditioning system low to preserve the samples."

"The doctor and his sample are frozen stiff."

"Okay." Mark Howard was breathing hard. "You have got to be careful here, Remo."

"I know."

"If Dr. Alcieni did what he hoped he was doing, he preserved whatever contaminant was in the water. That means it's virulent when thawed."

"I know."

"If you warm it up—"

"I *know.*"

"Look into the microscope."

Remo hated it; he felt inadequate to look into a microscope. Dammit, he didn't know what he was looking for in a frigging microscope! You were supposed to have scientists to look into the damn microscope! But here he was, Remo Williams, Sinanju Master and well-known dim bulb, and it was up to him, of all people, to look in a microscope and describe what he saw.

What he saw sent a chill through him. How that was possible he didn't know.

"Uh." Remo looked at Chiun. Chiun asked a question with his ancient Korean eyes.

Remo looked again, and some of the chill lessened. "I see it, Junior. It's not quite what I expected." Well, he thought, that sounded kind of stupid. He wasn't known for his scientific knowledge. What would a brainiac like Mark Howard care about what Remo *expected* to see in a microscope?

"Describe it, please, Remo," Mark said.

"Tentacles. Ten of them." Remo felt the Master Emeritus tense up nearby. "At first glance it's sort of a Su Mangsang Mini-Me, but it has a definite mechanical look to it. There's little tentacle hinges. The torso is kind of like a rivet holding the limbs together. It's not moving, by the way."

"It's frozen, not deactivated," Mark Howard explained. "Now let's see what happens when you start it up again."

Remo said, "Okay. Here goes nothing." Then he leaned over the microscope and gently breathed on the slide. His body heat made a mist of steam, and when he looked into the eyepiece again, the tiny robot with the tentacles was moving.

"Junior, you're not going to believe this. It's not building a clone of itself. It's tearing itself apart. Now I see more of them. They're ripping into one another. They're helping one another. What the hell is this?" Even as he watched, the thin layer of water was again freezing and locking the little entities in their crystals, halfway through their self-dismantling.

"This is what we suspected, Remo," Mark Howard

said. "Their programming includes a predetermined life span. Once the time is up, they self-destruct as completely as possible. Most of the remaining fragments settle in the water supply, so all that shows up in the tests is normal-looking mineral sediment."

"So letting the room warm up right now would be the right thing to do?" Remo asked doubtfully.

"It would give them the opportunity to perform their final function," Chiun observed.

"All of them?" Remo prodded.

"Maybe," Mark Howard said.

"Understood," Remo said, but he had squeezed the phone flat before he finished the word. "I didn't want to give them the chance to say something stupid, like, maybe we should keep the little buggies around to study them," he explained to Chiun.

"For once, you have made a profoundly wise choice, Remo Williams," Chiun said. "This is perhaps the most despicable killing tool the Western world has ever devised. It is less honorable than the poison that a coward places in a rival's wineglass. It is more cowardly than a boom dropped from the clouds to decimate a city."

"You're right, Little Father," Remo said. "You know what worries me? What if some of these buggies are programmed not to self-destruct? Like, maybe just one in a million is supposed to stop working for a while, then maybe get going again in a week or a month or a year."

Chiun gestured with his hands. "Then the waters of Ayounde are populated with these waiting no-no-buts."

"It would still feel good to make sure that all of them in this lab are permanently killed," Remo said.

Chiun raised his eyebrows. "This would give you solace?"

"I just feel like burning stuff up. Yeah, I guess that means I would be solaced. Besides, the doc deserves better than just rotting here until somebody comes to clean him up." He nodded at the frosty corpse of Dr. Alcieni.

26

Mark Howard saw the connection monitor blink off. He swore, an almost silent hiss, and began tapping out commands to reestablish the connection.

"Don't bother, Mark," Dr. Smith said. "The phone was likely destroyed. Remo would not want to hear any more from us."

"What is he thinking?" Howard asked. "This is no time to be out of touch."

"Make no mistake, Remo will thoroughly destroy the lab and its contents. He will not allow any of the nanobots to survive. He's probably thinking we would ask him—I would ask him—to preserve samples."

Mark looked at the old man behind the big desk. "Would you have?"

"Only for a very compelling reason," Smith said. "But Remo doesn't want to be reminded about my orders regarding the colonial governor of Ayounde."

Mark nodded. "You knew he would ignore them."

"I assumed he probably would," Smith agreed. "But there was a more important and compelling need to send him than to not. We have ascertained that it was nanotechnology at work in Ayounde, and we can assume it was nanotechnology stolen somehow from Loch Tweed Castle. That may be the link we need to trace the masterminds behind this mess." Smith sighed. "Let's try to accomplish that before we have repercussions from whatever Remo is about to do."

Mark Howard looked curious. "Do you know what he's planning?"

"He's probably not *planning* anything," Smith said. "But he'll definitely *do* something."

THEY WATCHED the College of Natural Sciences become engulfed in flame, giving a clean end to Dr. Alcieni and all the other unfortunates who had died within those walls.

It was made all the more strange by the lack of response from the city around it. There should have been fire trucks wailing and people gathering, but there was only stillness. The sound of the burning College of Natural Science was like the crackle of a campfire.

A small band of brave looters appeared for a moment, watched the blaze and returned to the task of removing jewelry from the corpses. It was best to get that job accomplished now, before the hard-core decay set in. Later on they'd get to work on the shops and homes.

"The mariner's helicopter comes to the park over there," Chiun said, pointing in the opposite direction from which Remo was now headed. "Alas, you go now to disobey the Emperor who pays you in gold. You are as a predictable as a schoolboy who cannot be cured of smoking tobacco. What mischief are you headed for now, Remo Williams?"

"You already guessed it. I'm going to have a few cigarettes before Uncle Sam comes to get us."

"You go to the mansion of the colonial governor to exact some sort of vengeance."

"Maybe. You can wait in the park," Remo answered. "I saw some nice benches there—just move the bodies."

By this time he was a block away, but he didn't need to raise his voice to be heard. Especially in this hauntingly silent city, their voices carried to the well-tuned ears of the Sinanju Masters. Remo expected he would soon hear the virtually silent padding of Chiun's sandals accompanying his own footsteps, and he wasn't disappointed. It occurred to Remo that, although he wasn't exactly the man in charge when it came to all things Sinanju, he was learning how to better turn the screws on Chiun.

"Do not think that you have berated me into accompanying you, Remo."

"You going to try to stop me, then?"

"Not exactly," Chiun said. "That is to say, yes, I am going to try to stop you."

"Fat chance."

"I shall accomplish this by appealing to your sense of duty, as the Reigning Master of Sinanju."

"Uh-huh." Remo walked faster, but he would never be able to outpace Chiun.

"Consider that the recolonizers may be the natural evolution of governments around the world, Remo," Chiun said. "It would appear to me that there are those in the Western world who are becoming enlightened. There are those who have the backbone to help forge a new government that might actually endure."

"What do you mean?" Remo demanded.

"What I mean is simple enough. An empire must be dominated by an emperor. A dictatorship will always be stronger than any democracy. Look at the mess that has been made of your own nation of North America—it is because there is no one in charge, with power enough. You have one face after another, spouting identical slogans devoid of meaning."

"We've had some okay presidents," Remo said.

"You have had many presidents—so many that some were bound to be less reprehensible than others. None of them took the reins of power firmly in hand and held on to them," Chiun complained.

"He'd be lynched if he did. We like having a variety."

"You insure that nothing ever gets accomplished," Chiun said.

"We make sure none of the stinkers last more than eight years," Remo said.

"You steer me from my point with your meaningless subtexts," Chiun said reasonably. "You must agree that a monarchy is always better for Sinanju than a democracy."

"Huh. I don't agree. Neither do you."

"Do not tell me what I think, Remo Williams."

"Let me put it this way. Has Sinanju ever made more over the long haul than it has working for the U.S.? You're one of the greatest profit-making Masters of all time."

Chiun couldn't help himself. He broke out into a huge, silly smile. "Remo, that is such a compliment."

"And it's sincere," Remo said. "Right from the heart."

"I can tell."

"And you did it by working for a democracy."

Chiun was still taken aback by Remo's uncharacteristic praise, so he conceded the point without further argument. "Still," he added, "there would be few options should Smith one day decide not to renew the contract. But if there was a new empire…"

"Yeah?"

"A new British Empire," Chiun added.

"What? Are you saying it would be a good thing?"

Chiun huffed. "Of course. It would be a *wonderful* thing. Such an empire would serve as a counterpoint to the United States, but a friendly one. Friendly rivalries are historically the most profitable. When there is animosity between two nations, one defeats the other or simply wears it to exhaustion, but when two nations competing in a game of put-one-up-the-man's-ship…"

"What?"

"The game in which one nation tries to be better or richer or more powerful than the other."

"One-upmanship?"

"As I said. These are the rivalries in which huge sums

of gold will be paid to a careful assassin, who in turn might adjust the situation himself to help retain the balance of power."

"And keep himself employed indefinitely."

"Perhaps."

Remo stopped suddenly and faced Chiun, a strange look on his face. "Aha!"

"What?"

"It was you, all this time, you old faker. For years and years and years, it was you who invented all these problems just so Smith would keep you around and keep paying you more and more gold."

"You speak nonsense!"

"Do I, Chiun? Or did *you* give crack cocaine to the youth of America and get the War on Drugs going? Did *you* help organize the gangs?"

"Of course I did not, and know you do not believe it, either. You are being oaffish."

"You did it all just so we would have work, you and I. It all makes sense to me now. You masterminded all that organized crime and you even arranged for us to have worthy foes to fight. Mr. Gordons was something you came up with, right?"

"Of course not."

"Friend, too? And Sam Beasly?"

"Please cease speaking."

"That bitch Judy with the chemistry set?"

Chiun stared balefully at Remo, who was on a roll.

"Now that I think of it, you had a pet squid in the

tanks when we lived in Boston and one day he's gone, poof, and years later—"

"Enough!" Chiun surrendered, his voice like fingernails on a chalkboard.

"I think some of the Ayoundes winced just now," Remo said, nodding at the litter of unaccessorized corpses piled up nearby.

"If so, it would be because they find you insufferable," Chiun exclaimed. "As do I. Truly amazing it is how quickly you can go from being kindly to being heartless and cruel."

Remo felt himself slump, at least on the inside. "Just trying to ease the gloom some, Little Father."

"At my expense!"

Remo wanted to point out that Chiun took shots at him all the time, but he didn't. He didn't know what to say. Chiun walked away, then looked back. "Well? Are you coming?"

"THERE IS A NOBILITY to the act of conquest, Remo," Chiun said.

"Bulldookey."

"The European's practiced nation conquering for centuries," Chiun pointed out. "It was considered noble."

"Now it's considered to be terrorism," Remo said. "The recolonizers are just terrorists, too, in my book."

"Your book is new and not researched well," Chiun remarked. "A book of history indicates that taking control of a nation is a noble deed. Recall that your own nation has done such nation taking recently."

"With good reason the first time and probably the second time," Remo snapped. "Maybe the second time. We had a good reason the first time—I'm sure of that."

"No one who ever took over a nation did so claiming they did not have a good reason for doing so," Chiun replied, passing judgment by acting nonjudgmental.

"You think we should let the terrorists keep their colonies, don't you?" Remo said.

"It is legitimate for the conqueror to hold the spoils of his conquest," Chiun said.

"It's giving in to the demands of terrorists," Remo responded. "The country that pays Sinanju its gold doesn't do what terrorists tell it to do."

Chiun said nothing. The silence was disturbing. Remo made a conscious effort to think along different lines. Why was Chiun trying so hard? The old Master wasn't laying down the law this time. He was really trying to convince Remo of something important, wasn't he?

Abruptly, Remo knew what it was. "This all about profits, Chiun?"

"We established that long ago, did we not?"

"I guess so. Wait." Remo changed his mind. *Now* he knew what it was. "This isn't about profits at all. Why didn't I figure it out sooner?"

"It is about gold and nothing but gold."

"Not gold. You're shilling for your sweetie!"

"You speak nonsense words and expect me to know their meaning."

"I'm talking about the queen of England. You know, the lady with the little black purse that she carries everywhere she goes? I know what's in that purse, Chiun."

"You know nothing."

It hadn't been that long ago that Chiun and Remo had been in the presence of the queen of England, during the Time of Succession. Although Remo long ago achieved the rank of Master of Sinanju, through the Rite of Attainment, he was not the Reigning Master until he went through the Rite of Succession. Both were ancient Sinanju rituals, and as far as Remo was concerned the succession was a lot of stuff to be done because it had always been done that way. The procedures of the Rite of Attainment were more cold-blooded, and more practical in that they greatly benefited the new Reigning Master at the start of his career.

The ritual required that each designated head of state—be he monarch, despot or bureaucrat—be sent an invitation to participate in the ritual. As a way of welcoming the Sinanju Master to his commanding role, each nation leader would allow the new Master into his court and offer him the challenge of battling the greatest assassin the country had to offer.

It was a battle to the death. The Sinanju Master won—always.

Not only did this serve to remind the world of the glorious Sinanju dynasty, and prove to all doubters that the new Sinanju Master was up to snuff, but it also effectively removed the competition.

Remo's succession challenges had been sidetracked, but not before his ritual audience with the queen of England. Truth be told, they had rubbed each other the wrong way from the moment they laid eyes on each other. He called her "hairdo"; she tried to stab him in the neck with a poised needle the size of tent stake.

Still, there was no excuse for engaging in royal purse-snatching, which is just what he did next. He stole the queen of England's purse and dumped its contents on the floor of the dingy old room in the moldy old palace. "I've always wanted to know what the hell's so important you gotta schlep this around all the time."

To his surprise, the only thing that came out was a tiny, framed picture of a much younger Chiun.

If she'd chosen that moment to try to stick a poison dart in his aorta, she just might have accomplished it. He was flabbergasted. It still made him wonder—and made him realize again that the old Master of Sinanju had done a lot of living in the seventy-odd years before he began training Remo Williams.

"You still have a thing for your little queenie," Remo said aloud. "That's why you're all in favor of giving the power back to the throne of England."

Chiun's face grew redder and redder. "Wrong."

"I knew it."

"Wrong. I say you are wrong. Please respect me when I say to you that you are wrong."

"I'm not wrong. Sometimes you say I'm wrong and I'm sure I really am wrong and sometimes I say I'm wrong and I think that maybe I might be wrong and sometimes I say I'm wrong and I know I'm right but I think that maybe after I stop being mad about what I'm right about I might stop and reconsider and realize I was wrong all along but sometimes I know I'm not wrong."

"Sometimes you babble like an infant."

"This time I'm not wrong, and I know I'm not wrong. You want your sweetums to get her empire back."

Chiun walked along glum and silent and pink-cheeked.

"Are you in cahoots?"

"I am in my robe and sandals."

"Are you in cahoots with the queen of England, I mean?"

"Certainly not! Do you speak of novelty underwear for sex-crazed couples to wear together?"

"Cahoots means working together. Are you and the queen of England scheming together to make this whole British Empire business happen?"

"No. I am doing nothing with the queen of England."

"Not even pining?"

"Remo, you know nothing of the matters of which you speak. Kindly quit speaking of them."

Remo shrugged and nodded. "Okay, but I was right about being right, so how am I right if I'm not right about you cahooting with the queen? What I'm saying is, you think this whole recolonization effort is a good idea."

Chiun was simply relieved that the conversation was steering in a new direction. "Of course. Any right-thinking watcher of the world understands the power of empire. Empires endure. Egypt. Rome. England. Each provided stability that can never be matched in a world of democracy."

"We've been going strong for about 230 years."

"Egypt endured for three thousand years."

"Egypt got a head start. Check back with me in 2,770 years and then we can compare oranges to oranges."

"Fah. Democracy is an experiment, Remo. It is like the highly polished automobiles that are created by the car companies for the one and only purpose of trying out a new kind of screw-pipe or agitator. Once the experiment is done, the car is abandoned. It was never meant to last."

"Well, guess what, America is lasting."

"America throws itself into chaos, deliberately, every four years for the purpose of rotating out the leaders it installed just four years before. These leaders express themselves in quips no more intelligent or meaningful than the screeches from the bird from the village of the People in Brazil."

"True."

"Think what would happen if the conquerors of the old British colonies were allowed to hold on to their possessions."

"They'd rule them."

"Yes?"

"They couldn't possibly do a good job. A race-car driver and an archaeologist?"

Chiun opened his hands. "How are they less qualified than a professional politician?"

Remo chewed the inside of his lower lip. "You got me there. But they're bad guys."

"Because they aggressively took power that they wanted, using devious means?"

"Yeah."

"And this cannot describe any elected one of the Americas?"

"Sure, it can. Now you've got me all confused."

"Now I have shown you the failure of democracy and the reason why an empire might be a good thing for the world."

"And Sinanju," Remo said. "The bigger the empire, the more gold and the more threats that need to be dealt with to keep the thing chugging along."

"True."

Remo sighed. "Here we are." They had come to the end of a street to an intersection. Across the street was a decorative chain around the vast grounds of the Ayounde Government House. It was the dwelling place of the prime minister and the place where all national government business took place. It was known that Sir Michele Rilli, self-appointed governor of the recolonized African nation, was inside the complex. So, presumably, were the hostages who ran the nation until a few days before.

"You are violating the edicts of the Emperor and this you must obey. Disturb not the colonial governor, lest more vengeance be taken upon the colonial people."

"Must've missed that memo. Don't worry. Nobody will ever know I was here."

27

"Hello?" Remo called out. "It's me! Anybody home?"

"You are certainly insuring that no one will know you are here," Chiun said.

"Don't worry about it." Remo slammed the door behind him. The twenty-foot-tall brass door normally took two men to open and close. The boom reverberated through the quiet chambers. If nothing else attracted the attention of the two guards at the front entrance, that would have done it.

"Hands up!" They were in Ayounde National Police uniforms, but they spoke as if they had slunk right out of a dingy London alley. "How'd you do that with the door?"

"How'd I do what?" Remo took a single step, or so it appeared to the men in the police uniforms, and he went from being all the way across the room to being right in front of them. With a grin he snatched each by the shoulder, turned them to face each other, then clapped them together with a whack on the back.

They smashed together only after their assault rifles skewered each other, much to their surprise.

A hail of machine-gun fire came from the end of the vast, richly decorated receiving hall. Chiun and Remo slithered toward the gunners, moving deftly to avoid the bullets that ripped the air around them.

"Most ingeniously stealthy, this method of entrance," Chiun remarked.

Chiun drifted everywhere except where the bullets were, then rose up underneath the attackers before they knew he had arrived. Chiun's fingers pinched the gun muzzles as if he were snatching the earlobes of two rascally boys, and the guns blew back. One of the blasts was fatal. Another was less immediately fatal.

Remo questioned his own trio of victims, then finished them off by flinging them offhandedly into a convenient marble pillar. "He know anything?" Remo asked of Chiun's lone survivor.

"Why not ask him yourself."

The dying man gave them a general vicinity in which to hunt for the governor. Sir Michele Rilli had opted not to take up residence in the prime minister's quarters and instead was housed in the bomb-proof emergency quarters underneath the meeting chamber of the cabinet of ministers. They left the informant to finish dying and went in search of the cabinet chamber.

"This will only result in more deaths," Chiun pointed out. "That is why the Emperor insisted we not touch the governor."

"Don't worry. I have a plan."

Chiun considered that. "Who devised this plan?"

"I did."

"I see."

"You *will* see. Here we go."

More taunts were shouted at them from a pair of machine-gun-toting toughs who were definitely not Africans. "Come and get a piece of this, you mothersucking Yank!"

Remo dodged their fusillade and snatched them by the chin, lifting and pressing them high up against the wall.

"I really get mad when people insult my mom," Remo said, and pushed harder—until the heads broke and the corpses collapsed alongside the heavy door into the chamber.

The door consisted of a decorative wood layer atop an inch of tempered steel. Tapered steel bolts were shot into the frame from the top and bottom and both sides of the door. It would take a bazooka blast to break it open.

Remo didn't have a bazooka, but he had ten Sinanju-trained fingers. He tapped lightly against the wood surface and found that it was an exceptionally well-made door. The imperfections in the subsurface steel were few and difficult to isolate.

Behind him, Chiun was doing his own tapping—on the floor, impatiently, with the toe of his sandal.

"Hold your horses." Remo found the weak seam he wanted and knocked carefully along it, creating a deep vibration that was at exactly the right frequency. The door spiderwebbed down the middle like a windshield hit by a rock. Remo pushed in, creating an opening that was immediately used as the exit point for blasts from a combat shotgun. Remo waited for the buckshot to go by like a kid waiting for the cars to pass so he could cross the street, then he slid through the gash. In the chamber he observed a trapdoor swinging into place in the floor.

He reached the trapdoor and grabbed the lip just before it was closed, and lifted it open again. The man who had been closing it was standing on a ladder with his hand still extended, and Remo grabbed the hand and lifted the man out of the hole, rattling him until he dropped his smoking shotgun.

"Sir Rilli?"

"No! He's down there!"

Remo broke the shotgunner and tossed him away like a banana peel.

"Hello?" Remo called down the tunnel. "Saddam, you down there?"

He waited, listening to the hushed voices from deep inside the chamber. He grew a grin. Chiun looked expectant and not quite tolerant.

"We're takin' over, you bleeding wankers!" Remo shouted, doing a bad British accent. "It's me, Nigel Grollman. Me and John Surah, we're taking over Ayounde for ourselves."

Chiun rolled his eyes. "Need I ask the meaning of this?"

"They're on the phone to whoever it is organizing this takeover circus. Now they're telling them that Nigel

Grollman and John Surah are trying to conquer the conquerors."

"And these names you mention?"

"Two of the guns-for-hire we squashed out front," Remo explained. Then he shouted again down the hole. "You bleedin' cowards come out of there now or we'll bomb you out!"

"You do not sound British," Chiun said.

"I sound British enough." Remo walked a slow circle around the chamber, found the place he wanted and stamped his foot. The room vibrated. He moved over a fraction of an inch and stamped again.

The building shook and the floor under their feet experienced a powerful tremor, actually bouncing. Cries of fear came from below, but one more foot-stamp was required from the Reigning Master of Sinanju. This time the concrete cracked and they heard chunks of the bomb-proof ceiling falling down inside the chamber.

Men scrambled from the exit tunnel and had their weapons and cell phones removed before they could commence firing or phoning.

Michele Rilli was the last man out. "What in blazes is going on?"

"Cabinet is in session," Remo announced. "Everybody is ready but you."

Rilli couldn't believe what he was seeing—all his personal bodyguards were in desks around the circular presentation floor. They had their hands folded on their desks and they were just sitting there. Then he was lifted and deposited in one of the desks himself, at the end of the line. Something was done to his neck and now his arms and legs became stiff as boards—but unmovable. The rolling eyeballs of his security staff told him that they were also completely paralyzed. Unlike his soldiers, Rilli could still talk.

"You're not Grollman." Rilli rolled his eyes at Chiun. "You're not Surah."

"I certainly am not."

"So who are you?"

"Never mind about that. I'm going to be asking the questions now," Remo said. "Question number one— the hostages are hidden away in the *blank.*"

"You are in violation of British law. This is an act of war."

"Wrong answer earns you a *zoink,*" Remo announced, and he poked a finger into the head of the first man in the circle. *"Zoink!"*

The man was now a corpse who toppled halfway out of his seat and hung there, eyes wide, gore seeping from the wound.

Sir Michele Rilli tried to make his body work, but he couldn't move anything below the jawline.

"Question number one again," Remo said. "Hostages are in the *blank.*"

"Let me move my arms, please!" Rilli had nightmares about being paralyzed while horrible things happened to him.

"Mmm, sorry. 'Let me move my arms' is not an answer at all. Another *zoink* for you." He poked the next man in line. *"Zoink!"*

"Jesus Christ!" Rilli shrieked hysterically as another man died. This time the corpse leaned forward in its desk and stared right at the great grand prix driver.

"I think you see where this is heading." Remo swept his hand in lovely Vanna White fashion to indicate the circle of desks, with two corpses at the end. "Now I have a lot of questions for you, young man, and the *zoinks* are getting closer and closer. I'd try hard to avoid the nasty old *zoink* if I were you."

Rilli tried to move. He screamed and screamed until the little old Chinaman adjusted something on his neck and made the panic go away but not the fear. He was still horribly afraid.

"Please no *zoink!*" Sir Rilli pleaded.

"Now, now, the *zoink* is something *you* control. Just *you,* you foolish little race-car driver. I think you know how to not get a *zoink,* don't you? I thought you did. Let's try it again, okay, and we'll see if you really understand about the *zoink.* Pay attention." Remo leaned in close, inches away from the red, streaming eyes of the Honorable Sir Michele Rilli. All of a sudden, the goofball American transformed into some sort of a Satan in human form. "Where are the fucking hostages?"

Michele Rilli had been afraid before, but now, now, now. What was it in the eyes of that man? What *was* he?

There was something shining red and livid and alive and it could suck his soul right out of his body.

"Basement. High-security wing for state prisoners. I reset the biometrics so only my voiceprint opens it up."

"Let's hear it for him. He has earned no *zoink!* Question number two."

"How many questions are there?" Rilli cried.

"I dunno. Eight or ten."

"Oh God no!" There were only five living men left to be *zoinked*. Michele Rilli couldn't care less about any of them—but he was in line to get *zoinked*, too.

"I'll answer them all truthfully, I swear!"

"Great! Question two is, who did this? The whole stupid knights-of-the-round-table thing—who organized it? Who put you up to it?"

"But I don't know that—"

"Remo, this is tiresome," said the old Chinaman.

Rilli had forgotten about the old Chinaman. Maybe he would help Rilli escape the madman with the *zoink* finger. But no, the Chinaman was simply bored.

"I don't know the answer—please understand," Rilli pleaded.

"'I don't know' is the same as getting the answer wrong."

"No, it's not! How can I answer if I don't know the answer?"

"My game, my rules. *Zoink!*" Another man died with a hole in his head.

"I don't deserve this!" Rilli screeched.

Remo stepped before him. "Hey, Rilli, even before you killed most of the innocent people in this city, you deserved this. So, once again, you are wrong."

"That was a statement, not an answer to a question!" Rilli protested.

"No matter. *Zoink!*"

AYOUNDE'S GOVERNMENT House had a very secure prison vault in its lowest level. Prime Minister Shund Beila estimated that he and his cabinet had been locked inside for about two days. They had food and water enough, but it was hell being in there, cut off from his people, not knowing what was happening.

Then they heard the vault doors crack and scream. Metal tore apart and a flash of light pierced the seal. There had to be some sort of a huge machine being used to break inside. That could only mean rescue.

He and his men gathered expectantly as the shattered door gave up and swung inward on its giant, creaking hinge. A man stood there, white, sullen. Behind him stood a tiny Asian man of immense age.

There was no sign of a machine.

"You're free."

"Wonderful!" Prime Minister Beila exclaimed. "What of the rat Rilli and his murderous soldiers?"

"All dead. No more threat."

"Oh, yes! Thank you! What a happy day!"

The white man's eyes seemed to sink a little deeper into his skull. "I guess you guys have been out of touch."

"Yes. We've heard nothing since they put us inside." Shund Beila's stomach flopped. "Why? What has happened?"

The American seemed to be trying to make the words come, but they wouldn't come.

"Please, tell me."

The man shook his head, and the prime minister of Ayounde knew that whatever bad thing had happened, this man simply couldn't bring himself to put it into words.

"I gotta go." That's what the man said, then he whisked away like a breeze, the old Asian vanishing with him.

"That was them," said the minister of finance. "They were fighting off the flamethrowers, remember, in the square. They were the ones trying to stop the killing."

Of course it was them. Prime Minister Beila had not seen them up close, but those two were distinctive enough. While locked in their prison, Beila and his cabinet had spent the hours discussing at length the two men who had been doing wondrous things in National Square in defense of the Ayounde people. What extraordinary exploits they had witnessed.

"Well, whoever they are, they finally saved us," said the minister of internal security. "I wonder what they did not want to tell us."

"Let us go and find out," the prime minister said, and up they went.

28

Remo Williams was supposed to phone his office.

"I'm supposed to call Smitty when I'm on my way back," Remo remarked as they were heading back to the park for the rendezvous with the Marine helicopter. "I'm not going to Folcroft. I'm going to Hong Kong."

"I see."

Remo's mind was far away. All the way back to the Sierre Leone base he was distracted and distant. Only when his chartered jet was reaching cruising altitude did he look over at the seat across the aisle.

"I guess you decided to come with me," he observed.

Chiun nodded without taking his eyes away from the window. "I have been at your side all along. Should I be flattered when you become aware of this?"

"I've been thinking about Luzuland, Little Father." Remo said it as if he were asking for forgiveness, which he was.

"Ah."

The Masters of Sinanju had been in the East African nation of Luzuland when it became a gathering place for the world's organized-crime figures. The plan was to create a criminal friendly government, sort of a safe haven for every organized-crime element on earth. CURE went in to put a stop to it.

While in Luzuland, Remo learned of weapons that were planted under the city with the intention of wiping out most of the world's top criminals in a single moment of havoc. A different set of criminals planned to take over the crime outfits that would be left leaderless.

Remo decided to let the bombs do their work. Even if innocent people in Luzuland were annihilated, too, the price in lives would more than balance out. After all, killing those criminals would prevent countless future murders....

And then Remo changed his mind. He and Chiun raced to find and disable those weapons before the horrible deed could be done.

"There I almost did it myself. Wiped out the whole city. On purpose," Remo recalled. "But in Ayounde, I couldn't stop it from happening."

Chiun nodded again. His eyes were locked on the wing of the private jet. Chiun knew the little wing was brittle as kindling and likely to crumble like shattered wood planks at any moment.

Chiun said, "There is more. The fire in Turkey. Children were killed. You did not save them."

"Not the same thing."

"Why not?"

"Because I wasn't in Turkey. I wasn't involved in any way."

"Because you are involved means you are responsible for any catastrophe, foreseen or unforeseen, preventable or not?" Chiun turned to him. "I think perhaps you are not suited for the role, Remo Williams."

"You've told me a million times you should have picked somebody else to be the next Sinanju superassassin."

"You are suited to be an assassin and a Master of Sinanju. That is not what I speak of."

Remo's patience ran out. "Okay, fine—what am I not suited to be?"

"A good-doer."

"A do-gooder?"

"Exactly."

"Someone who does good?"

"Yes."

"Why do you care? You don't want me doing good things unless there's a profit in it."

"It is you who care, and it is you who are unsuited for it."

"Oh, criminy, Chiun, you're the only person I know who could give me a headache, even after you trained me not to get headaches."

Chiun said nothing.

"Fine, so tell me, why am I unsuited to be a do-gooder? Because I always screw it up?"

"Screwing it up is something you perform with equal frequency, whether while doing good-doer deeds or while doing the deeds assigned to you by Emperor Smith. I speak of temperament. You have the temperament to be an assassin, and yet you cannot handle the burden of doing good deeds."

"You've totally lost me."

"Regard yourself in the mirror of your response and tell me what you see. What happens to Williams when he is sent to be a Sinanju Master—to assassinate a cartel cretin who desires to franchise his narcotics in American cities? The one, Burgos, in the jungles in Brazil, for example."

Remo thought about it. "I did the deed on him and his whole entourage. What's the problem?"

"None. Then you helped to rebuild the village of the People, but you left feeling poorly for doing it."

Remo shook his head. "I was ticked off because that villager started saying I was some other demigod or demonoid that I didn't want to be."

"You were angered by something," Chiun said. "You were angered in Ayounde the time before."

"Because I wasn't allowed to do my job."

"You were angered in Jamaica, where you *were* allowed to do your job."

"Because I should have been doing my job in New Jersey."

"You were angered because Smith advised that you not return to the Castle on the Loch, although you were alternatively sent to deal with the threat of Sa Mangsang, which would have had graver consequences if ignored."

"I can't tell which of us sounds more like a broken record," Remo said. "What's your point?"

"Thank you for recognizing that I do have one. The point is, you have a choice. Your decision is your own. The direction you go from here is also your own."

"I see."

"You don't."

"You're right."

Chiun pursed his lips as he watched the wing. He held up three fingers. "One, continue on this course. Do the deeds you know are good and feel bad about it, regardless of the specific reason—there will always be a reason for guilt if you search it out."

"That doesn't sound like a good choice."

"Two, continue doing the good deeds and give yourself credit for making the best decisions you can make, allowing yourself to *not* be burdened with guilt."

"Huh."

"Three, stop doing good deeds. Concentrate on your role as Master of Sinanju. Do what is asked of you, fulfill your responsibilities to the village and waste no concern on the troubles of the world."

The stewardess came out with cups of water. Remo glared at her so fiercely she ducked back into the kitchenette, but he was looking through her, not at her. "The third choice is not a choice."

"Because of your compulsion to fight for truth, justice and the way of the American?"

"Not really. I'm not seeking out good deeds to do. It's

that I'm in the right place at the right time to do some good and stop some bad—because I am Sinanju and working for Smitty. When I'm in those places, I *have* to go the extra mile if it will mean a big difference. See?"

"Yes."

"So as long as I'm doing the Sinanju thing, I'll feel compelled to do what I can to help people out. That's not too schmaltzy, is it? So I have just two choices. Keep doing those things and feel bad about it, or keep doing those things and not feel bad about it. The second choice is the obvious way to go, all things being equal. I see it. I really do. Thanks, Little Father."

"You are welcome."

"So how do I do that?"

"It is easy. It is very difficult. You must simply choose to be at peace with what you can and cannot do."

"Oh. Well, that's great. That's really helpful. I'll get right on it. Thanks a lot."

"You are welcome."

29

Hong Kong was afraid. You could smell the fear in the streets.

"Always knew the Commies would screw up Hong Kong," the cabbie complained. "I'm Chinese and British put together, and I know which one of them can run a country and it is not the Chinese. I'm just surprised it took them so long to bring it all crashing down."

"Hush, blatherer!" Chiun snapped.

"See, what they were doing was sowing the seeds of their future failure," the cabbie explained bitterly. "I guess they wanted Hong Kong to collapse completely, no if, ands or buts, so they put everything in place to make it happen."

Chiun refrained from slicing the cabbie's throat with a single, deadly fingernail and peered sharply at Remo. "Does the cretin believe the Chinese truly wished for this to happen?"

"He's being sarcastic. You know, Sheldon Jahn might turn out to be a better leader than the PRC. Ever thought of that?"

The cabbie snorted. "Right, bub, a sixty-year-old flaming fagula. He can't even write good tunes anymore. When's the last time he had a hit?"

Remo didn't know the answer to that. "Seems to me his credentials are as good as any other world leader I can think of. Drop us here."

The cabbie stopped, just now realizing where his fare was headed. They were a half mile away from the infamous Ministry of Financial Logistics. A ring of Chinese military encircled the facility, but they made a show of being nonaggressive. The last thing they wanted to do was alarm the nutcase inside.

"Why are you coming to this place?" the cabbie demanded.

"He's a huge Sheldon Jahn fan." Remo jerked a thumb at Chiun.

Chiun regarded him curiously. "What kinds of music is practiced by this Sheldon?"

"Pop music. If you ever listened to the radio during the seventies you probably heard his stuff."

"I listened little," Chiun said with a look of distaste.

Cordoning off the entire city block around the Ministry of Financial Logistics were vehicles belonging to the Hong Kong police and the Chinese military, fronting rolls of barbed wire.

"Halt," barked a Chinese guard with suspicious eyes, issuing a stream of orders in Chinese.

"Speak Svedish?" Remo asked in a heavy, poorly executed Swedish accent. "Or English?"

"Who are you? Why do you come here?" the guard demanded, without missing a beat.

"United Nations inspectors." He presented his credentials. "Dr. Remo Octavius. My associate is Mr. Kar Sano. We're expected inside."

"Can you not see that the entrance is not here? Besides this, no one will be allowed inside."

"We will be allowed inside. The UN says we will."

"You must speak to my superior officer."

"Are you trying to keep us out?" Remo demanded.

"There is no entrance here," the guard insisted, waving helplessly at the rolls of barbed wire that created a barrier around one of the most expensive blocks of real estate in Hong Kong.

"There's going to be hell to pay. Sanctions. Resolutions. Next thing you know you'll be unilaterally invaded and it will be all *your* fault."

"I am only pointing out the fact that the entrance is not at this place!" the guard exclaimed, unsure if he should be extremely worried or simply amused. "Speak to my superior officer, please." He summoned them to the nearby financial office building, now requisitioned as a field headquarters. They guard spoke hurriedly to the building guards, who phoned ahead.

"We will take them," growled the headquarters guard, who led Remo and Chiun to the stairs.

"Elevator not working," the guard explained. "Chief of this operation just twelve floors up."

"They lie about the elevator," Chiun whispered in

Korean too soft for their escorts to even hear. Their escorts were talking Chinese and chuckling. "They seek to play a cruel joke on an old man," Chiun translated.

"They're really going to have mud on their faces when we reach the twelfth floor and you're not even breathing hard."

"Someone will be breathing hard," Chiun said, and he was gone.

One of them happened to glance back as they plodded up the concrete fire stairs. "Where did the old man go?" he queried.

"He couldn't stand waiting for you slowpokes. He went on ahead."

"That is a lie!"

"Now, why would I lie?"

"How much longer shall I be forced to stand waiting for lazy Chinese soldiers?" called a distant squeaky voice. The Chinese soldiers peered incredulously up through the stairwell, where they caught a flash of Chiun's red-accented robe.

"It is a trick!"

"Naw, it's just that you guys are so slow. It's another side effect of communism."

"Untrue! Chinese soldiers are very fit. This is a trick."

"Oh, yeah—want to race?" Remo glided up the stairs before the guards could answer. In seconds he was standing alongside Chiun listening to the stamping of combat boots.

"Just about everybody else has figured out that communism doesn't work," he lectured loudly. "When are you guys going to catch up?"

"Trickery!" panted one of the guards, but their gear and their guns wore them down and they were heaving.

"Let us proceed," Chiun said. "We need not wait for those twin tortoises."

In the twelfth-floor hall they heard activity at one end, but most of the offices were dark. Business could not proceed when a military operation had taken over the premises. Chiun chose a closed office door and turned the knob. It was locked, but the lock mechanism snapped. They entered and closed the door behind them. Another twist jammed the doorknob.

At 120 feet up, the window glass wasn't supposed to open. Chiun opened it with his steellike fingernails, which scored a deep oval in the glass. The scorings were deeper at the apex of the oval, and shaped to affect the balance of the glass as it broke, so that the oval leaned into the office accompanied by the tinkle of cracking crystal. Chiun was now standing aside, hands in the sleeves of his robe. He looked at Remo as the glass panel rushed to the floor.

"I'll get it," Remo said sarcastically, and he deftly scooped up the glass panel.

"I know."

Remo put the glass in a safe place between a desk and a wall. It was thick, tempered crystal and Chiun had created an opening much bigger than was strictly necessary. The noise of it shattering would have alerted everybody in the building.

"I still think my way would have been easier," Remo said as he stepped out on the window ledge.

"You would have had us traipsing through sewers." Chiun was already making his way to the corner of the building, traversing the two-inch ledge as if he were strolling a city sidewalk. Chiun's small size made it relatively easy.

Though Remo was much taller, he could still achieve a kind of balance on the thin, flush-mounted surface, but he had to keep a grip on the building to do it. "Taking the sewer would have been faster and we wouldn't have had to deal with all the Chinese military types."

"These inconveniences are minor compared to your scheme of wading through underground filth." With that, Chiun strolled away on a long, flexible aluminum pole that was meant to hold large fabric banners. The pole didn't even dip under Chiun as the ancient man reached the end—and leaped off.

Out he sailed, unnoticed and unseen by the throngs of guards below. From this height, his long leap easily carried him over the wide stretch of barbed-wire ground cover. In fact, he had enough momentum to carry him to a fourth-floor ledge of the Ministry of Financial Logistics building.

Remo followed him. Jumping powerfully from a thin rod not designed to support a man was a tricky maneuver. It involved the displacement of weight—but Remo preferred to think of it in Sinanju terms. He thought like a bird and hopped like a bird, then leaped into space and allowed the wind to carry him like a bird.

Sinanju training could do a great deal to enhance a human being far beyond what was considered normal, but it could not make a man fly. The best Remo could do was ride the air currents for a moment and allow his body to be carried by them.

His feet touched the ledge of the financial logistics building without a whisper of sound.

"Little Father, you were right," Remo said. "This is a much neater than wading through the sewer."

SHELDON JAHN WAS SLEEPING in his cot in the secure inner office at the ministry when one of his new loyal supporters phoned him with the news.

"There is disturbance outside, Governor Jahn. There are sirens and searchlights." It was Wei, an accountant who specialized in information technology systems. He had been a quick convert to Sheldon's new colonial government, and Sheldon was thinking of making him deputy governor.

"Is it some sort of an attack?" Sheldon asked sleepily.

"I can't tell. If I did not know better, I would say some person has attempted to break into the grounds of ministry."

"Oh, really?" Sheldon had been warned of the tactics that would be used by the devious Chinese government to extricate him from his seat of power. These intruders could be Chinese agents. He turned on the exterior security cameras and watched the show of criss-crossing spotlights and scampering soldiers. "Looks like a circus show's about to start."

But he didn't see any intruders.

AN ALARM SHRILLED from the security cubicle—someone was breaking into the building. Correction, had broken in already.

"Knock, knock," Remo said.

The Chinese guards were grim-faced and silent. They stood inside the glass security panel that was slid in place at the front entrance. It would stop small-arms fire, even explosives. The guards had no fear of the two intruders. In fact, they were hoping for a good show when the pair of lunatics were picked up by the PRC military. The building security staff had just radioed the military commander to come get the weasels who had slipped through his perimeter.

Remo looked at Chiun. "I'm sure they can hear me."

"Quit playing silly games."

"I said, knock, knock," Remo told the guards through the glass. Remo knocked on the glass lightly with his knuckle, and he kept knocking. He patterned his gentle knuckle-taps to perfectly exploit this weakness. In seconds, the perfect, fatal vibration was created in the one-ton slab of glass, and it vibrated noisily. The guards inside were alarmed for the first time, and then the whole thing shattered. The bulletproof pane became a pile of glimmering rubble that filled the entrance.

"I said," Remo said, "knock, knock. What are you, deaf?"

"They are worse. They are Chinese," Chiun explained.

When Remo and Chiun began strolling over the hillock of broken crystal the guards overcame their amazement and grabbed their weapons. They triggered a brief burst of gunfire.

The old Asian man seemed to whisk to the side for an eye blink. The young man simply made a face. The guards couldn't believe they could have missed. It was a corridor just five feet wide. They were trained to fire a side-to-side sweep that should have cut down the intruders without fail.

"Next time somebody knocks," Remo said as he glided effortlessly around the automatic rifle and tapped his deadly knuckle on the forehead of a guard. He never finished what he was saying. The guard was too dead to hear it, his brains crushed. The second guard felt a jerk and looked down. His gun barrel was now inside him. The old man had done it. He died before he figured it out.

Military vehicles were swarming toward the front entrance of the ministry, orders pouring out of a bullhorn. "Hold on," Remo said. "Let's give them something to think about."

"For what purpose?" Chiun asked.

Remo's hands flickered, the motion too fast for any human eyes to follow, save Chiun's, and Chiun thought it was a waste of time. Remo was snatching up shards of glass from the pile and flinging them out into the night.

"Childish," Chiun complained.

There were cries and shouts, and the assault vehicles rolled into each other or simply halted. Commander Whui was shouting for an explanation.

"No sniper could have taken them out that fast," he snapped. "We'd have heard the weapon!"

"It might be suppressed," his second stated stupidly.

"You know of any silenced weapon of any kind that could have pierced that armor?" Whui was livid as he stomped to the reconnaissance truck. In the overheated truck, screen after screen showed the details of the perimeter and the ministry building from various mounted cameras. "What can you see?" he demanded.

"We're not certain yet," the crew chief admitted. "Take a look for yourself."

Whui gargled his rage as the screen before him changed to a close-up of the stalled assault team. The vehicles were crippled by flattened tires and the drivers were dead in their seats. The tires and the drivers were identically impaled with glittering daggers of shattered glass.

There was movement. The back of one of the transport vehicles fell open and a pair of special-forces soldiers teetered on the tailgate. One had a foot of bloody glass protruding from his hip front and back. He collapsed to the ground, driving the glass back out by a few inches, then he began crawling with the heavy crystal trailing behind him. His companion was still on the tailgate, pincushioned with shorter daggers of glass that he was yanking out angrily. He never should have removed the one in his thigh. Blood started gushing down his leg by the pint. Seconds later, he collapsed from the tailgate and he didn't get up again.

Sheldon Jahn watched the same show, but his view was better, watching it from the cameras mounted on the outside of the building. He had also seen the perpetrators of the killings. Well, *maybe* they had killed the Chinese soldiers. But *how* had they done it?

Who were these two? An old man in an outfit so flamboyant even Sheldon wouldn't wear it onstage—except maybe at the Hollywood film awards. Anyway, they weren't going to get past the internal security systems.

"Hi, guys." Remo waved at the knot of gun-toting men in gas masks. The gas masks waited until Remo and Chiun let the door close behind them, then they dropped their grenades. Even as the metal cylinders toppled to the ground, Chiun and Remo filled their lungs with clean air and stopped breathing. The grenades popped and clouded the room with grayish gas.

Remo allowed the tiniest taste of the gas to enter his nose. Familiar, deadly, but only if he inhaled the stuff. It wasn't going to eat at his exposed skin. Chiun made the same determination and they stepped through the clouds, removing the gas masks from the surprised guards. There were gasps and cries. Only one of them had the forethought to clamp his own nostrils shut and run for the exit. Chiun slipped in front and raised his flat hand. The runner slammed into the hand, which felt like an iron plate bolted to a concrete slab. His chest was compressed and the air forced from his lungs, which left him gasping involuntarily on the floor, and dying alongside his comrades.

Remo was tapping his chin and looking at a sign on the wall. It was in Chinese, so he made nothing of it. Chiun glared at him and they left the noxious corridor for the cleaner air in the next hallway. When it was safe to breathe again, Remo said, "I think we go this way."

"It is the only way one may go," Chiun pointed out, "and the sign merely informed one to not smoke on the premises of the ministry."

Remo shrugged. "Guess the bunch back there couldn't read Chinese, either."

Sheldon Jahn was getting worried for the first time since becoming governor of Hong Kong. There were two unarmed men breaching his security. Who were they? One of them looked American and spoke American English. The other one spoke English, too, but with an Asian accent. A joint Chinese-U.S. special assault team of some kind?

There was a blip of noise and blur of motion when the pair walked directly beneath the security camera, hidden in the wall on the ground floor. Sheldon had a sick feeling in his stomach as he rewound the digital video feed and played the blip again. Then he slowed it. The digital recording wasn't good, but it was good enough.

At 1/64th speed he saw the young American turn to the camera, wave his hand and say, "Nobody's going to be saving your life tonight, doofus."

"Why must you taunt? Does it inflate your pride, like the child who bullies all other children in the village square?"

"Just trying to put a little bit of play into my day," Remo said.

"Play? My comparison to the young bully holds true."

"Why does killing people have to be serious all the time?" Remo asked. "Why not brighten things up with a little good-natured kidding?"

"This has nothing to do with our discussion on the plane, I hope. If so, you misunderstood magnificently."

The way to the top floor required passing through the lower-level workspace where twenty desks sat abandoned, and the doors on the far side parted swiftly. A two-man crew spun out a portable, wheeled blast shield and another man standing inside poked his gun through the narrow turret. The barrel was too big for a gun, too small to shoot a grenade.

"Look, it's the rocket man," Remo said.

With a flash of flame, a tiny missile shot out and zeroed in on Remo. Watching it travel in the direction of his chest, he could tell what it was. Not heat-seeking. It didn't waver with the lightning-fast adjustments a computer would make as it sniffed out body warmth. It did waver more slowly. It would be following the aim of the shooter, who had a red laser dot on Remo's chest.

Remo stepped aside when the rocket was less than a yard from his chest, and he snatched the thing out of the air. It was the size of a spring roll and wiggled in his hand like an electric eel. He showed Chiun the flaring white flame shooting from its backside. "Rocket. Man. Get it?"

"No."

Another tiny jet flared to life and the next little rocket sped at Chiun. He stepped aside at the correct moment and allowed the rocket to crack into the wall with a sharp explosion. Remo's rocket used up its propellant, and he held it in his fingers and tossed it across the room. It made a satisfying hollow-tube noise as it neatly entered the gun barrel from which it came, just as the next rocket was flaring to life, and they detonated against each other with force that blew the barrel open. The gunner's transparent mask was torn off and his face with it.

"Must you always throw things?" Chiun said. "You looked like a lager-quaffing British pub patron hurling darts for amusement. I should have known better than to train an unreformed gun-toter."

"It's not like I'm using a weapon." Remo grabbed the pair of cart-pushers and sent them flying into nearby walls, where they flattened and stuck like swatted flies.

"It is precisely as if you are using a weapon."

"What I mean is, I do not have to use a weapon. I didn't have to use the little missile back there. I could have just as easily gone in and poked his lights out. You know it and I know it."

"Why did you not do so?"

Remo thought about it. They were in the elevator that

had disgorged the rocket-firing man. It appeared to be the only way up short of scaling the walls. Remo pushed the button for the top floor and they ascended.

"Their captain is not so fantastic or he would have thought to turn this thing off."

"Answer the question. Why did you throw the tiny missile?"

"It just seemed like an interesting thing to do, I guess."

"You did it for the novelty of the experience?"

Remo nodded. "Yeah. What's wrong with that?"

"What is wrong with adhering to the noble tradition in which you are trained?" Chiun shot back.

"I do."

"You don't."

"I usually do."

"You often don't."

"So what?"

The elevator stopped between floors and Remo wordlessly jumped up, punched away the emergency hatch in the ceiling and followed it out into the darkness of the shaft. He landed on the roof, and Chiun emerged beside him. They started up the ladder rungs bolted into the wall. They were twenty feet above the elevator when Remo felt the tiny trickle of static in his fingers. He pushed away from the rungs as the electric charge grew to levels fatal to humans. He was now hanging by the elevator's safety chain, and when he looked between his feet, Chiun was also gripping the chain and looking perturbed.

The chain clanked and the elevator started rising toward them.

"This becomes tiresome," Chiun announced. He released the chain and allowed himself to fall back to the elevator roof. Remo landed beside him, and they hurtled toward the ceiling, where the building designers had overlooked including any sort of safety hollow to keep hapless elevator topsiders from being crushed.

The elevator rose to its apex with a brake-squealing halt, its rubber bumpers thumping against the interior roof.

Remo and Chiun were already inside again. Before the elevator could descend, Remo hauled open the interior door, then curled the exterior doors inward. The elevator groaned but the interior doors were heavy steel. They weren't budging.

"You want to take me to the pilot?" Remo asked the surprised gunners, whose guns were being removed from their hands and returned, mangled.

"Even I don't know what silliness you spout," Chiun said. "More novelty?"

Remo just shrugged. "Where's the pop star?"

One of the guards pointed down the hall on the right.

The two Masters glided into the corridor, their senses tuned to whatever final assault would come their way, and stopped, shoulder to shoulder. They could feel the electric charge building up in the wall in front of them. The wall was metal. The decorative copper inlay wasn't there for decorative purposes. Something was wrong.

Remo's mind whirled. What was he missing? There

was some sort of an electric charge in the wall. It would strike them if they ventured between the copper electrodes. He sensed it and Chiun sensed it, but *something was wrong.* Chiun looked at him curiously, sensing his tension, and Remo made the connection. There had been copper discharge plates in the adjoining hall and through the surge of static coming from ahead of them he felt the trickle of another charge building behind them. In the heartbeat it took for him to experience his doubt and understanding, it became too late to flee, but he tried anyway. He bolted, signaling Chiun to come with him, and they moved like swift shadows toward the elevator again, where the uncertain guards saw nothing more than streaks of color.

Then the world filled with blinding, sizzling electricity. The guards were directly in the middle of the twin-mounted pair of discharge plates and they were grabbed and shaken and cooked alive by the extreme voltage. When the artificial lightning bolts vanished, the guards dropped with their flesh sizzling and gaping pits where their eyeballs had been. Then nothing moved but the wafts of steam rising from the corpses.

30

His flesh crawled. But he was alive.

There had been no time to figure out how to channel the electricity, and channeling it would have been impossible. It had come like lightning strikes, dancing erratically, and the jagged bolts had crisscrossed simultaneously from all four copper panels.

Remo and Chiun sped down the hall and around the corner into the intersecting hall, where Remo half expected to see a third pair of copper electrodes. But there was none. This hallway should be outside the danger zone, more or less. The static bolts ricocheted in the main hallway and seemed to turn corners, like deadly white fingers seeking them out. It shocked Remo's system and took him down hard. Now he struggled into a sitting position, his head reeling.

What about Chiun? Had he taken a worse hit? In fact, where *was* Chiun?

"Little Father?" Remo croaked, turning, leaping up and into the intersection of halls in front of the elevator. There was a flash-roasted pile of security guards, but no old Asian. "Chiun!" Remo exclaimed in rising panic.

"Here." Remo's gaze was drawn up, where Chiun was casually gripping the framework of the ceiling panels with his fingers and the toes of his sandals.

"What are you doing up there?" Remo demanded.

"Enjoying the spectacle and avoiding the shock." Chiun dropped noiselessly to the floor. "You would have been well-advised to come up, too."

"Didn't even occur to me. Were you hit at all?"

"Just a few stray twigs of lightning came my way."

"Huh." Remo was still reeling from the hit. His skin felt like it wanted to crawl off his body, and there was a persistent sizzling in his ears. "You could have suggested it."

"There was no time. I thought you would understand the ground-loving nature of the beast and come up with me."

"I'll pay closer attention next time."

"A wise ambition," Chiun said seriously.

SHELDON JAHN HAD ONE last tool under his control, and he threatened to use it. "Don't touch that door or I'll shut down the entire Chinese financial system, for good."

The knocking on the door turned to pounding—three fast blows by the bare fist of the young one. The old man was just watching. The steel high-security door cracked up the middle. Sheldon saw it all on the security camera. Then, live and in person, the security door crashed inside the Information Technology Center in two pieces and the pair of agents strolled in.

"Hard to hear you through that door," Remo said. "Don't touch what, now?"

"Not one step closer! I'll pull the switch and shut down the entire system. It'll take days to get it running again. The PRC will loose billions." Sheldon paused, then asked breathlessly, "Who are you people?"

"I'm Benny. He's Daniel."

"The guards are all dead. It's you who should be dead!"

"We're still standing. As for you—"

"Goodbye, English imbecile," Chiun said, removing Sheldon Jahn's finger from the controls and slinging it into the corner.

"My playing hand!"

"Who's pulling your strings?" Remo asked.

"No one!"

"Somebody is handling the logistics of your little nightmare. Who?"

"I don't know!"

Chiun grabbed the pop star's hand and removed a second finger.

"Doesn't that hurt?" Remo inquired.

"It hurts like the devil! I don't know who's behind it! I swear to God! Please don't let him cut off more of my fingers!"

"You've gotta know *something*," Remo said impatiently. "Was he British?"

"Yes!" Sheldon exclaimed. "English royalty, sounded like, from the way he talked."

"One man?" Chiun asked.

"I only spoke to one man, but he always talked like he was the head of a large movement."

"Which was named what?" Remo asked.

"I don't know that."

"Do you know anything about any of this or are you just a dimwit pop star who became famous for his on-stage foppery?"

"Oh, well. The foppery. To be honest, it was the foppery. And the songs! The songs were good!"

"Somebody else wrote them, though," Remo said.

"I write some of the words. Sometimes."

"Doesn't qualify you to be the governor of Hong Kong," Remo pronounced.

"But being a knight of the realm *does* qualify me," Sheldon protested. "It's a part of British law."

"Blah, blah, blah. I've had enough of you knights and your rights to last me forever. Tell me something meaningful. You'll live longer if you do."

Sheldon Jahn was struggling to make his brain offer any tidbit of knowledge that would earn him a reprieve. He didn't know any names or anything. Except, wait. "Rowester."

"Rowester?" Remo asked. "Who's that?"

"Not a who, but a place. That's where the bloke is from, I think. The one I talked to all the time. The one who set this up for me and gave me all the instruction manuals and such. He called me a hundred times and the number was always blocked so I never knew where he was calling from, right, but two times he happened to call me from a phone in Rowester. Sounded like a house phone. Your man lives in Rowester, I bet."

Remo was suspicious. He'd never heard of Rowester. "Tell me about it."

"Nice place. A bunch of old families with some money and they needed to keep out the undesirables, you understand? They set up their own sort of unofficial city, but they made it kind of official in all the ways they knew how to make it. They got their own phone codes and all that, and they managed to make it a gated community, you know, keep out the rabble. Just the kind of place our man would live, if he's from one of the old families with old money."

Remo considered that. "So maybe we know the city our man comes from. That's not exactly narrowing it down."

"Wrong, mate," Sheldon said quickly. "Rowester's big on property and money, but there's damn few people actually living there. Just the uppermost crusts, so to speak. Maybe a thousand people. Maybe even less."

31

"Not much, but it's the most he could give us," Remo told Harold W. Smith.

"Remo, this could be enormous," Smith answered.

"It could?"

"Mark's already combed Mr. Jahn's phone records for the past several months but without knowing what to look for. Now he's zeroing in on the calls Mr. Jahn mentioned. Looks like he's found them. Here we are. Sir James Wylings."

Remo was suitably impressed at how fast the information was isolated. "Still, sounds like the kind of place where everybody is a knight or a prince or a duke of earl. We don't know that Wylings is *the* guy."

There was silence. Remo heard quick exchanges between Smitty and Mark Howard. Those two bounced data off each other like silver marbles bounding around in a pinball machine. "You want me to call back."

"It's him," Smith breathed. "Sir James Wylings. He's the one."

"What? How could you find him guilty so fast?" Remo demanded.

Smith began rattling off bits of data. Parliamentary insider. Boyhood friends with Andrew Dolan and Geoffrey Sykes, both members of parliament and actively opposed to the parliamentary efforts to condemn the recolonization efforts. Wylings had friends in high places all over the government. Including -yes, he knew Professor Roland R. Gill. Was the last one to see him alive, in fact. Gill was the mastermind behind the nanotechnology project at Loch Tweed Castle. Got drunk and drove his car into the Thames.

"Or Wylings drove him in, after learning a thing or two about Loch Tweed Castle," Remo remarked.

"This is vital. The man is a trusted parliamentary insider without actually holding any government positions. He's a part of parliament's International Terrorism Defense Support Initiative. They use classified information to identify weaknesses in the infrastructure of foreign countries—ways terrorists might get in and do serious damage," Smith explained.

"How convenient," Remo said.

"There's more," Smith added. "His travel schedule. He was in Sierre Leone two days ago on unspecified business. After landing in Africa he took another short-range helicopter transport to an unknown destination, returned shortly and headed directly for England again."

"He planted the nanobots in the water in Ayounde," Remo stated. "He's the one."

"He's in New Jersey now. The nature of the trip is un-known. His private jet is scheduled to return to London within the hour."

"We'll be in London to meet it," Remo said.

Smith was quiet. No key tapping. Just breathing. "I'll call the President and have a state of emergency de-clared in New Jersey. Wylings may have planted nano-bots there—more likely, he staged them to deploy remotely should more global arm-twisting be required."

"Yeah," Remo breathed.

"Are you sure you don't want to be in New Jersey?"

"No, thanks, Smitty. If Wylings is going to London, I'd like to go to London, too. London is one of my fa-vorite places. Can we get there before he does?"

The answer was no. The plane chartered by Remo and Chiun was just as fast as the plane owned by Sir James Wylings, but they were farther away. "It all depends on when you leave and when Wylings leaves Newark. You still have to wrap up things with Sir Sheldon Jahn."

"That's—wait a sec—that's wrapped up."

The body of Sheldon Jahn fell heavily. Smitty heard the thump.

"We're on our way." Remo and Chiun hurried out of the secure communications hub, descended and emerged from the front of the building.

"Halt!" commanded an infuriated Chinese general.

"She's all yours, Commies," Remo announced. He and Chiun glided into the disordered attack formation of military vehicles and troops and vanished.

32

Wylings was taking his leave of the colonial governor of New Jersey, posing for the camera so the reporters could see that this was a legitimate visit between two legitimate statesmen. Perception was everything, and it was imperative that the world understand fully that the newly reconquered colonies were now irrefutably a part of the British Empire.

The governor of New Jersey had welcomed him as a fellow knight, as a high, influential member of the British government and as a supporter of the empire movement. Maybe the governor even suspected that Wylings was the one behind it all—the mastermind— but they never discussed it openly. Their conversations were limited to organizing the new trade coalitions between New Jersey Colony and England.

As he entered his limo, Wylings turned on the news and received the shock of his life. In a matter of hours, two of his established colonies had been knocked over. Ayounde had fallen when, according to reporters, there was a rebellion by the mercenaries who had helped Sir

Michele Rilli conquer Ayounde. A call for help had been overheard during the fighting. Later, the ministers and prime minister managed to break their way out of a holding cell in the basement of Government House and had only then learned of the devastation that had befallen their largest city.

Minutes ago, another catastrophe. Sir Sheldon Jahn was dead and the financial ministry in Hong Kong was back in the hands of the People's Republic of China.

Devastating losses. Ayounde had petroleum resources worth billions. Hong Kong, serving as the financial powerhouse behind the People's Republic of China, would have channeled billions more into the coffers of the British Empire.

Something was happening. The scheme was discovered. Maybe Wylings himself had been identified. It was time to accelerate the schedule and it was time to turn the screws on Her Majesty the queen. Wylings would force the British government to come to its senses.

James Wylings knew how to make that happen. As with everything else, his scheme was already mapped out. The tools he needed were in place. He held the power of life and death over the heart and soul of the British Empire. London. Soon the British Empire would be acting according to his wishes—or London would be a vast and silent graveyard, full of rotting corpses.

The main city of Ayounde was just three thousand people. London's population was considerably larger.

Aboard his private aircraft, bound for London, Sir James Wylings placed a phone call to a very private number.

"Sir James Wylings calling. May I speak to Her Majesty at once, please? Oh, yes, the matter is quite important."

33

Mark Howard knew that royal marriages were often arranged for reasons that had nothing to do with love or romance, even in the enlightened twenty-first century. Still, this had to be one of the least-romantic marriage proposals ever.

"James Wylings is threatening to annihilate half the population of London if he doesn't get what he wants," he reported from his computer screen. The speakers, hidden in the desk, connected their conference call to the chartered Learjet, which was now transporting the Masters of Sinanju away from Hong Kong. "Wylings called the queen of England personally. Get this—his conditions are that she marries him, immediately."

"Hold on a second," Remo said.

Mark Howard and Harold Smith heard Chiun and Remo conversing in Korean. It was difficult to read their emotions in the language, so unlike American English. Still, Mark thought Chiun sounded tense.

"Didn't take him long to figure out we were on to him," Remo complained. "What's he trying to accomplish?"

"He's to be crowned king of England during the same ceremony," Mark said.

A burst of noise cut off further explanation. Mark Howard and Harold Smith looked at one another across the office. It sounded as if somebody was breaking up the furniture. Strangely enough, it sounded as if Chiun was doing the breaking.

Remo said, "He can't *do* that. Can he?"

"He is doing it," Harold Smith said. "He more or less came right out and admitted he was responsible for the genocide in Ayounde. Who's going to argue with him?"

"Emperor Smith," Chiun asked, "do you mean to say that Her Majesty will bow to his vile wishes?"

"She did not state her intent. When she received the call she was understandably, er, shaken," Smith said. "Wylings informed her that he is en route to London and will proceed from the airport directly to Buckingham Palace. He intends to force the issue without delay."

"She'll go along with it," Mark Howard added. "That's just my gut feeling, but she'll marry the son of a bitch and name him king of England if it means sparing her city."

"Yes. She will do this." Chiun sounded tense. "How could she not?"

"I agree with Mark," Smith said. "No one, royal or governmental, is going to put up a resistance. They'll let it happen and deal with the consequences later—whenever later is." Smith and Howard were busy monitoring other communications lines, just in case Wylings used another method of reaching out to the world. Mark was trying to figure out how to get the Masters' aircraft into England first—and finding few options.

"But it's a sham," Remo said on the phone line. "Can't they have it annulled and voided once the nano-bots are found?"

"Such is not the way with royalty." It was Chiun who answered. "The queen will give her word and then break it? Even if she faces extortion, it mars her credibility to renege. A king is crowned and then the crowning is nul-lified? Many will say a coronation cannot be nullified. If these ceremonies are allowed to proceed, they cannot be undone without chaos."

"This guy has been riding this wave of kinda-sorta legitimacy long enough," Remo said. "A law isn't a law just because he pretends it is, no matter how many peo-ple agree to pretend along with him. A king ain't a king just because he makes somebody say he's king. It doesn't work like that."

"It does work like that," Smith responded. "No mat-ter how blatant the lie, a segment of the population will call it truth if they are told it is truth."

"It's stupid."

"This is beside the point," Smith added. "Wylings has got England under his thumb, and the rest of the world as well. Until and unless the threat of the nanobots is removed, he calls the shots."

"Not for long will he be calling shots," Chiun squeaked. "I will pursue the pilot of this sky needle to accelerate his pace."

Chiun was gone in a flash, leaving Remo sitting alone at the small sofa booth in the rear of the aircraft with the speakerphone. "He's up front, telling the pilot to step on it."

"I've already given your pilot air clearance for a more direct route and he's at top speed," Mark Howard said. "If he goes any faster, his gas mileage decreases and he'll risk running out of fuel short of the British Isles."

Remo heard shouting from the cockpit and a yelp. The Learjet's speed picked up noticeably. "Maybe somebody had better do some smoothing over with the charter company," Remo said.

"Remo," Smith asked, "does Chiun have some sort of a personal involvement with this Wylings?"

"No. Absolutely not. Why would you even ask such a thing?"

Chiun was, naturally, within earshot and returning to the booth.

"Our estimated time of arrival has been revised," Chiun announced. "We will land in three hours, eighteen minutes."

"Oh," Mark Howard said. "That would be advantageous and somewhat amazing."

"Then you shall be amazed," Chiun said. "The pilot has given his word that it shall be done."

"Unfortunately," Mark added, "that will still be an hour later than Wylings's arrival. He's got a lot less distance to travel."

Chiun nodded and said, "I will see how much more motivation can be applied to the pilot."

"No, that won't be needed," Smith insisted. "The pilot is performing admirably. We show your airspeed is at the maximum design limits of the aircraft now."

"Design limits are simply numbers on paper," Chiun said. "They can be ignored by a skilled joystick-toggler."

"There's a risk," Remo pointed out before Chiun could scamper up front to apply his motivation. "The wings."

"What of them?" Chiun demanded.

"The engineers make them to go a certain miles per hour, you know," Remo said. "Any faster—"

"They will come off?" Chiun gasped.

"Almost never."

"What knowledge of engineering is there in your swollen white head?" Chiun demanded. "The wings will *not* come off if we exceed the design speed. Emperor?"

"Correct, Chiun. The wings are made to withstand stresses much greater than the design speeds of the aircraft. It's unlikely that the wings would lose structural integrity."

"Quite unlikely," Mark Howard added.

Chiun squinted at Remo, at the small electronic box of the phone, back at Remo. "We are traveling quickly enough."

"I think so, too. What do we do in the meantime?" Remo asked. "Can you guys stall Wylings? Can you divert his plane? Anything?"

"We're not going to risk setting him off," Smith said. "We don't even know what kind of personality we're dealing with here."

34

"Oh, heavens!" Wylings had never fainted in his life, but the spectacle of the royal parade almost made him swoon.

Built in 1798, the Wylings family coach was a jaw-dropper back in its day. Old Edward Wylings III spared no expense to hire Britain's best carriage-smiths and to have gold plating applied to every filigree and detail. More than two centuries later, Sir James Wylings hired equally capable carriage-smiths to carry out the restoration, and he poured more than a million pounds into gold plating the *complete* exterior.

He hadn't stopped there. Gold-and-silver baubles, gemstones and platinum rivets decorated the bridles of the horses and the coats of the twenty-four horsemen. The drive was lined on both sides with standard-bearers holding twenty-foot wooden poles displaying the Union Jack. Every article of textile, from the flags to the coats to the horse blankets, had dangling gold fringe. It was truly a royal procession that was staged in front of the Heathrow Airport terminal exit.

The orders had reached the street cops. There was no

police resistance to the unscheduled jubilee, and they were organizing the crowds like any other royal event. The police were making room for the media, even providing priority access for Wylings's staff.

Wylings had expected this. The queen and the other powers that be were not going to risk intimidating him—not when he had the power to burst his WMDs in the streets of London, symbolic heart of England. The more England's people appeared to be a part of today's events, the more legitimate would be the coronation. With police escort, this parade would look as it should look—like a royal procession. The ceremonial arrival of the king of England. This parade and the festivities that followed would convince the world that he *was* the king of England. Once the people of the world believed it, his opponents would have to change the people's minds, and that was always the hard part.

Wylings's hired band played. The police struggled to hold back the crowds, and four attendants—four, count 'em—came to perform the act of opening the doors from the airport terminal to the drive. Delightfully, it was an automatic door and the assistance was purely ceremonial. This was getting grand indeed!

Of course Wylings was paying for all this attendance, just as he paid for the carriage restoration and rented the horses and hired the standard-bearers and even purchased the big Union Jacks they were carrying. He spent a mint on the virgin-red cad carpet upon which he strolled from the terminal doors to the waiting carriage.

The people threw confetti, which he had paid to purchase and distribute. He waved, with one hand, showing royal restraint, and gripped his thin briefcase in the other hand.

The world was watching it all on their televisions—even if they did not know what they were watching yet. There would be rumors flying, because Wylings had himself tipped off the media.

Maybe Buckingham Palace would confirm the rumor and maybe they would demure. They were probably trying to think their way out of this situation in a hurry. They wouldn't be able to. Wylings had planned everything too carefully. He had even had a hand in writing the speeches of support to be delivered by his comrades, Dolan and Sykes, after the coronation festivities.

For now, the royals would be keeping mute—but they would not risk denying the rumors. That was as good as a confirmation. The media were receiving the carefully prepared portfolio on James Wylings, which emphasized that he was a royal insider and even had distant blood ties to the royal family. Given his position in English royal society, marrying the queen of England would seem like a reasonable explanation for Wylings suddenly rating a splendid royal processional,

Wylings relaxed into the seat of the carriage as the parade began to move, away from Heathrow and toward London. It was going to be a slow trip, certainly, but even that was a part of Wylings's strategy. The media frenzy needed time to build into a mountain. There would be massive efforts underway to get teams into London capable of covering an event as major as an impromptu royal wedding and coronation. Wylings wanted them to have all the time they needed. The whole world should be watching when he achieved his station.

The trouncing was awful and the cushions were designed to be decorative, not comfortable. His tailbone was getting bruised. He tried to adjust his behind, but there just didn't seem to be a comfortable place for his royal butt.

"I'm getting a royal pain in the ass!" he mumbled to himself, and he had to restrain himself from snorting aloud as he passed a bunch of cheering old ladies on the curb. Snorting was not the dignified behavior of a king of England, but the private joke was funny.

Wylings, old man, take control. You're getting giddy.

Well, why in blazes couldn't he get a little giddy? He was about to become the king of England! *Nothing* could stop that now.

But blast, his rump was sure complaining.

35

The private jet landed smoothly, braked to about fifty miles per hour, and the hatchway flew off as if blown with explosives.

"What the hell?" demanded the air-traffic coordinator in the control tower. Something flashed in front of his vision and twisted. Was he seeing things? Was it a figure with a pale, raisin face in a brilliant, multi-colored robe? It was moving so fast he couldn't be sure—it slipped from the still-speeding aircraft and flattened, rolling under the aircraft and between the landing gear. It was like a squirrel trying to make a dash under a large truck going one hundred kilometers per hour on the autobahn. There was only one possible outcome.

But the Learjet Challenger was still rolling down the runway and there was no crumpled figure left behind on the tarmac. The figure was gone now. *Where had he-she gone?*

"Did you see—?" asked another controller, who was monitoring what seemed to be trouble aboard the chartered jet. The pilots didn't seem to know why the hatch had popped off.

Another figure appeared in the hatch, then he stepped out of the Learjet, which put the bloody fool right where the wing should have chopped him in two. But the man hit the ground running—and he was running as fast as the jet was rolling, which was impossible. The man increased his speed, zipping up and alongside the cockpit. He seemed to be shrugging to the flight crew, as of to say he was sorry for the trouble.

Then—then he *ran around the front* of the Learjet and was gone. He should have been run over. He should have been squashed. But he was gone. No body, no nothing.

Funny thing. As amazing as it was, all the air-traffic control coordinator could think about was how much paperwork this was going to require, just to try explaining.

"YOU'RE SUPPOSED to leave your seat belt on and stay seated until the aircraft has come to a complete stop," Remo pointed out. "Where we going?"

"To London." Chiun was setting a quick pace, determined to make up for the time lost to their late arrival. Every British television channel they could receive on the aircraft—even Eurosport—was covering the procession as their on-air reporters struggled to make sense of it.

Wylings had opted to make a royal parade of his journey to Buckingham Palace, and that gave Remo and Chiun some breathing room.

As soon as they came across some shops, Chiun headed into a storefront electronics store. Remo was four steps behind him, but Chiun met him coming in. Chiun's hand was wrapped around a small silver gizmo of some kind or another, and it made the store's alarm system screech.

"Uh, boy." Remo jogged inside and tried to settle down the excited shopkeepers.

"Did you see that? That old fart had the fastest fingers I've ever seen!" The clerk was dialing the police.

"This'll cover it," Remo said, dumping a wad of bills on the counter.

"Those are American dollars," the clerk pointed out.

Remo spread out the wad, so the clerk could see just how many American dollars there were. Many, many of them, mostly twenties. "Will that cover it or not?"

"And then some."

Chiun reappeared, stepping up onto the counter and holding the clerk by a fold of skin pulled from his buzz-cut scalp.

"Batteries or death, cretin," Chiun snapped, and shoved the little silver box into the clerk's face. To his credit, the clerk managed to reach for the shelf behind him, find the correct package of batteries by feel, and hand them up to the little old man. Chiun snatched the batteries, ripped open the package and had them inserted in the electronic device before the clerk completed his messy landing behind the counter.

Then Chiun was gone again.

"Will this cover the batteries, too?" Remo asked.

REMO CAUGHT UP to Chiun and found the old Master running and watching the screen of his tiny portable TV.

"His procession moves slowly. We will reach him soon," Chiun announced. "We may be thankful that the fool has a grand ego and wishes to make himself the center of a spectacle before he comes to the palace. The people come to see him and he is caught up in their great numbers."

Remo looked. Sure enough, there was a tiny image of a street swarming with people and the little gold dot in the middle had to be Wylings's carriage.

"I think he got more than he bargained for, Little Father," Remo said.

"He shall soon," Chiun said.

36

Sir James Wylings couldn't help but be amused at the predicament. He was a victim of his own success.

Londoners were in a frenzy. The queen was marrying. They were getting a new king. *Today.*

Every royal watcher knew this was highly unusual. No sort of protocol was being followed. The queen didn't just *get married*—not without long courtship, at least a full year for the engagement, and months of planning for the royal wedding. As for crowning a king on the very day of the wedding—outrageous!

And yet all the officials who should have been crying foul were not. It looked as if this was truly going to happen. The people certainly thought so; spectators were pouring out to greet the new monarch, and Wylings's procession had been slowed from a brisk march to a slow walk. Wylings could be patient. If only his bottom weren't in such blasted agony.

He drew the curtains and fumbled for his cell phone, flipping it open and saying, "The queen."

It dialed the queen. She never, ever answered her

own telephone, but that was fine. "This is Sir James Wylings. To whom am I speaking?"

"This is the queen's personal attendant, Alfred Herlingwythe."

Wylings chuckled. "Herlingwythe, I know for a fact you're with the queen's special protection detail. Never mind. Is everything being prepared?"

"Just as you requested, Sir Wylings." Herlingwythe's teeth were making grinding sounds as he spoke.

"Everyone has received my instructions as to what is to occur and what is not to occur?" Sir Wylings asked.

"Yes, sir."

"I'd like to remind you of the consequences, Herlingwythe, should anything go wrong. The consequences would be most dire. The very phone I am speaking on can release any one of my weapons or all of them. Have you been informed that I planted four weapons within the city of London?"

"I have, sir."

"They'll release themselves if I don't send the correct signal every two hours. You'd best remember that I need to stay in good health and good humor."

"I understand, sir."

"Does everyone else understand? I imagine you have ten or fifteen people listening in on this call."

"We all understand, Sir Wylings."

"Just to be absolutely sure you understand, I will tell you what will happen. Five or six million Londoners will experience agonizing death. Is that *perfectly* clear?"

"Quite perfectly clear, Sir Wylings."

"Good! Glad to hear it! I'll be along eventually. Bye-bye."

Wylings clicked off the phone.

"And hello."

It was an odd experience for Sir James Wylings when he heard the voice of another human being. It was inside the carriage with him. But there was no one inside the carriage with him. It was as tight as a confessional in there and thus easy enough to be aware of others.

But when he looked up from his phone he found not one, but two other human beings in the carriage with him. The side door was still tightly closed. Even the curtains remained drawn.

"What in blazes?"

"Shh," said the younger one, who had an American accent. "You had best just not say anything. We're both pretty mad at you right about now. I don't now which one of us is more ticked off."

Wylings tried to fling his arms out and dash madly from the carriage, but the young one had a hand on his shoulder and Wylings wasn't going anywhere. He tried to scream, but the man clamped his mouth shut, and that hand wasn't moving with a crowbar.

Wylings got a good look his captor, a slim man of indeterminate age and unexceptional looks. In fact, only his wrists were distinctive. They were abnormally thick, as if they were excessively muscled.

The other one was quite unusual. He was ancient,

Asian and tiny, with hazel eyes and wisps of yellowing hair over his ears and a few yellowing threads of a beard.

When the hand come off his mouth, Wylings gasped, "Sinanju."

"Hey, you're a fan."

"I never really believed it could be true. I believed Sinanju was just a fairy tale."

"You're the one riding around in a gold carriage, princess," Remo said.

Wylings straightened in his seat. "I will not suffer the insults of any man, no matter what skills he possesses. Leave me be."

The small, old Korean spoke for the first time, and in Wylings's sight he transformed from being a bent, frail old man to be someone dignified, noble and powerful. "You shall see your tongue taken from your own mouth before you die, usurper," the old Master said with barely contained fury. "You shall witness your own lifeblood streaming from your body."

Wylings was filled with fear such as he had never known—but he sensed something amiss in the elder Master. The old Korean was holding back, and it was difficult for him. Wylings knew he had these Masters of Sinanju just where he wanted them—just where he had everyone else.

"You won't harm me. I hold the key to four weapons primed to infect this city. They will strike this city down when I command—or automatically, if I fail to transmit the proper codes on schedule."

"We heard. What some guys won't do to get women," Remo said.

"He shall never have the queen and he shall never have England," Chiun spit. "You will tell us the place where these weapons are hidden, and then we will grant you the mercy of death."

Wylings sniffed haughtily. "Who'd have thought? The legendary Master of Sinanju is just an old fool."

Chiun moved, though Wylings never saw him move. Even Remo almost missed it. Chiun snatched Wylings's hands in his own and lifted them above his head and squeezed the ball of each thumb.

Wylings opened his mouth, and the sound that started coming out was a foghorn blast. Remo quickly pinched the man in the neck, locking up his voice box and freezing his body in position.

Chiun kept squeezing.

Inside of Sir James Wylings, a lifetime of civilization and humanity was erased in a blind, burning, dismal wall of agony that was so immense it seemed impossible even as he was feeling it. No source for it, just pain everywhere that went on for an eternity and made him into a madman.

Remo winced. Chiun was giving Wylings a king-size jolt to the nervous system—worse than was necessary or even wise. "Little Father, we want him to be able to talk, at least."

Chiun stepped away. Wylings was still locked in position, his face wet with tears, his breathing labored.

Remo cranked his neck and the arms fell and the man began to whimper like a wounded terrier. It was the word "no," breathed out over and over again.

Remo got worried. "Wylings? You still in there?"

"No no no no no no."

"Talk to me, Jimmy."

"No."

"Yes."

"Not again. Don't let it happen again. I can't stand for it to happen again."

"Hey, snap out of it, Majesty." Remo stimulated the nerves along Wylings's spine, provoking a jolt of adrenaline that brought him back into the real world.

"Now you know the gift Sinanju can give," Chiun said. "There are many more coins in our treasure chest."

Remo wasn't sure when he had last seen Chiun so vengeful. When Chiun really wanted to kill a man, he usually just did it. This time, his hand was stayed, and he was practically vibrating with his wrath. "That's right, Wylings, you want to avoid a repeat performance, you cough up the goods. We want to know where your nanobots are tucked away."

"I can't tell you. It would ruin everything!"

And then, Wylings experienced it again, the pain of a thousand hells—the reprisal of a Sinanju Master angered.

37

They left him in the carriage, and they left him alive.
Slipping unseen from the golden coach, they blended
into the crowds who were disappointed at being unable
to see inside. The curtains were now drawn back, just a
little, on each side, and the people caught just the brief-
est glimpse of their new king. He was sitting in the carriage, watching the world go by. His waving hand had
to have gotten tired.

THE ELEVATED WALKWAY was sparsely traveled, and in
fact most of the city was empty of pedestrian traffic as
the Londoners gathered in homes and pubs to watch his-
toric events unfolding.

"That's a lot of people sitting around watching a
slow-moving stagecoach," Remo observed.

Chiun replied by vaulting lightly over the side rail of
the walkway and vanishing. Remo leaped after him, his
feet touching down on an irregular, broken stone wall,
part of a small complex of ancient Roman ruins nestled
on grassy lawns.

"Begin searching this place quickly!" Chiun said. "It is in a high crevice!"

Remo stepped down into gap between a pair of free-standing stone walls, his eyes piercing the shadows and the bricks and the hollows in search of the thing Wylings described—a thin steel tube inside of plastic outer casings, with a small black charge adhered to the end. The blast was designed to discharge the nanobots in a deadly mist that would carry far on the breeze.

It was difficult to picture the device. When they found the first one, they would know what to look for.

It occurred to Remo he was looking in the wrong place. He was in the center of the ruins. Wylings would have put the device somewhere that he would have been able to reach when he paid his ha'penny and was roaming the grounds like any normal sightseer. He wouldn't have tried sneaking into the off-limits interior of the ruins.

Remo made his way out of the craggy corridor and stood examining the grounds. All Wylings said was that it was in a high crevice in the ruins.

His eyes wandered to the admissions hut. It was also of brick, but constructed in the past century or so. It stood beside the gated entranceway.

"Why are you wasting time when time is so precious?" Chiun demanded as he slipped like a shadow among the alcoves of the ancient labyrinth.

"There." Remo bounded down from the bricks and across the lawn. In a high crevice in the brick building, just under the eaves, was the plastic container he had spotted. He withdrew it with care as Chiun arrived alongside him.

"Heat must be used to destroy them," Chiun said. "Remove the metal tube from the plastic. Create heat with friction."

Remo looked at him.

"It is not the first time I have had to destroy these same entities," Chiun explained.

"Oh, really?"

"Do it."

Remo used his one long fingernail to slice the plastic housings away as if they were sandwich wrap being cut by a straight razor. He held the cool steel tube in his hands, feeling the movement of liquid inside. He began to rub the surface with his finger. He adjusted his skin contact to minimize the friction against his flesh while the friction against the steel increased and the surface became hotter. In moments he could feel the bubbling of the solution inside the tube, and he allowed it to boil a full minute.

Then he gingerly unscrewed the two halves of the steel tubes and revealed the glass tube inside. There was clear liquid and tiny specks of floating crystal.

"They are dead," Chiun said. "But that is one of four."

"Can we cover the entire city before Wylings arrives at Buckingham Palace?"

"We should have ended his miserable life," Chiun said angrily.

"We can't take the risk of not finding all of them,

Chiun. Until the nano-things are cooked—and I mean all of them—Wylings has to stay alive."

Chiun didn't agree, but he didn't disagree. "Then let us find them!" And he was racing away through the ancient city of London.

38

James Wylings couldn't move. The carriage ride through the streets of London seemed endless. He was paralyzed, so that he could not even shift a little from this exact sitting position, and his bruised derriere was in screaming agony.

Soon enough, the time would come for the weapons to receive their signal. The Masters of Sinanju knew it. They would return and they would be forced to release him, and then Wylings would once again be the one making the demands. They would not trust their torture to force him to send the correct code, would they?

Or would they find the weapons and return before the top of the hour? Unlikely, he thought. Even just one of those devices had the power to wipe out two million people. That kind of power was *true* mastery.

"Hey, Yer Majesty, lookit what we found."

Suddenly, they were back. The Masters of Sinanju were inside the carriage on either side of him, and the curtains were drawn tight.

"Your coward's weapons are disabled," the old one

reported. He pulled his arm from the sleeve of his robe and displayed four glass tubes. There were little specks of glass floating in them. The nanobots were melted.

"Oh, damn!" Wylings said, and noticed he could speak again.

"I was going to ask you about the others," Remo said. "But I don't think I need to."

"You do not?" Chiun asked.

"The other weapons are scattered around the world in my colonies," Wylings reported. "Sixteen of them remain. You will never find them all."

"Noisy contraption you have here," Remo said. "But not too noisy." He pulled Wylings's briefcase out of the felt-lined drawer beneath the seat. It was thin and covered with a rich, dark leather. "Pretty sloshy. Are you packing Red Bull?"

Remo opened the briefcase. "I count sixteen plastic containers," he announced. "But they're not energy drink."

"They certainly are not," Chiun said.

"I'd say Mr. Wylings has used all his bargaining chips."

"I believe Mr. Wylings had best be prepared," Chiun said. "He must be presented properly to Her Majesty the queen."

THE WORLD WAS WATCHING as the gold carriage closed in on the grand drive, where it was to be received by the queen herself. A hundred uniformed security men were stationed in the street, on the buildings and flanking the queen's honor guards. None of them knew what to expect. Few were briefed as to why this insecure reception ceremony would even be permitted.

The ceremonial carpet was laid out from the street and between a stern double column of Grenadier Guards, divested of their firearms but chosen for their ability to fight hand to hand. They were armed only with ceremonial glaives. They were supposed to look strictly ornamental, but the guards were instructed to be ready to lay down their lives for the queen. The glaives, however, would be useless in a fight—long poles with short, curved blades mounted atop. Packed so tightly together that their shoulders touched, the Grenadier Guards would have no room to use such weapons. Truth be told, none of them knew what to expect.

Even the media was given contradictory and confusing statements as to the purpose of these events.

The crowd grew hushed as the long line of Sir Wylings's standard-bearers appeared, and then they heard the clopping of many hooves. The procession made its way between the police barricades, and the brilliant gold carriage came to a stop. Her Majesty the queen stood atop a rise of steps and waited—only she had an uninterrupted view of the gathering.

For a moment, nothing at all happened.

Then Sir James Wylings emerged from the carriage—airborne, clawing at the air, screaming, shouting, and he rose to an impossible height. The cameras followed his high arc and the people gasped in unison.

Then Sir James Wylings came down again, and his girlish screams ended as his body was impaled on the purely ornamental glaives of the Grenadier Guards.

There were cries and the crowd recoiled, the defense teams shouted at one another in instant mayhem. Whatever they had been prepared for, *this* was not it.

As the pandemonium grew all around her, Her Majesty the queen caught sight of movement beyond the hideous corpse and the dripping gore. There was someone barely visible to her inside the carriage. A small figure was there, looking back at her.

The queen recognized the figure, which explained well enough how the situation had reversed so suddenly. She picked up the sides of her lips in a rare and somewhat sad smile.

Then, as if she had been hallucinating the figure, the interior of the carriage was empty.

Epilogue

The London parade coverage was interrupted on New York television by a breaking story from Hong Kong.

Seventies pop star Sheldon Jahn was dead!

"The much-beloved performer has most recently been busy composing the soundtrack for the new animated feature film version of *Bomba the Jungle Boy,* as well as holding the government of China hostage in an attempt to recolonize Hong Kong," the entertainment anchor reported. "Sheldon Jahn will be missed, and we can only pray that his work on *Bomba* was complete."

"A sad day for us all, Sheila," said the anchor in New York. "Now, back to London, where we can confirm that the queen of England will *not,* repeat, *not* be getting married this afternoon. If you're just joining us, here once again is the video of the queen's fiancé as he left the carriage and, as far as we can understand, tripped onto the spears of the queen's personal guards."

Harold W. Smith couldn't seem to drag his attention away from the coverage by the inane anchors, although he had seen the "accident" footage a hundred times already. He concentrated on other intelligence feeds coming in from around the world.

CURE had instantly passed along the news to the President when he heard from Remo and Chiun that the nanobot weapons were all accounted for and destroyed. Twenty minutes later, when the armies showed up in New Jersey, the colonial governor couldn't surrender fast enough.

"We're back to having fifty states again—whew!" the news anchor said, pretending to mop his brow. "What a strange, weird trip *today* has been. Also, we've received word that the occupying forces in New Finland have ceased their occupation. It is unclear whether they were forced to abandon their takeover, or if they just left."

"It's Newfoundland," Mark Howard replied to his own video feed.

IT WAS EARLY MORNING when Mark found another tiny blinker on his display and followed the alert to a news item from the *Chicago Tribune*. The article was a short piece from the entertainment section of the newspaper—and it was unrelated to any of the wrapup coverage from the Colonies.

The article, *Leggy Attraction Closed Due To Gigantic Indigestion,* informed the reader that the Chicago Aquarium's most popular display was closed temporarily.

The Chicago giant squid, the one and only living giant squid in captivity, was off its feed. The article said, "Given the rumored pressure put on the aquarium president to keep the display open to the paying public, at the expense of scientific research projects, one has to wonder about the true nature of the closing."

Howard did wonder about the nature of the closing. He wondered and he worried. Maybe the scientific community had finally flexed some muscle and gained access to the one-of-kind cephalopod. But scientists never had the finances to stall the accumulation of profits. That's why they had been relegated to studying the creature only after public hours. Since the squid's environment was controlled to keep it active for the ticket-buying attendees, the researchers were stuck staring at a snoozing squid for hours at a time. This limited their ability to learn much from the creature. But if the scientists hadn't engineered the shutdown, then the squid must be *very* ill. It had to be more than a little stomach upset.

Mark Howard felt weighed down with his nameless thoughts. The squid was just a squid, but he had worried about the thing even when it was first captured and transported to Chicago, when the world was going haywire under the influence of Sa Mangsang. Whatever Sa Mangsang truly was—and Mark Howard wasn't ready to believe Master Chiun's assertions that it was an elder god bent on the earth's destruction—the thing had spread its mental disturbances around the world. Mark Howard had felt the influence more acutely than anyone else, for Sa Mangsang had sought him out as the most receptive mind close to the Masters of Sinanju.

Sa Mangsang used the squid for its dirty work. The big squids had swarmed to the surface by the thousands during the crisis. That was how the Chicago Giant was captured. Now Sa Mangsang was in slumber, or hibernation, or comatose, depending on how you looked at it. So the giant squid in Chicago was just a giant squid. Magnificent, but completely natural. Right?

Howard had tried telling himself that there was nothing to worry about—and he wasn't very convincing. He kept an eye on the Chicago Giant, and set up alerts for news about the creature.

Now the Chicago Giant was ill, maybe even dying, if he read between the lines. Shouldn't that be good news? When the thing was dead, he wouldn't have to worry about it anymore.

Smith looked up to find Mark Howard sitting rigid in his chair and even rocking slightly. The young man was as pale as death and didn't seem to know Smith was there.

"Mark?"

Mark's eyes flitted in Smith's direction, then back to the screen.

"What's the matter?" Smith demanded. He strode behind his assistant's desk and glared at the open window. *Chicago Tribune.* The captured giant squid.

"What of it?" Smith demanded.

"I don't know."

"What about this concerns you?" Smith pressed, unsatisfied.

"I don't *know*." Howard was pressing his fists into his abdomen. "I think I'm going to be sick."

Smith wordlessly handed Howard the plastic-lined wastebasket. As Howard wretched into it, Smith leaned over him and scrolled through the article. When Mark sat up again, he hit Smith's chest with the back of his head.

Smith retreated to his own desk thoughtfully. Mark Howard was wiping his mouth with the back of his hand.

"Hurts. I feel like my stomach is full of ball bearings."

"This is related to the item on your screen?"

Mark Howard nodded slightly, eyes dancing as if he were trying to avoid mentioning it. "Somehow."

"Is it nerves? Or is this something that is, uh, meaningful?"

Mark Howard made a sort of sickly smile, like the last grin of a dying man who was shot under ironic circumstances. Mark left in a hurry, heading for the washroom, and met Mrs. Mikulka coming in. The old dear was in early. Smith's secretary wasn't supposed to arrive until 9:00 a.m., but her old habits died hard. She didn't get a chance to say good-morning before she got a whiff.

"Oh, dear, poor Mark." She took away the wastebasket.

Smith was deep in thought. Did Mark just have a case of stomach flu? Was he being nervously affected by the news from Chicago because it was related to the traumatic crisis in the Pacific Ocean? Or were his unique abilities communicating to Mark that there was some sort of impending crisis related to the squid in Chicago?

Smith was uncomfortable discussing Mark's abilities. They were so undefined, so unquantifiable that one could only use terms like extrasensory perception and precognition to name them. Those terms had been applied for years to charlatans and quacks. Smith was unsure about the nature of Mark's abilities—although there was nothing fake about them.

In the same way, Smith had never satisfied himself about the nature of the crisis in the Pacific Ocean. An elder god of the lost continent of Mu? It was the stuff of bad documentaries from the 1970s. Still, Master Chiun's myths of Sa Mangsang had held true throughout the crisis, including the worldwide mental disturbances that worked destructively on Mark Howard.

Smith felt sudden alarm as he made the connection. Could Mark's nausea and emotional distress be coming, again, from Sa Mangsang—*whatever* Sa Mangsang was?

The Masters of Sinanju had assured Smith that the gargantuan creature was withered and weak, and had gone down with its ancient island into the Pacific waters to begin again the aeons-long restorative sleep. But how could he trust their understanding of this creature? Chiun was superstitious. Remo, at times, was less than brilliant.

And Sa Mangsang—whatever Sa Mangsang was—had been an influence on the world even through its period of convalescence. Minds around the planet had always been affected by the creature.

Maybe Mark Howard just had a virus.

The giant squid in the *Chicago Tribune* article hovered before Smith's vision. A squid eye was visible. It didn't look intelligent, the way the eyes of a marine mammal can look intelligent. There were those who claimed cephalopods were extremely intelligent, and that man was simply too limited in his creative scope to find ways of communicating with the more alien cephalopod mind.

Smith idly wondered what kinds of thoughts were inside the mind of the Chicago Giant. Was it suffering in its confinement? Was it capable of being angry at its captors? Was it smart enough to have an agenda?

Smith, not a superstitious or imaginative man, knew the creature had been following some sort of a command or signal when it was captured. Were the signals broadcast in real time through the oceans, or were they orders—given, received and remembered by the squid?

Was the Chicago Giant still waiting, even now, to carry out the orders of Sa Mangsang?